I0820024

# "THE STEREOSCOPE" AND OTHER MYSTICAL TALES FROM ST. PETERSBURG

# Cultural Syllabus

**Series Editor**
Mark Lipovetsky (Columbia University)

## Other Titles in this Series

*Dostoevsky's "Crime and Punishment": A Reader's Guide*
Deborah A. Martinsen

*Culture and Communication: Signs in Flux. An Anthology of Major and Lesser-Known Works*
Yuri Lotman
Edited by Andreas Schönle and translated by Benjamin Paloff

*Permanent Evolution: Selected Essays on Literature, Theory and Film*
Yuri Tynianov
Translated and edited by Ainsley Morse & Philip Redko

*21: Russian Short Prose from an Odd Century*
Edited by Mark Lipovetsky

*A Dostoevskii Companion: Texts and Contexts*
Edited by Katherine Bowers, Connor Doak, and Kate Holland

*Russian Science Fiction Literature and Cinema: A Critical Reader*
Edited and introduced by Anindita Banerjee

*For more information on this series, please visit:*
*https://www.academicstudiespress.com/cultural-syllabus-series/*

# “THE STEREOSCOPE” AND OTHER MYSTICAL TALES FROM ST. PETERSBURG

Edited by Dan Ungurianu
Translated by Elena Ungurianu

ACADEMIC STUDIES PRESS
BOSTON
2025

Library of Congress Cataloging-in-Publication Data

Names: Ungurianu, Dan editor | Ungurianu, Elena, 2003- translator
Title: "The stereoscope" : and other mystical tales from St. Petersburg / edited by Dan Ungurianu ; translated by Elena Ungurianu.
Description: Boston : Academic Studies Press, 2025. | Series: Cultural syllabus | Includes bibliographical references and index.
Identifiers: LCCN 2025013329 (print) | LCCN 2025013330 (ebook) | ISBN 9798887197647 hardback | ISBN 9798897830268 paperback | ISBN 9798887197654 adobe pdf | ISBN 9798887197661 epub
Subjects: LCSH: Short stories, Russian--Translations into English | Fantasy fiction, Russian--Translations into English | Russian fiction--20th century--Translations into English | LCGFT: Fantasy fiction | Short stories
Classification: LCC PG3286 .S74 2025 (print) | LCC PG3286 (ebook) | DDC 891.73/00815--dc23/eng/20250520
LC record available at https://lccn.loc.gov/2025013329
LC ebook record available at https://lccn.loc.gov/2025013330


ISBN 9798887197647 hardback
ISBN 9798897830268 paperback
ISBN 9798887197654 adobe pdf
ISBN 9798887197661 epub

Book design by Lapiz Digital Services
Cover design by Ivan Grave
On the cover: Evgenia Smirnova-Ivanova, illustration for Alexander Ivanov's "Stereoscope" (St. Petersburg: Sirius, 1909).

Published by Academic Studies Press
1007 Chestnut Street
Newton, MA 02464, USA
www.academicstudiespress.com

# Contents

# Preface

The following tales date back to the Russian Silver Age, a fascinating part of the European *Belle Époque*, with its renewed interest in mysticism and intense apocalyptic premonitions on the eve of World War I and the revolution. Their action takes place in St. Petersburg, Russia's magnificent imperial capital. A fantastical city par excellence, it generated enduring mythology and provided ideal settings for supernatural stories. As the twentieth century was dawning, such stories combined traditional plots with signs of modernity, from high-tech media and virtual reality devices to phone sex and celebrity culture. Each tale includes some commentary, in the form of endnotes, on relevant allusions and historical details. Also included is a selection of contemporary reviews on the centerpiece of the collection—Alexander Ivanov's "Stereoscope" (1909), a forgotten gem of fantastic literature and a pioneering museum adventure tale, which also happens to be an early example of fiction about photography. Whenever available, illustrations from the original publications are reproduced. Just like the texts for which they were created, they range from the ordinary to first-rate, such as the exquisite drawings for Sergei Auslender's "The Night Prince" by Mstislav Dobuzhinsky, a prominent member of the World of Art circle. The concluding article places these tales into the context of the literature of the Silver Age and also into the larger tradition of the fantastic genre in Russia. In the main body of the collection, the more common English spelling of Russian names is used, while the bibliography follows the Library of Congress transliteration (for example, Alexander vs. Aleksandr, Alexey Tolstoy vs. Aleksei Tolstoi). None of these tales have been published before in English translation.

Figure 1.1. Evgenia Smirnova-Ivanova, illustration for Alexander Ivanov's "Stereoscope" (St. Petersburg: Sirius, 1909).

Alexander Ivanov

# The Stereoscope

(A Twilight Tale)*

## I

I smashed my stereoscope. It did not merely contain simple optic lenses. It was a kind of door, to some world inaccessible to us. But I have firmly blocked this mysterious portal. It was someone's great invention, but whose I do not know, nor will I ever know. Doors were unlocked for me to those realms which humans are forbidden to enter, into which they can only glance. The uncrossable boundary between that world and ours disappeared for me. But on that memorable night, in a fit of terror I took up a hammer and smashed the lenses of the stereoscope to establish once again that boundary between myself and its dreadful world.

Have you ever noticed that photographs have a strange charm to them? All of them, simple ones and the double ones used for a stereoscope (these can be on paper, or transparent, on glass), they all mysteriously draw you in, and the older the photograph, the stronger the effect. A whole world, peculiar and secluded, looks out from them. It is mute, dead, frozen and immobile. It has no living colors. Dull brown and its shades rule over all, as if everything has faded. This is the ghostly world of the past, the kingdom of bygone shadows. What you see in the pale image was once but a moment in our living world. Then our world irreversibly outlived this moment. And now, the only thing left is its double, hiding on a little piece of paper or a glass plate, frozen, silenced, and faded. The ghostly doubles of things forever in the past look at you from old photographs, a mysterious sadness and a quiet terror emanating from them. And the older the photograph, the deeper its charms.

And so, when we examine old photographs, we are peering into their secret world. But we are only looking—no one can penetrate this world. At least, that is what I used to think. But now, when I look at the fragments of the stereoscope lying on the table, I know that it is possible. And yet, I know that humans should not enter there, even though we can. A living person should not disturb that dead, frozen world, should not invade its depths. Then, the mysterious balance of those depths becomes disrupted, their sacred and ancient peace is troubled, and the impudent stranger pays for the invasion with a crushing horror. It was in a fit of such terror, trying to save myself from it, that I smashed my stereoscope on that night.

It came into my possession so unexpectedly and served me for so short a time. I was walking down G-ya Street on a frosty morning, the dawn all dressed in white.[1] The sky was gray and the air, a pale blue. Numberless white clouds of winter smoke rose from the chimneys and tried to stay upright, but the sharp eastern wind knocked them sideways and ripped them to shreds, making the whole city fume ominously. Upon reaching the Auction Warehouse, I stopped in front of its large windows, as I had done many times before. On the low, wide windowsills were many different objects, crowded together and in no particular order. Some had numbered tags on them, most likely showing their price, and others did not. But they all, it seemed, had been lying around for too long, and had therefore been put up for sale.

I liked looking at this junk, at these heaps of objects, old-fashioned for the most part, and long since gone out of use. These old things, which had ended up in the warehouse, had once belonged to someone. They seemed to have absorbed the life of the bygone people who once surrounded them, and this now emanated from them like a gentle and melancholy breeze. In the large seashells used on desks as paper weights or decorations, the past sound of their native seas, where they used to lie, lives on eternally, hidden in their depths. The life at the center of which these things once dwelt is long gone; only quiet rustles and whispers of the past emanate from them as they lie in the windows of the warehouse. There were strangely shaped candlesticks, ancient lamps, inkwells, worn-out binoculars—even the shell of a huge lobster in a glass case: bizarre, whitened with time, and of no use to anyone . . . I had seen all of this already many times in these wide windows. But now I noticed one object which had not previously caught my eye. It was a small box of polished wood with two elevations in the form of a tetrahedral prism. I took a closer look. It turned out to be a stereoscope, its large bulging lenses strangely reflecting the light. It came to my mind that I had long wanted to obtain a stereoscope.

Figure 1.2. Evgenia Smirnova-Ivanova, illustration for Alexander Ivanov's "Stereoscope" (St. Petersburg: Sirius, 1909).

Isn't looking at photographs through a stereoscope such a simple, childlike pleasure? And yet, there is a strange magic behind it, and the soul gladly surrenders to its charms. Here is a photograph. In it is a world of frozen phantoms. You put it into the stereoscope and look into it, and suddenly, that world seems closer to you. The flat image has deepened and gained an enigmatic perspective. You are no longer merely looking; instead, you seem to penetrate the depths of this ghostly world. You have not passed into it yet, but there is already a hint of this entrance. The first step has already been made. You feel how the mysterious terror and sadness emanating from the photograph have grown in strength, as if they have come closer to you.

The impression I had the first time I looked into the lenses of a stereoscope will remain with me until the day I die.[2] This happened very long ago, in my childhood. A friend of my father's brought it. "Hold it with your hand," he told me, "and look here." I looked into it, and one of the realms in that strange, alien world opened up to me. It was (as I found out later) an image of the Abu-Simbel Colossi.[3] The gigantic figures of Ramses, carved into a cliff, loomed over me like brownish ghosts, protruding into the air. The air itself was as lifeless and photographic as the statues. The ghostly double of an Arab, who had once lived on earth, was seated on the enormous hand of a Colossus. The perspective and three-dimensionality of this inaccessible realm instantly and unconsciously struck my imagination. I wanted to climb onto the colossus, to walk on its ghostly stone knees, to slip into the caverns hidden from view by its gigantic hands, to pass behind the seated Arab. Everything there was so silent, so frightfully still. The figure of the once-living Arab was as eternally unchanging as the stone faces of the pharaohs, with their sharp protruding beards. How sad and eerie everything was there! Then new images passed in front of us, one after the other: the Colossi of Memnon, views of Rome, the tomb of Napoleon, a square in Paris . . . And for us children, the magical world of the stereoscope was opening further and further. It was new to us, but at the same time felt familiar, strangely reminding us of our childish dreams. All day we couldn't stop thinking about it, and that evening in our nursery we sat remembering and sharing our impressions, speaking quietly, for the sadness and horror of those mysterious lands had already permanently settled in our souls.

That same excitement gripped me when I looked at the small device lost in the heaps of auction rubbish. It was of an old design and seemed similar to that first one I had seen in my childhood. I thought I might buy it if it wasn't too expensive. My legs, freezing in the cold, pushed me into action. I opened the door and entered the Warehouse. There was a vast room, completely filled with racks holding fur coats and other pawned clothes. The corners, like the windows, were packed with old objects. Paintings and portraits hung on the walls. Two men were sitting behind the counter. One of them rose inquiringly to meet me.

"You have a stereoscope on display," I began. "Is it being sold? Right there." The clerk walked up to the window and took it from the windowsill. He looked at the tag stuck onto the side of the stereoscope. "Two rubles," he said, and gave it to me.

The device was unexpectedly heavy, as if there was something else inside it. The lenses also caught my attention: they were unusually convex and reflected the light strangely. I looked at it from all sides. It was clear that it was old and used. The polished wood was badly scratched, and in some places the polish had come off completely. Then a further peculiarity caught my eye—the box was sealed. It did not have the usual slot where photographs are inserted. The back side was made from matte glass, but the wood was tightly fitted everywhere and there were no signs of any openings near it. I mentioned this to the seller. He turned the stereoscope around in his hands a few times and tapped it with a finger, but he found no explanation. He brought the device up to his eyes—and then told me that it already had a photograph inside it. I also looked into it, and saw a picture of one of the halls of the Hermitage. I immediately recognized it as the hall of Zeus the Olympian. An especially strong magic, long familiar to me, blew into my soul. The perspective in this old stereoscope was astonishingly full and deep. Evidently, the lenses had been made to perfection and masterfully placed. I realized that the transparent photograph was tightly embedded in the box, placed flush against the back wall, and not visible from the outside through the matte glass. The whim of the unknown optician—to dedicate the entire device to one photograph—seemed strange and absurd. I hesitated. I mentioned this to the seller, but he was not very amiable. He hinted that he was not terribly concerned whether I bought the device or not. I thought it over for a bit and decided that the back wall could be redone somehow, if need be. I took out my money and the purchase was made.

I returned home only late in the evening. The clock on my neighbor's wall (he rented the adjacent room from my landlady) struck ten as I was lighting the lamp on my desk. For some time, I sat in my armchair, resting and absent-mindedly listening to the muffled sounds coming from the kitchen at the end of the hall, where old Marya was washing the dishes before going to bed. Then I got up and unwrapped my purchase, still cold from the frosty air. And once again, it occurred to me that this stereoscope vaguely resembled that first one I had seen in my distant childhood. I brought it up to the lamp and looked through its lenses into the hall of the dead Hermitage. The photograph must have been taken a very long time ago. I came to this conclusion from several indications that are difficult to describe. I could see that a special method had been used to take the photograph, one no longer used today. Then, I thought I saw that the top right corner had some kind of date written on it. The stereoscope was heavy, and my hands trembled while holding it. So I stacked three large dictionaries, put it on top of them, directed it toward the light of the lamp, and sat down at my desk. Then, comfortably leaning on my elbows, I brought my eyes closer to the lenses. The numbers of the date became more visible, but they were still unclear. I strained my eyes, and it seemed to me that it said "April 21, 1877" or "1879."[4] Did this really mark the day this faded photograph was taken? Even from its appearance it was clear that it was taken long ago, perhaps even at the same time as this stereoscope had been made. "Was it really that long ago?" I asked myself joyfully.

Then the incredible passage into the secret realms of the stereoscope happened. I was sitting, leaning my elbows on the table and looking into the lenses. Before my eyes lay the hall of the Hermitage, familiar, but at the same time a bit alien and frightening, the way familiar rooms and chambers appear to us in our dreams. The double of this hall was somewhat smaller than the original, and of a photographic color. My old excitement grew as the magic of the past overcame me more and more. I wanted to stroll through this dead hall, to wander between its statues and sarcophagi. I wanted to slip into the next hall, which quietly looked through the tall door. Suddenly, it seemed as if the faint smell of my lamp's kerosene was fading, being replaced by some other smell I recognized from elsewhere. Soon, I realized that it reminded me of the smell characteristic of the lower halls of the Hermitage. I watched, transfixed. The ghostly outlines of the hall and its objects started to grow. The hall seemed to be approaching me, taking me in, surrounding me with its walls from behind, from the right and from the left. I already felt I could see them if I only turned my head. And now this hall of the past Hermitage had grown equal in size to the hall of the present Hermitage. All of a sudden, I realized that I was no longer sitting, but standing on the floor. My elbows were no longer propped on the desk, and I lowered my unimpeded arms. Any doubt about the magic that had just occurred finally disappeared. I was standing inside the ghostly hall, which up till now I had only seen from afar through the lenses. My room, desk, and lamp had disappeared. Even the stereoscope itself had disappeared. I was inside of it.

It was dead silent. Only the nervous beating of my heart and ticking of the watch in my waistcoat pocket could be heard. I took a few steps forward, and a strange ringing sound came from under my feet and then died, echoing somewhere in a corner of the ceiling. This sound was familiar to me. It was the sound of footsteps on the stone slabs that make up the floor of the lower Hermitage. Only here it was dull, like the walls and everything else in this world of faded apparitions. I looked to the right. A ghostly light poured into the hall from the windows, high up near the ceiling. A courtyard, roofs, and the colorless photographic sky were visible through them. The weather in this frozen moment was clear and sunny. I looked to the left. The statue of Zeus with an eagle at his feet rose up in its expected place.[5] I had recently been in the Hall of the Olympian, in the real Hall, and I remembered suddenly that behind a wall ledge there should be a bust with a Phrygian cap. I walked forward a little, awakening the dimly whispering echo, and looked behind the ledge. The bust was there, its bygone double. I reached out and touched it. It was cold and hard. This phantom of the past was corporeal. A quiet terror was growing in my heart. With an inexplicable feeling I moved among the urns, statues, and sarcophagi: everything familiar and at the same time alien.

Suddenly, I shuddered, realizing I was not alone. Out of the corner of my eye I saw a dark human figure standing behind me. And it was not a statue. I quickly turned around. A person in a dark frock coat was standing motionless, his gaze focused on the wall, his hand strangely thrown back. Next to him stood some tall object. It was a camera on a tripod. I froze in silent fear. A few seconds passed. He did not move, did not sway or make a single gesture. He stood just as silent and unmoving, in that same strange pose, with the same expression on his face. Then I saw that it was just a phantom, faded and frozen, like everything around it. Suppressing my terror, I walked up to him and looked into his face. His ghostly features were motionless. Seconds passed, then minutes, one after the other, but his eyes and lips retained that same dead immutability. My gaze fell on the apparatus on the tripod, and I saw now that it had two lenses. "It's a stereoscopic camera," I thought. Then it suddenly dawned on me that this was the person who had taken the photograph of Zeus's Hall. This was his sad double! Here he was, a silent and faded, but still corporeal phantom, standing and photographing this bygone hall with his apparatus. He has been doing this already for twenty-eight years, motionless, and will continue to photograph it eternally! Everything that was in that distant moment around the photographer, including himself, had been inexplicably replicated on a thin glass plate, becoming a world hidden in the depths of a stereoscope.

I wanted to touch this silent figure, but for some reason could not make up my mind to do so. I walked around it and went to the adjoining room. It was almost dusk there. I could vaguely discern and recognize the familiar statues sitting here. The large window in its depths barely let in a brownish light, and through it, like in a dream, a wall of the Winter Palace was visible.[6] A new human figure could be vaguely discerned by the window. Walking past it, I saw that it was the double of an usher, standing motionless, with his back turned to me. The dim light from the window reflected strangely on his bald head.

And so began my wanderings through the lifeless rooms of this stereoscopic world, through these irretrievable halls of the Hermitage that had long since floated into the past like a dead and frozen moment. I went from hall to hall, the dull echo of my footsteps ringing in the corners and by the ceiling, dying down behind me every time I neared the doors to a new room, and being reborn once again in front of me. And everywhere there was that distinct smell of the lower Hermitage. Here and there I came across mute and motionless human figures, which looked like faded wax dolls. These were the past visitors to the museum, guards of these irretrievable halls. Each kept his own unchanging pose, glassy eyes fixed in one eternal spot. Sometimes I would catch their gazes on me, or I would look directly at them. Then I would shudder. They stood still, a dead light pouring over them. From them, a mysterious sadness and fear flowed into my soul.

Soon, however, I grew used to this fear and learned to suppress it. I began to grow accustomed to the lifeless forms of the doubles, and, walking past them, I forced myself not to avoid them, but to calmly look into their faces. I even built up the courage to touch one of them. It was a tall, elderly man dressed in a style no longer worn today. He was standing in front of a case filled with ancient weapons and equipment, looking at a small book in his hand. My fingers slid over the rough cloth of his collar and touched the phantom's neck. The skin was not cold like that of a corpse. It retained some sort of warmth, as if it was the faded warmth of a living body. I quickly withdrew my hand. The book he was holding was a catalogue of the antiquities of the Bosporus, an old edition. I carefully turned over a page and heard the soft rustle of the ghostly paper. I shuddered as I saw another figure, sensing something familiar in it. In the real version of this narrow hall of the Bosporus, with its echoing wooden floors, I used to see and sometimes talk to that old usher. He disappeared a few years ago. He must have died. And now, in the gloomy past hall of the Bosporus, I recognized my old acquaintance in the faded figure seated before me. Only his double was a lot younger, not yet a gray-haired old man. Thus he was when I first met him, long ago, as a child, when my father brought me to the Hermitage for the first time and we entered into the narrow hall that kept the antiquities of the Scythians. I walked away, deeply astonished.

So I roamed through this inaccessible realm. At times I would stop, my footsteps would die down, and then the silence of these strange halls became inexpressibly dead and deep. It cannot be compared to any other silence. And these irretrievable chambers were so full of shadows, so mysterious, terrifying, and sad. It is never particularly light in the halls of the lower Hermitage, even on brightly sunny days, and the dim radiance from the sky of the stereoscopic world poured over the brownish halls only a hazy mysterious twilight, which especially thickened in distant corners and nooks. Now and again, submitting to that pull which arises in us toward the unknown and frightening, I purposefully went to these dark corners to identify them and remember them. In them, I would vaguely discern a once-familiar vase on a stand, or a case with Tanagra statuettes. At times, I also met mute motionless human figures, irresistibly eerie in the deep twilight of the solitary corners. I had now fully conquered my fear, and though it remained lurking in my heart, a hitherto unknown bliss permeated me more and more. I thought about how inexpressible and insatiably strange this all was.

Figure 1.3. Evgenia Smirnova-Ivanova, illustration for Alexander Ivanov's "Stereoscope" (St. Petersburg: Sirius, 1909).

I reached the vestibule. The grand staircase leading to the upper halls opened before me, and it became lighter. The same puppet-like, long-gone people stood by the coat racks. I briefly saw the brown face of a porter holding a coat, and the glassy eyes of the person he was motionlessly helping into his coat. For a moment their gaze fell on me as I walked past. I began, slowly, to go up the sloping steps. I remembered that day, long, long ago, when I ascended the marble staircase of the Hermitage for the first time, with my father. I once again lived through the bewilderment I felt in front of an endless series of steps, and the strange strain in my legs. And now, standing in the depths of a moment frozen thirty years ago, looking at a faded phantom of the staircase, I thought to myself, "Maybe only last night, I, as a boy, with my father, walked up these stairs for the first time? Or maybe, I will walk up them for the first time today, in half an hour?" Then I asked myself whether I was perhaps asleep. Was it in my dreams that I was seeing this incredible realm of the stereoscope? I ran my hand along the glossy wall and clearly felt its hardness and smoothness. I pinched my cheek and pulled my hair a few times, thinking I would wake up, but I did not.

The upper halls of the Hermitage were brighter, though the light coming through the windows and glass ceilings was still ghostly and gloomy. The parquet floor gave rise to footsteps more resonant and lingering than the stone slabs of the lower levels. The ghosts of familiar halls were revealed to me one after the other. Rows of paintings, familiar, but devoid of their living colors, watched me from the walls. There were notably more deceased visitors up here than down below. There were crowds of them everywhere. It was as if I was present at a ghastly gathering of human-sized wax figures. They stood, fixing their lifeless gazes on paintings, some with their heads slightly tilted back. Some looked at their catalogues, or silently conversed with one another, their mouths eternally opened, making their faces look strange and at times ugly. Others were sitting on chairs and couches. Some old man, it seemed, was trying to explain something to two ladies (both from the past, just like him!) and his eternal pose was bizarre. He was somewhat crouching down, leaning slightly to one side and spreading his arms, his unchanging face at the same time terrifying and funny. I was the only one alive amongst these faded, ghostlike figures; I alone had entered their irretrievable dwelling! But fear seemed to have left my soul completely. The magic of the past completely took possession of it: those old premonitions of this strange bliss had come true.

Suddenly it occurred to me to disturb the silence of these halls of the past. I let out a loud, drawn-out yell: "A-a-a-a-a!" How can I describe my impression of this yell? It quickly sobered me from my ecstasy, and once again instilled a gnawing terror in my heart. The sound hit the wall and ran across the cornice, faded and frightening. "A-a-a!" it rang from the next hall. "A-a!" "a-a!" it echoed further and further through the vast ghostly chambers. And it seemed that the echo went through all the dead halls above, went down to the gloomy chambers of the lower level, and dimly continued even there. Upstairs and below, listening to it were only the unanswering doubles, frozen in their places. And when the last echo froze and died down, an inexpressibly deep and eternal silence returned to the ghostly halls. I didn't yell anymore after that.

My fear subsided a bit, and I once again wandered from room to room, bringing the colorless echo of my footsteps into their silence. I once again found myself by the staircase, its countless steps leading down to the brownish twilight of the vestibule. By the coat racks, I once again saw the double who was stiffly leaning forward, his outstretched arms catching the coat invariably being given to him. And once again, for a moment, his persistent gaze crossed my path. The semi-darkness and coolness of the lower Hermitage enveloped me once more.

The Egyptian Hall faced me, deeply familiar and at the same time alien in its ghostliness.[7] Even in reality the hall lacks lively colors and light, but here it enveloped me fully faded, brownish, and drowning in a deathly darkness. It was infinitely silent, frightening, and enticing. Assyrian bas-reliefs leaned against the walls in the mysterious dusk. Large, swaddled figures, with menacingly cheerful and secretive faces, looked out from glass cases. Sarcophagi stood in somber rows. The dark form of Sekht with a lion's head towered over me. Nowhere else was the strange dusk of the stereoscopic world so thick and gloomy as it was here. Especially deep shadows lay between the ledges of that wall, where up by the ceiling there were two square windows with winged figures. Something terrible emanated from those dark corners, where my eyes, still used to the brightness of the upper halls, at first could not distinguish a single thing. I stood motionless for a few minutes, listening to the dead silence of the distant past. A vague thought was going through my mind. "Perhaps only half an hour ago a boy and his father entered this hall for the first time, and for the first time the mysterious charms of Ancient Egypt, emanating from the dark stone sarcophagi and painted wooden coffins, washed over his soul."

Figure 1.4. Evgenia Smirnova-Ivanova, illustration for Alexander Ivanov's "Stereoscope" (St. Petersburg: Sirius, 1909).

Then I walked over to one of the round display cases and looked into it. There were amulets and sacred scarab beetles, large and small, in all shades, light and dark, of a gloomy brown. I looked at them, and suddenly had the thought to retrieve one of them from the case. This thought was frightening, yet enticing. Mechanically, without thinking about what I was doing, I pressed my fingers against the glass. Suddenly it crunched strangely, and a piece of it fell into the case. A piteous ringing sound swept through the hall. The opening in the glass was still too small, so I started to take out another piece. I stood bent over, but out of the corner of my eye I could vaguely discern a dark crevice to my left, between two ledges of the wall. Soon my hand entered the case, and I took out one of the scarabs. Marveling, I felt the cold hardness of the ghostly stone.

Then a sudden fear entered me, as I felt upon me a fixed, heavy gaze. It was coming from the darkness of that crevice I had noticed to my left. I quickly looked over. There, in the corner behind a small white statue, a short dark figure stood in silence, looming out of the darkness. It must have been staring at me from the moment I reached the display case. And now, as I turned in its direction, not yet raising my head, my eyes met with its stubbornly fixed eyes, weakly reflecting the light. I straightened, stumbled back, avoiding its dead gaze. This was not the first time I had felt the frozen looks of the inhabitants of this world on me, but these eyes were especially frightening. I sensed reproach and threat in them, as if I had been caught at a crime scene. Then I suddenly realized that I had committed a mysterious sacrilege by plundering the case that held the scarabs' dark doubles. With the amulet in my hand, suppressing my growing fear, I started to approach the phantom. I saw that it was a decrepit old woman, short and hunched over, in an ancient dark coat, with a strange hat on her head. Stepping forward, she leaned on her umbrella, fixing her heavy gaze on a single eternal point. Vague thoughts and impressions were trying to form words in my head. "Almost thirty years ago, some strange old woman, God knows why, wandered into the Hermitage and roamed through its lower halls. And, having entered the Egyptian Hall, she stopped in a corner, and from there looked straight ahead, slightly above the case with the scarabs, pointlessly and mysteriously, with her old eyes. And from that moment her frozen double in the inaccessible realms of the stereoscope eternally guards, with its glassy gaze, these dark amulets, and with them the deep secrets of these realms. Then I came in, and with my audacious theft, encroached upon these secrets . . ." That is what I said to myself about the old woman.

I walked up to her from the side, avoiding the dead stare of her eyes. I walked behind her. I forced myself to touch her coat. I lifted up its edge, let it go, and then watched it weakly sway and move, until it became motionless again. She looked like an ugly and terrifying mannequin. I could get a good look at her now. A dry, bony hand convulsively gripped the handle of the umbrella. I could see the phantom's wrinkly cheek, and the brown tones of its face. Its thin hair began above the ear and went under its old-fashioned hat. I already wanted to move away, but a strange force pulled me to look into her eyes once more. I bent down and resolutely looked into them. And now I could closely see, only half a yard from my own face, that which had frightened me from afar. For a moment I saw all of the frozen details of the eyes before me, and I stumbled back with a shiver of horror. Then, something hideous and frightening happened: the mannequin rocked forward, and started to lean slowly to one side, then more and more, until it finally collapsed on the floor, softly, almost soundlessly. The umbrella fell from its hand and hit the tiles of the floor with a pale sound. With a scream of terror, I jumped back and froze, looking at the double. It was lying in a dark, motionless heap, and the echo of my scream ran across the ceiling, dimly dying in the silence of the ghostly halls. I stood like this for a few more moments, then turned, and ran out into the vestibule.

I ran for a long time. Then I finally stopped, a cold sweat on my forehead, my heart pounding violently. I tried to come to my senses, to understand what had just happened. Why did she fall over? Did I snag her inadvertently? Or did one of the tiles on the floor shift under my feet? It seemed, and I was becoming convinced, that the old woman was guarding the faded Egyptian Hall, and with her fall, the terrifying secrets of the ghostly hall and the whole irretrievable world were disturbed. The mysterious terror in my heart, hitherto conquered, now broke free and took possession of it. And for the first time the thought came to my mind: "How do I return? How do I get out of here?"

Only then did I realize what despair awaited me. I was a lonely living being, lost in these dead realms, cut off from the world of life and the present by an impenetrable border. I did not know how I had entered here. How could I possibly find the way out? And even if I could find the exit eventually, how much time would pass before then? What if before then something happens to the stereoscope, standing on my desk under the lamp? Am I doomed to stay forever in this dull world inhabited only by eternally immutable doubles of the past, where, in a dim hall, there motionlessly lies a silent phantom with terrifying eyes? I was bathed in a cold sweat, and my heart whimpered in fear and confusion.

Then I decided to not allow this fear to fully take me over. I tried to consider everything rationally, to think about what I should do. Looking around, I saw that I was standing not far from some large bookshelves. Ten steps from me rose a huge head on a high pedestal, faint and familiar. To the front, back, and left of me, faded expanses of vast chambers receded into the distance. I positioned myself in the dark corner between the wall and the bookshelf, and pressed my back against the wall, so that none of the silent visitors of the hall would be behind me. There I stood silently—as if I myself was someone's quiet double—and tried to gather my thoughts. But for a long time, I was unsuccessful. My eyes only aimlessly and semiconsciously studied the veins on the marble of the ghostly wall, half a yard away from me. And in my head, arbitrary lines of verse floated pointlessly and persistently, and God knows why they popped up in my memory: "And as if with a groan in the dark abyss it echoed and died, echoed and died . . ."

Then my heart started to beat more calmly, my thoughts cleared. And suddenly, almost on its own, the answer to this frightening question appeared. I realized there was only one path on which I could try my luck: I needed to find that spot on the floor from which I made the first step in my journey through the depths of the stereoscope. I needed to stand there and wait. What else could I do? Perhaps that same miracle which brought me here would carry me out of this world and back to life and the present. I left my hiding spot and headed toward the hall of Zeus. I walked carefully, trying not to wake an echo with my steps, not stopping, and not looking at the sparse figures keeping watch in the dusk. I passed one hall, then the next. Here, the usher, my old acquaintance; there, the tall double with the catalogue in his hand. The long row of ghostly halls turned left, and at the end of it, the Hall of the Olympian became visible; at its center, the unmoving figure of the photographer came into view. There was the small half-dark room, the bald man still standing facing the window, light dimly reflecting off his head. And here, finally, was the hall of Zeus.

I walked up to the photographer and moved as close as possible to his apparatus. The lenses were only an inch away from my face, right at eye level. Then, not moving from my spot, I turned around and carefully touched the back of my head to the lenses. I froze like this, only slowly and slightly turning my head left and right. Finally, it seemed, I had found what I was looking for. From this point, at this angle, the picture of this hall was taken—thirty years ago, by the phantom now standing quietly behind me. I was standing in the exact spot where my feet had first touched the floor of this past hall. I waited, but nothing was changing, and despair once again started to take over. But then, with a joyful stopping of my heart, I felt something. I felt that I was freeing myself from the depths of the hall. Its walls shrunk, as if they were moving back into the distance. The smell of kerosene once again entered my nostrils, and I again heard the muffled chiming of the clock behind my neighbor's wall. Then I grew conscious that I was sitting, as I was before, in my room in front of a lit lamp, leaning my elbows on the desk, and touching my brows to the prismatic tubes of the stereoscope. The ghostly hall, visible through the lenses, again seemed distant and external.

Joy swept over me. With a sigh of relief, I stood up and paced my room, hardly daring to believe my senses. I tried to think some things over, to understand something, but my head was heavy and spinning, and my thoughts were confused. I turned off the lamp, staggered into bed, and lay down without getting undressed. I didn't notice when I fell asleep.

## II

My sleep was heavy but dreamless. When I awoke, a new frosty day had already risen and was peeking through the gaps in my blinds with bluish rays. I lay there for awhile, and then suddenly remembered. Everything that had happened the previous night seemed like a dream to me. "What a strange dream," I thought, "just like in my childhood! I must have fallen asleep in front of the stereoscope last night." In that same moment I felt a dull pain in my side—that is to say, I turned my attention to it, for it had vaguely troubled me before. In my right pocket there turned out to be some kind of hard object, and, lying on my side, I was pressing down on it. I propped myself up, and from my pocket, I took out a thick disk about two inches in diameter: a stone, by the feel of it. I rushed to the window, ripped open the blinds, and looked at it by the light. What had happened last night was not a dream! I put the scarab on my desk, examining it in disbelief, and telling myself: it is from the past! It was the same as it was when I took it out of the case in the mysterious hall: dark brown, rough to the touch, and rather heavy. It was still warm from being in my pocket, and was slowly cooling down, like a real stone. I must have unconsciously slipped it into my pocket during my wild flight.

Then my gaze fell on the stereoscope. It was where I had left it at night, on a pile of books. I sat down at the desk and peered into its convex, strangely shiny lenses. Like in a dream that is being dreamed a second time, I saw the dark walls, the white sarcophagus in the distance, the ledge, hiding the head in the Phrygian cap, all looking out at me. The floor on which I had walked was still shining. The adjoining halls were visible behind the door where I had wandered yesterday, where now the frightful double of the old woman lies. I shuddered and looked away from the lenses, fearing that this dead hall would approach me again and swallow me into its depths.

My door cracked open, and Marya poked her head in. "You're already up?" she asked. "But your clothes haven't been cleaned, and your boots . . ." She looked at the desk. "Why are you wasting kerosene? You left the house last night but left the lamp on. As I was going to bed, I saw a light. The door was unlocked, I looked in: you were not there, only the lamp was burning. I wanted to extinguish it, but saw you had things stacked on your desk. I thought I might get scolded, so I didn't touch it." "That's alright, Marya," I said. "I only left for a short while, and it's good that you did not touch anything on the desk. As for the clothes, I think today they can go without cleaning." "Alright, well, if they don't need it. It's already past nine." And she left. I wondered what she would have thought if she had looked into the stereoscope yesterday during my absence, and suddenly saw me, exiting through the doors of the strange hall hidden behind its lenses. Or, if Marya had really decided to extinguish the lamp on my desk, what would have happened to me? Black darkness would have spilled over the chambers where I wandered. And I would have been left alone in them, staggering about in horror and despair, stumbling upon frozen doubles in the darkness and knocking them over! This thought made my heart freeze.

I sat at my desk for a long time, recalling what I had experienced in the night. It was coming back to me: its images, feelings, and vague thoughts. I thought of the world of the past, which dimly echoes the footsteps and voice of the intruder but is itself eternally silent, this past world which is like a faded ghost of real life, but at the same time strangely corporeal and tangible. I thought of its inhabitants, and it seemed to me that maybe they are not fully dead. They are unmoving, and their faces are unchanging, but perhaps there is a semblance of feeling buried in them, as frozen and faded as they themselves are. Are they not the source of the great and quiet sadness that the world of the stereoscope is so full of, which seeps from the walls, from the ceilings, from every object, from the pale sky itself, into the soul of the person who has looked into its lenses? Are they not silently and eternally mourning that which has irretrievably passed with them? Or maybe some of the doubles are filled with a deathly malice when living eyes from our world look into their realms. For the realms in the stereoscopic depths are frightening and terrible, especially where the dusk has fallen more thickly. Is it not the anger of those doubles at being observed, having their realms invaded, that fills the walls, ceilings, galleries, and ghostly chambers with horror? Is it not this terror and fear that flows into the heart of the person looking into the lenses? Then, the frightening image of the old woman reappeared in my mind.

Suddenly, amid my thoughts about her, there appeared a distant, long-forgotten image, some kind of old, old memory, buried in my soul without a trace for many years. Perhaps it was a snippet from a dream I had in my distant childhood! It seemed to me now that somewhere in the murky past I had already met with or dreamed of this strange image of the old woman. And even more hazily, even more vaguely, I remembered meeting her in some vast and gloomy room. My imagination began to weave its fabric, trying to reconstruct the parts of this fragmented vision that had disappeared without a trace, trying to establish the new, mysterious connections. Then it prompted me: almost thirty years ago, a boy and his father stood in a hall of the Hermitage, then still a living one, and the majestic mysteries of Ancient Egypt entered the boy's soul for the first time. And it was then that his eyes prophetically met, for a brief moment, the decrepit eyes of some old woman. They parted ways, and he never saw her again; the frightening memory of her did not stay long. On that day, after their encounter, she wandered aimlessly through the vast galleries for a long time, and again entered the Egyptian Hall, and was there in the moment frozen in the stereoscope. And now her double in the faded hall became the eternal keeper of secrets of past worlds.

I finally awoke from my thoughts and daydreams. The stereoscope was on the desk in front of me. I was looking at it with a strange feeling, in which fear was intertwined with an old attraction. I decided to put it away. I wrapped it in newspaper and hid it in my closet. It was time to go to the department. I locked the scarab in my desk, got dressed, and left the house.

The whole day I was in a fog, enveloped by the impressions from my nighttime wanderings. At the department, I only sat idly, oblivious to the papers spread out in front of me, immersed in the incredible memories. The thought of going *there* a second time did not cross my mind for a long while. My soul still harbored the remnants of my nighttime fear. But hours passed, and the ancient, enticing charms of that world, which would not leave me, finally gave me that thought. And I told myself that it was shameful to fully give in to fear, that having felt it during my first wanderings, I can cross the boundary of the lenses a second time with a greater calmness and grip on myself. Then I suddenly remembered: I already knew the way out of *there*. I felt a giddy excitement. The danger of being stuck eternally in the woeful realms of the past no longer threatened me. That obstacle to the mysterious temptations of the stereoscope disappeared. I already thought more calmly about the old lady, and once again, from the depths of my memory arose the vague vision, perhaps from a dream, of that first distant encounter with her. I marveled again at the many hidden ties in the fates of men. Time, usually so slow, quickly passed in emboldened daydreams. I imagined what would happen if I decided to enter there again . . . I would not only stay in the halls of the Hermitage. I would reach the front door, open it, and go out and roam the streets of the past . . . Then the thought came to me that it would be colder on the streets than in the halls. I remembered the date in the corner of the photograph: "April 21," the end of April . . . and I thought that I should bring my coat and hat . . . I tore myself away from my dreams. The blue frosty day was fading outside the windows. Electric lamps were already casting their light on the desks and walls, and the ceiling was immersed in the shadows of their lampshades. Amid the tobacco smoke, brightly illuminated heads leaned over desks, and the sounds of restrained conversation and the rustle of paper were heard. The world of life and the present overcame me so forcefully that I asked myself whether I had not lost my mind, and was thinking nonsense. But remembering the scarab, I pressed my fist into my right side, and the dull pain convinced me that it really had been in my pocket this morning.

As the day went on, I did not stop thinking about it all: not when leaving the Department, nor at the restaurant for lunch, nor at the house of a friend whom I visited on some business. When I finally returned home around nine, I had already made a terrifying decision. I lit the lamp, retrieved the stereoscope, and put it on the stack of books, like I had done the night before. Then I lowered the blinds and locked the door, so that Marya in her diligence would not cause a disaster. Seating myself at the desk, I checked whether there was enough kerosene in the lamp. Then I remembered, stood up, and got my coat, scarf, and hat. Fully dressed, I finally sat down at the desk. My heart was stuttering with a vague, aching terror, but I resolutely brought my eyes closer to the lenses and began to look.

About a minute passed, and then the previous day's feeling returned, and the magical crossing of the terrifying line was completed. I was once again standing at the center of the dead hall. I turned around and intently gazed into the face of the motionless photographer. Stiffness distorted his features, but still it seemed inspired and significant, and the lifeless eyes had sadness and depth. He looked to be in his fifties, his temples visibly gray. Was this man, whose double remained here as the quiet photographer, perhaps also the maker of the stereoscope itself? Was this not perhaps the ghost of the man who had found the forbidden passage into the lands of the past, standing here in front of me, mourning bygone days? That's what I said to myself about him.

I then headed to the vestibule, taking the same path around again, through all of the lower halls, for I was afraid to pass through the Egyptian Hall. And again, the echo of my steps rang out dully and died by the cornices. The mournful dusk still reigned over the vast chambers, and the inhabitants stood here and there, like wax dolls, keeping watch from dark corners. Some were secretly angry at me, others mourned what had passed. And again, an incomparable, dead silence ruled whenever I stopped. And so, I reached the vestibule. I was right by the front door, but, submitting to a strange impulse, I paused. Then, I slowly and carefully walked to the entrance of the Egyptian Hall, took about three steps past its threshold with a coldness in my heart, and stopping there, looked around. Everything was as it had been the day before. Only now at the end of the hall I could make out in the semidarkness two ghostly figures I had not noticed before. I turned to the case with a gaping hole in the broken glass, stood up on tiptoe, and peered over it into the space behind it, under the windows. There, in the dead twilight, I could see a dark object, resembling a pile of rags. Having satisfied my terrible curiosity, I quickly turned back, walked up to the front door, and pulled it. The door opened softly and soundlessly. And here I was, standing on the long-gone porch, surrounded by gigantic atlantes.[8]

I saw a street going left, familiar and at the same time alien and frightening, the way well-known places can sometimes appear to us in dreams. The huge square opened up to the right, the Column in the center, which I had seen so many times already, but here it was distorted in the way of an oneiric reverie. Everything here was a deathly brown shade—the pavement, the sidewalks, the long rows of houses, the misty cathedral in the distance, and the dull sky above. I left the porch. The pavement was dry, but in some places, there were puddles, some with motionless ripples, others smooth as a mirror. These clearly reflected the ghosts of houses. The surrounding air was still. But it was a lot colder than in the halls, and I did not regret bringing my coat and hat. I came across various pedestrians, frozen in strange poses, one leg put forward with the foot pointing up, the other leg back. Observing them, I realized that a strong wind was incomprehensibly frozen in the deathly stillness of the air. Their coats waved and billowed motionlessly, and some people were leaning forward, holding their hats. It was a wind from the past.

I quietly wandered through the wide, sorrowful space. This was how people had seen the living square thirty years ago. Some things had changed on it since then. And it seemed strange to me that no eye now would be able to see the square like *this*, and that like *this* it is forever gone. The dark, dead façade of the Winter Palace stretched out in front of me, ending to the left, allowing me to freely see the distant crowds of ghostly houses across the river. This was how things used to be. Marveling, I thought that from this spot in the living square, no one will ever again be able to see those buildings: the high railing of the new garden in front of the palace covers them.[9] A terrible silence reigned, not a sound to be heard, except for the faint echo of my footsteps, disappearing without a trace in the open expanse. I looked up, and saw, for the first time, in the colorless sky, a ghost of the sun, illuminating this monstrous world. It was still quite high up in the sky, but it was much dimmer than the living sun. One could look at it without squinting. It poured a sad light over this strange, dead city. Somber shadows fell from the Column and buildings. And the shadows of lone pedestrians and rare carriages, with horses frozen on the run and silent riders, were just as motionless as the figures themselves. The huge needle shone dully and lifelessly above the familiar white tower. The gold in its radiance had faded and died. The rays of the long-gone sun weakly but noticeably gave some warmth.

Then I went out onto a large, wide street, which I recognized as the Nevsky Prospect of the past.[10] It was flooded with silent inhabitants of the faded city. I passed some, overtook others: men, children, on their own, in pairs, or in whole crowds. On the wide sidewalks it appeared as if they were walking, but not leaving their spots and not moving. Many of their frozen poses were bizarre, at times ridiculous. Some seemed to be carelessly strolling, while others hurried forward, a strange look of concern on their faces. On the opposite side of the street, they were also moving in a dark, continuous line. Their cabs, coaches, and carriages motionlessly rolled along the pavement in both directions. It was the height of traffic, as if the people from the past rejoiced at the bright radiance of their ghostly sun, poured out onto their Nevsky, and sadly and horribly played the game of life. And it seemed to me that they were all hiding something from me, and that they secretly mourned that which had irretrievably passed with them.

The rows of houses that went off into the distance were familiar to me, but monstrous, as in a deep dream. I kept walking forward. Sometimes I would look ahead into the vast faded avenue, and as far as my eyes could reach, darker and darker, infinite crowds of ghosts thickened along it. From a distance they looked more like living, moving people. But whenever I approached, I could see that these were only frozen doubles of people that had once lived and moved. There, in the distance, was a group of phantoms. They seemed to be walking towards me, their faces directed to me. I got closer and closer to them. Their faces were visible more clearly, they were motionlessly staring forward, and I already felt their dead, stubborn gaze on me. Some were turned towards each other with frozen smiles. Now we were on the same level. I could closely and clearly see their faded features, either strange or frightening. Then I passed them. Then came new strangers, new crowds, and everything was frozen and colorless, and a great sadness emanated from everything and entered my heart. Everyone was as silent as the dead. They remained speechless by the temple with the dull colonnade, as well as here, across from the receding mass of the Theater, leaving entrances, crossing roads. There were no voices to be heard, no whispers, no laughter, no noise from the carriages, no droning of a great city. There was only eternal and terrible silence, disturbed solely by the quickly fading echoes of my steps. A quiet, mysterious fear beat loudly in my heart, but it was under control . . . And I kept thinking that no one else on the living Nevsky will ever see the things hidden here. And I looked, marveling, at the clothes of a long-gone style on the phantoms, at the past stores, and forgotten signs . . .

That is how I walked, alone, with only my silent shadow on the colorless stones as my companion. A lone living person was walking further and further, drowning in the depths of a vast dead city, lost among its hundreds of thousands of houses, each one inhabited from top to bottom with silent ghosts.[11] Around me, streets crossed each other and stretched out for miles, squares spread out, and on them stood the silently frozen doubles of once-living people. Everything in the city was insatiably strange, and sadness and horror emanated from every corner. I was reminded of an old Arabic tale about the City of Brass, which Emir Musa and Sheikh Abd-al-Samad had once entered.

I somehow ended up in a dark, narrow street. I was walking down the sidewalk when I suddenly shuddered and stopped, my heart pounding. I remembered, I recognized this place and the ghost of an old gloomy house on the other side! In the world I come from, I know this street well. For many, many years I have walked on its stones. Life and the present imperceptibly transformed it from year to year, subtly changing its appearance. Then they destroyed that house and put a new one in its place. And this old, forgotten street, and this gloomy house, hidden in the depths of a stereoscope, drifted deeper and deeper into the past. But now I had once again entered here, and I stood looking at the infinitely familiar windows of the fourth floor, where I had lived as a child!

I walked up to the entrance with trepidation. Yes! There were the two dark crooked steps, those same steps! I remembered every detail of them. And there, the old glass front door: I recognized it, I recognized it again! There it was, the deserted, forgotten, and again infinitely familiar staircase! A gloomy dusk reigned, just like back then, and a faint smell of gas was perceptible, just like back then! Then comes the inner glass door. It slammed shut behind me, and a sad ringing sound, once often heard, passed over the ghostly stairs and for a few moments filled it from top to bottom. In my soul, in a hazy stream, childhood memories flowed one after the other, one after the other. To the right under the stairs was a narrow stone platform, and I wondered how in the span of all these years I never once remembered it. In the past, my childlike imagination would dwell in its darkness. There was the first flight of stairs. I counted the steps. There were thirteen, like back then. My gaze paused on the third one from the top. On its left side it had a large crack. Something stirred in my memory, then joyously awoke, and now I remembered this completely

Figure 1.5. Evgenia Smirnova-Ivanova, illustration for Alexander Ivanov's "Stereoscope" (St. Petersburg: Sirius, 1909).

forgotten crack in the stone, I remembered all of its branches. I stood on the platform, and saw the gloomy courtyard through the wide window, and the inner wings of the house. And everything appeared to me as if in a reverie, like something dreamed before that I was dreaming again. The rows of windows, the roofs with chimneys and windvanes, the distant merging mass of a ghostly city . . . Everything was like it was *then,* but faded and long-gone. I went up the stairs, and their silence was disrupted only by the sound of my footsteps, returning to their deep silence whenever I stopped. I went from one floor to the next, and on each platform, there was a vaguely familiar door. And my memories, waking up from a long sleep, recognized, in the dim twilight, the outlines of these doors, the little windows above them, the rows of upholstery nails, the plaques with the names of the residents, and joyously whispered:

"Just like back *then*!" I looked at the plaques. The names on them, the names of our neighbors, which I used to hear as a child from the adults in those long-gone days. Here, behind these ghostly doors, now lived their doubles, silently and mysteriously. The plaques shone with a dead brilliance, the living radiance of the brass faded. And their shape was the same as before: rectangles with cut-off corners.

I finally reached the last flight of stairs and looked up. Dear God, there was our door! Excitement and fear gripped me. I went up the stairs to the platform. There, on the door, was the plaque with my father's name, and the letters, once carefully studied by my eyes, and deeply forgotten! There, the narrow windows at the top. Through the windows I could see the ceiling of the entrance hall and the top of the mirror standing against the wall, submerged in the dusk. I could see the doorbell. Its outside handle was here, in front of me. I touched it with my hand. Not knowing why, I pulled it, and behind the door rang out a sound, long-forgotten and faded, yet familiar. And the ghostly bell, visible through the glass, swayed as it used to.

Then I noticed that the door was not fully closed. One half was ajar, forming a gap. I pushed the door. It gave, and then stopped. Something was holding it from the inside. Of course! There was a chain there. Someone forgot to lock the door, but the chain was put up, stopping it. I put my hand through the gap and felt around until it touched the cold chain. I could hear how it released and hit the door with a muffled sound. The door opened slowly, and the entryway from my past appeared to me, like in a dream! There, in the dusk, were the coat racks, where I would hide playfully. The smell of the place seemed to spill around me, filling my nostrils, joyfully recognized in the uncharted depths of my memory. And in the semi-darkness, my eyes once again followed the pattern of the wallpaper and the cornice, mysteriously confirmed by the depths of my memory: "It's just like it was!" There was the old mirror by the wall. Who was looking out of it at me in the quiet darkness? It was myself, in a coat and with a hat in my hands, reflected in its ghostly depths. Me, a living person, in a phantom mirror. And everything around me was faded and filled with a sadness for the past.

There was a doorway to the right: my father's study. My heart stopped as I looked in and recognized the dark walls, the round stove and ceiling. I made up my mind and entered the room. It was resurrected before me more clearly and terribly than in my dreams! My God, who was sitting there at the table by the couch? A motionless phantom of a person . . . It was him! I approached it, painfully and eerily recognizing those dear features again. I walked around the chair, looked at the crown and back of the head, at the hands lying on his knees, and the agitated voices of my memory confirmed every detail of what I saw. I remembered him the way he was before he left us forever, fifteen years ago. And now his silent double sat before me. His face was motionless, and had no living colors, but I could still see that the face of the double was younger than his last face in the world of the living. His expression was lighter and there were fewer wrinkles, the mournful folds around his lips were not as deep yet. He sat as if deep in thought, and I watched him, insatiable. Thirty years had passed since then! I sat down on the faded sofa across from him, and we sat together like we had in those distant golden days, here, in the same spots. I again felt the long-forgotten springiness of the couch, and again smelled the faint scent of tobacco smoke inherent to this room. The desk, the paintings on the walls, the bookshelves, all were like they used to be, and surrounded us like back then. The courtyard, once so familiar to my eyes, was visible through the window. Everything was as it had been in those distant years, when I sat as a boy with my father in his study. But alas, we cannot return what has passed. I am no longer a boy, and across from me is just the sad double of my father. Everything

Figure 1.6. Evgenia Smirnova-Ivanova, illustration for Alexander Ivanov's "Stereoscope" (St. Petersburg: Sirius, 1909).

was ghostly and long gone: the desk, the bookshelves, the paintings, the old courtyard outside the window. Everything was filled with an aching sadness for the past. And my father too, it seemed, silently mourned that the past would not return, would never return. And I mourned with him. Strange tears welled up in my throat.

Then I got up and walked further. I entered the long-dead living room, and everything in it looked at me, once so familiar and now ghostly and forgotten. The dark wallpaper, the three windows with flower pots facing the wall of the opposite house, the two tall mirrors . . . The rays of the past sun fell on the floor and reflected off the parquet with dead brilliance. Then, I saw the ghost of a girl, sitting by the open piano, her fingers flying motionlessly across the keys. I bent over to her frozen, faded face, no longer asking myself who she was. And my memories, awaking from their long slumber, confirmed: these, these were her features when we were children and played in this room! All that had been lost and forgotten in my memory was confirmed and resurrected. I stood by the piano, and both of us, a dead double and a living person, were reflected together in the ghostly mirror by the wall.

A faded row of rooms opened up before me. My steps rang out dully as I walked through them. At the end of the row, a sad room mysteriously looked out at me. It was our past nursery, once so completely ordinary. Its former table was visible. Someone was sitting at it, his shadow on the floor, but he himself was not visible, hidden behind the door. I approached and looked in. A phantom of a boy was sitting there. He looked to be about seven or eight. Silently and motionlessly, he was looking through a book in front of him, on the table. Then, my heart stopping, I realized that this was my double! That dark little coat was mine; I used to wear it. And I had seen that book many, many times before, that old and tattered magazine. The dead book was open to a page with a large engraving depicting the head of a giant with closed eyes and earrings in his ears, two knights with swords, three ladies, and their gloomy surroundings.[12] I recognized an image in it, one that had been vaguely and incoherently stored in my memory from my distant childhood; now, I finally knew where it came from. It was the memory of this old book, not seen by me for many, many years. The double sat quietly and dolefully, its frozen eyes fixed on the engraving, and I eagerly looked into its colorless features, recognizing my own current face in them, already mysteriously hidden in them. I stepped back, went to the window, and once again, for the first time in thirty years, looked out at our old, dead street. It lay narrow and unwelcoming, like I had seen it as a child sitting by this same window. Pedestrians and cabbies were frozen down below in the brown shadows of its houses.

Figure 1.7. Evgenia Smirnova-Ivanova, illustration for Alexander Ivanov's "Stereoscope" (St. Petersburg: Sirius, 1909).

I wandered through the room, touching its walls, once so ordinary. I picked up my old toys, completely forgotten. In a dark corner I found my horse, which I had always had a vague memory of. It seemed so small to me now. A hole gaped in its side, and bending over, I caught the once-familiar smell of *papier-mâché* wafting from it. My old bed was at the end of the room. I walked up to it and had a strange idea. I lay down in it. It creaked and moved under me, and my legs did not fit onto it. I lay there and seemed to forget myself, and it seemed to me that I myself was from the past. From here I could see the damper by the stove with two round handles on it, which used to seem to me, from my pillow, like a pair of someone's angry, stubborn eyes. And above me, on the ceiling, I saw the round stucco decoration that I had once studied at every twist and turn on my pillow. How far these objects had sunk into the depths of my memory! Never in my life since had they floated to the surface. But it seemed to me that now, I myself had descended to those depths where they were concealed. That I myself had become a memory, and as I looked at their faded forms, marveling, the voices of my memory joyously exclaimed: "These are the memories you have forgotten for so many years!" I woke from my fleeting oblivion: I was alive, after all. I turned my head toward the windows. There, by the table, his back to me, silently sat he whom I once was—the doleful phantom of a boy.

Then I entered the other rooms, one after the other, in constant wonder. I walked through the dark corridor with the old closets along the walls. At the end of it usually gaped the dark bathroom, populated with my childhood fears. In the dim dining room, I saw the old wall clock and remembered again its forgotten form. It motionlessly showed the time as a little after three. I recognized again the lamp over the table, which had long since disappeared. I touched it, and it swayed slowly, creaking softly. Then I went back to those rooms where the quiet doubles of my family sat. And I was the only living one among them, all long-gone, visiting them in their irretrievable dwelling. I stood, lost in the bottomless silence of the past, mourning that it would never return. I cried in my soul that humans were not allowed to relive the same moment over and over, thousands of times. And at the same time, my heart filled with an inexplicable bliss. My old premonitions of the stereoscope's magic had come true! And I thanked God for his wonders and secrets. In deep awe, I got on my knees before those mournful phantoms, and for a long time stood in reverence before each of them, before the sacred doubles of the past. And they kept sitting, quiet and mute, silently mourning what had forever passed with them.

But then, imperceptibly, the first trickles of fear returned to my heart. I looked around, and it seemed that in this immutable world something had—it was barely noticeable—but still, had strangely shifted. And suddenly I realized that it had grown *darker* in the rooms since I entered. I looked out the windows. It seemed that the shadow, covering the wall of the opposite house, had also deepened. I thought that perhaps my eyes were playing tricks on me. But the fear did not leave me, melting away the bliss in my heart, and the doubles of my loved ones began to seem hostile. I went through all the rooms again, and took a last, parting look at everything. I went out on the staircase, closed the door, and put the chain back up, to leave everything as it had been. Then I quickly descended. The glass door slammed behind me once more, filling the ghostly staircase with a ringing noise, and I was on the street again.

I walked, still feeling some echo of the bliss I had experienced. However, as I looked again at the shadows of the houses and the gloomy lengths of the streets, I suddenly realized that my eyes had not mistaken me before. A mysterious darkening was indeed occurring in the world of the stereoscope, as if dusk was falling. My fear grew, took over my heart, chased away the bliss, and mysteriously merged with the oncoming twilight. I remembered the old woman again, lying on her back in the dark hall. And I shuddered. At that same moment a horrible premonition struck me: it was her deadly malice that had bewitched this twilight. Then, only one goal possessed me: to reach the Hermitage as fast as I could. I rushed past the crowds of silent apparitions, and my steps rang out hurriedly on the dead streets. The frightening image of the old woman rose before me. And again, I remembered my first encounter with her, the living her, held in my memory as an incoherent, distant vision, and I thought of all the connections in the fate of man. Had our encounter not happened on that very day? Marveling, I spoke to myself of my ghostly self, there, in the gloomy house. Maybe some dead, faded thoughts were hidden in him, and the boy, sitting there at the table with his book, silently thinks of the Hermitage, where he had been for the first time and just returned from, of the mysterious dusk in the Egyptian Hall, and of the strange old woman's decrepit eyes, which he encountered for a moment in that hall . . .

I hurried along, almost running. I was halfway there when I noticed with horror that the darkness over the city was even deeper. Now the brown tones in the vistas of the streets became more distinct, and the shadows from the houses more frightening as pedestrians and carriages plunged deeper and deeper into them. Sad and foreboding was this brown dusk in the lands of the stereoscope. And yet the sun was not setting. It stood motionlessly in the same spot, and gradually darkened with the rest of its world. It became easier to look at it without squinting. A brownish hue spilled over the sky. The dead city and its countless hordes of doubles became more and more sinister. I quickened my pace and finally stepped onto the small, familiar bridge. The wide, darkened river briefly showed through the opening of the arch, built over the dreary canal. Exhausted, I ran up the porch with the gigantic atlantes.[13] The gloomy entrance to the vestibule washed fear over me, and for some time I stood still, not making up my mind to enter. Then I finally walked up and grabbed the handle of the inner door. It yielded easily and came ajar. I was once again in the Hermitage. I saw that the darkness reigning in it had thickened since I left it. The entrance to the Hall of Egypt was visible, pulling me to have a look, but, overcoming this pull, I turned to the Etruscan Hall. I walked quickly, my footsteps echoing. The brown dusk was deepening, ominously drowning out the familiar motionless figures.

There, the bookshelves, and the huge head on the tall pedestal. The walls of the vast mournful halls surrounded me on all sides. There, the corner where I had hidden from my fear yesterday. A sinister twilight had already taken over the turn in front of me. Suddenly I stopped, stood still. What was that? I heard somebody's footsteps ahead of me. Someone was coming my way! I couldn't believe my ears and listened keenly. Those were not the echoes of my footsteps—I was now standing motionless. The strange sounds were indistinct, almost imperceptible, but they still reached me through the boundless silence of the dead hall. They were shuffling steps, as if the person walking was dragging his feet. And immediately, their sound struck an inexpressible feeling in me; my heart dropped, and hideous conjectures arose in my mind. After a while the footsteps stopped. I could not bear the silence that followed; I dashed to one side and hid, waiting. Then the steps started again. They were coming from the dark turn ahead, getting closer, and becoming louder and clearer. I listened intently, and suddenly realized what had seemed strange about them: they did not resemble the steps of a living person. They were monotone and dead, as if a machine was walking. Frozen, I fixed my eyes on the dusk. Then, something was born from it, something emerged from it! A strange short figure with a bizarre hat on its head! I recognized her in an instant: she had gotten up from the floor, and was now walking around, a puppet-like double, looking for me! And her movements seemed restricted by something, like those of an automaton, lifeless and horrible. Closer and closer. The strange doll was walking straight towards me, fixing its glassy gaze on me, hobbling along and shuffling its feet.

I screamed wildly, awakening a horrible echo in the halls, and scrambled to run back. I ran in large leaps, and quickly reached the dark entrance of the Egyptian Hall. But I did not dare enter there; I turned to the side to rush up the marble staircase, taking three or four steps at a time. Reaching the top, I ran along the colonnade that encircled the stairwell and stopped, leaning against the massive railing, above the chasm. My heart beat furiously, and my mind was racing with incoherent thoughts—about the mysterious balances disturbed through the entrance of a living person into the depths of the stereoscope. About the frightening changes in this eternally unchanging world. About the descending darkness. And about the deadly malice of the old woman. So this meant that disturbed doubles could move! The eternally motionless ghosts leave their spots, wander about sometimes, but they still cannot access the fullness of living movement. Their old stiffness does not fully leave their joints, and they merely become frightening automatons . . . I looked around. Even here, the brown dusk was entering through the wide windows. And leaning over the railings, I saw that the vestibule below me was already fully drowned in darkness, with an almost reddish hue.

Then I heard the steps again. They came from the gloom at the bottom of the large stairwell, growing ever clearer. Through the dark shadows, I could already make out the strange dark object climbing the stairs. Despite the automated quality of its movements, the phantom climbed the stairs with unnatural speed and agility. Soon it fully left the darkness. Then I saw how it stopped ten steps from the top, and suddenly turned its head in my direction. And our eyes met again. Then, as if it had confirmed that I was there, the silent automaton once again began to hastily and anxiously climb the stairs. It reached the colonnade and headed towards me. I ran along the railings, trying to get to the stairs as quickly as possible, but the old woman suddenly turned back, and we almost collided by the first step. I quickly jumped back and ran as fast as I could through the upper halls. Faded rows of familiar paintings flashed past me. My steps echoed off the parquet floors. The mournful, foreboding darkness spread all around, and the motionless figures, drowning in it, silently watched my wild flight. And behind me chased the strange mannequin, and I heard its rapid, monotone steps. While I was running through a small room with dull frescoes, my face was briefly reflected in a ghostly mirror, pale, distorted, and wrapped in darkness. And I knew that in half a minute the horrible phantom chasing me would also mysteriously be reflected in it.

At times the chase quieted down. Perhaps she was losing her way. Once, taking advantage of this, I carefully started to make my way to the stairs, to return to the lower halls, but entering one of the rooms, I saw the mannequin hobbling towards me from the adjacent hall, and I hastily turned back. Another time I first hid and listened for a long time to hear if there were any steps. For about a minute it was dead silent. Then, running on tiptoe, I made my way towards the stairs, but in some small, dark room I ran into her, face to face. In silent terror I grabbed her shoulders and stood like that, unable to take my eyes off her deadly wicked gaze. Then, with all my strength, I pushed her away from me. She swayed and fell backwards with a dull thud. I ran to the stairs—but stopped in indecision. Dusk had fallen so deeply that the stairwell looked like a dark void in front of me. However, I had no choice, and I rushed down the stairs into the dark abyss of the vestibule. On the last steps I turned around and looked up. I saw the silhouette of the automaton that appeared on the top platform and was descending the stairs! Without thinking, I ran to the right and hid behind a coat rack. The sound of the dead steps on the stairs came closer and closer. What if she looked behind my rack? But, oh joy, I saw the phantom hobble past me, as if it hadn't noticed me, and head toward the hall of Etruscan vases, disappearing in its gloom.

I realized instantly that I could reach the Hall of Zeus faster than the old woman, who was heading there through the long row of the lower halls. A shorter path lay through the Egyptian Hall. I carefully left my hiding spot, and rushed to the entrance of the hall, suppressing my immense fear of it. But having entered it, I stopped, taken aback by what I saw. Everything there was already covered in brown dusk, but through it I vaguely discerned a new figure, sitting on a dark sarcophagus in the back. It was motionless, only slowly turning its head in my direction. It was a ghostly visitor. He must have come alive following the old woman, started moving, and clambered onto the sarcophagus. I remembered the two frozen phantoms I had noticed here earlier. In the dark corner under a window, someone else was stirring and rustling. That must be the second one. Disturbed by the invasion into their world, they left their spots and started to make strange and horrible mischief in the darkened hall! But, quickly overcoming my hesitation, I started to run again, without looking back. There, the Hall of Zeus. Everything was covered in a thick dusk. The statues, formerly white, were now brown, protruding ominously in the darkness. And there, the photographer. His motionless face was now a reddish-brown, and frightening. I put the back of my head flush against the camera. I felt the tubes of the double lenses. The entrance to the adjacent hall was before my eyes, filled with a deep, dead dusk, and a faint light in the distance. And now again, somewhere in front of me, I heard the faint echoes of footsteps. The phantom had walked through the lower halls. Its dark, ugly silhouette had already appeared in the distance and was rapidly approaching me. But thank God! I felt how the hall seemed to distance itself from me. I had already crossed its border. The magical return to life and the present occurred again. I was once again sitting at the desk in my room. The lamp burned in front of me, and the stereoscope stood on the pile of books.

I leaned back in my chair, averting my eyes from the lenses, and sat like that for a while. My heart was still beating dully and rapidly, there was a terrible fatigue in my legs, and my fingers still retained the revolting feeling from touching the phantom's shoulders. Then I carefully glanced into the lenses, from a distance at first, not bringing my eyes up to them. I could see the darkened hall, but already small and distant. I was no longer in it, the border between me and it had returned. I boldly brought my eyes closer to the lenses, and suddenly saw, there, near the tomb in the back of the hall, vaguely visible in the brown dusk: the old woman was sitting on the floor, staring directly at me! Like a madman, I jumped up from my chair, knocking the pile of books away from me, and the stereoscope fell onto

Figure 1.8. Evgenia Smirnova-Ivanova, illustration for Alexander Ivanov's "Stereoscope" (St. Petersburg: Sirius, 1909).

the table with a thud, lenses up. A horrible thought went through my head. She could also cross the boundary and enter my room! After all, I could enter her past realms from my living world! And in my terror, not remembering what I was doing, I grabbed the hammer lying on the table, and one, two! I shattered both lenses. Their fragments fell into the stereoscope with a ringing sound.

I walked around my room for a long time before I calmed down a little. Only then I realized that I was still in my coat and scarf, but my hat was no longer on my head. I looked for it on the floor, but I couldn't find it. I must have accidentally lost it in the ghostly halls during my flight. Then I took the stereoscope, and after much effort, managed to break its back wall and take out the photograph inserted into it. My heart stopping, I held it up to the lamp. On it was the immensely darkened depiction of the familiar hall. It looked like those photographs which have been severely damaged by light. The hall in the picture seemed to be drowned in the reddish-brown dusk, but nowhere in it was there any trace of the figure seated on the floor, and nowhere could I find any traces of the old woman. She must have slipped out of sight just in time. The darkening of the photograph seemed to have stopped. The strange dusk no longer deepened. And I thought, maybe the doubles who had left their spots were frozen once again. I examined the glass plate from all sides. It was an ordinary photograph for a stereoscope, a double image of the hall, four inches long. In its top right corner, I could still make out the date, written in by hand: "April 21, 1877."

***

Thus I destroyed the stereoscope. When and how did it end up in the Auction Warehouse on G-ya Street? Who made it? Who opened the path into the faded realms of the past? Was it that tall photographer, whose double eternally stands in the ghostly hall? Or was it somebody else? If it was him, what had he felt when he first crossed the boundary of that world, and turning around, saw his double in the deep silence of the dead hall? How did he, having entered those mournful realms, manage not to disturb the peace of the silent phantoms, not to awaken a hidden terror, not to invite an ominous twilight? Perhaps it was not fated for him to return to life and the present, and some kind of strange cause buried him forever in the depths of the stereoscope. He could have had a heart attack on the streets of the dead city, he could have fallen down the stairs, or drowned in the waters of a ghostly river or canal. Or (who knows?) perhaps the maker of the stereoscope never managed to cross the boundary of the lenses, and out of all living people I was the first and last visitor to the depths of the past.

A long time has passed since that night. Whenever my hands fall on a stereoscope, I take it, look into it, and that old magic still blows into my heart. But I know that it is only an anticipation of that strange bliss, and that I will never again fully experience it. I, who once entered there, can now only look into that world. Through the round lenses I can see a pine forest with a narrow path going off into the distance; puddles from a recent rain glisten dully on it. And it seems to me that I am already there, walking along the damp path, walking deeper into the forest of faded dead pines. I see how they are reflected in the motionless, mirrorlike puddles. I make my way to a ghostly clearing, dimly visible through the tree trunks, and in the great silence of the ghostly forest, only the faint snapping of twigs under my feet is heard. Water droplets fall from the brown leaves of bushes, and there is a faint smell of pines after a rainstorm. But that is all my imagination. An uncrossable boundary separates me from that world. Other times, I see a deserted seaside through the lenses, and it feels like I am already walking there, on the moist, faintly crunchy sand, with the deserted lengths of the strange coast stretching out in both directions while in front of me the ghostly ocean stretches out like a desert: white, eternally frozen waves wherever the eye looks. And everything is sad and colorless. I stand and listen to the dead silence of the sea and its shores, feel the salty freshness and faint smell of silt. But this is all only a fantasy, and after a moment I remember that I am merely looking through a stereoscope, and a forbidden line separates me from this ocean of the past.

But that old device, the only one that truly opened the doors to the past, is no more. Only its frame stands on my desk. The fragments of its lenses are tucked in a box and put away. Sometimes I take out that double photograph from the stereoscope, with the darkened, "overexposed" image of the hall. I look at it again. The walls, the floor, the statues, and the receding line of rooms can still be made out quite clearly through the thick brown dusk. And this dusk has not deepened since then. Nothing has changed in the photograph, only that the strange world hidden inside it sinks deeper and deeper into the past each day. In it are hidden the halls of the Hermitage, drowned in an ominous gloom. They are inhabited by the quiet photographer, the silent visitors, the frightening mannequin which was once again frozen, and the two frightening visitors in the Egyptian Hall. There, in that gloomy hall, is the case with the broken glass, robbed by me, and somewhere on the floor in the dark lies my hat. A huge dead city hides there, covered in a menacing darkness, and in it my old familiar house and its rooms, inhabited by the doubles of my loved ones. They sit there, submerged in the dusk, disappearing deeper and deeper into the past each day. I will never be able to return there. The mysterious entrance is forever sealed.

Here, in our world, I often wander through the halls of the living Hermitage. And as I roam about, I try to see the ghostly past of these halls through the colorful present. Recently I was there on a dark winter day, one of those days when even the upper halls are covered in a dull gloom. A dreary light from a colorless sky poured through the windows, and the living colors around me seemed to grow pale and dim, allowing the faded past to stand out more clearly. It stood out especially clearly in those chambers where I happened to be alone, with no one else around. At times it seemed that the walls, the floor, the paintings, the decorations on the ceiling would fade completely, and everything would die and freeze, and I would again be reflected in the ghostly mirror, lonely, alive, and moving among the dead world of the past. Horror would come over me when, looking at the turn of a wall, or a group of statues in the shade, or a reflection of light on the floor, I would remember distinctly what happened to me in that place during my flight through the darkness of these irretrievable halls and stairs. And the past stood out even more clearly in the lower halls, where the winter day poured semi-darkness through the few, gloomy windows. At the spot where three vast halls met by the bookcases, I nervously recognized the place where I had first heard the horrifying footsteps, and the corner where I had hidden in fear the first night. I lingered for a long time in the Hall of Egypt. I stood full of strange thoughts in the gloomy space by the wall where I had first seen the old woman guarding the hall. Then I walked up to the case with the scarab beetles, and looked at the amulets lying behind the solid, untouched glass. Taking the object I had stolen from *there* out of my pocket, I compared it, like I had done many times before, to the green stone scarab in the case. And once again I was convinced that they were similar, like doubles. They were the same size, same shape, had the same part broken off at the bottom of their right wing. But my scarab was dark brown. And again, like many times before, I stood over them in deep amazement.

More and more often I think about who that strange old woman was, who wandered thirty years ago through the lower halls, and what she was looking at from her corner, in the moment captured in the stereoscope. And I tell myself, maybe she took a liking to the boy she met in the shaded hall, who was soon whisked away by his father. Unable to find them, she returned to that same hall, and gazed mysteriously and intently at the dark display case where he had recently stood. Then, that ghostly mannequin in the depths of the stereoscope began to guard the case of scarabs with its deadly gaze. For it was by this case that she had seen the child she had taken a liking to. And with this gaze, hiding behind it her faded thoughts of the boy, she guarded the eternal peace of my double in that distant house, jealously afraid that he would be stolen away from her mournful realms, protecting his secret and all other secrets of the past . . . I do not know, and am scared to know, who she was in our, living world, back when I met her in my distant childhood. But the ghost of the boy, now sitting in the gloom of his irretrievable room, can never leave the realms of her double. Those are my thoughts. The frame of the stereoscope stands on my desk, illuminated by the lamp. And before me lies the dark scarab, the secret of those mournful realms and my childhood double, stolen from the old woman.

*1905*

Figure 1.9. Evgenia Smirnova-Ivanova, illustration for Alexander Ivanov's "Stereoscope" (St. Petersburg: Sirius, 1909).

## Notes

* **Alexander Ivanov, "The Stereoscope. A Twilight Tale."** Dated to 1905, the tale was first published in 1909: A. P. Ivanov, *Stereoskop. Sumerechnyi rasskaz* (St. Petersburg, Sirius, 1909). The second (identical) edition appeared in 1918. Ivanov's tale shared the fate of all the other pieces translated here, which was to be largely forgotten for seven or eight decades and then republished during *perestroika* or the early post-Soviet years. This process had an ideological dimension: a passionate rediscovery of the previously suppressed or sidelined aspects of history, very much in tune with the restoration of the imperial state symbols and the renaming of Leningrad back to St. Petersburg. Equally important were the new possibilities for commerce, as such works did not have any copyright protection. The result was a veritable avalanche of republishing of all sorts of literary production from the pre-revolutionary era.

Ivanov's tale was republished in 1988 in a magazine. It also appeared as part of the anthology of fantastic literature from the early twentieth century that in many ways inspired the present collection: E. B. Belodubrovskii and D. K. Ravinskii, compilation and introduction, *Stereoskop. Antologiia peterburgskoi fantastiki* (St. Peterburg: Fond kul'tury, 1992); the second edition was published as *Nochnoi prints. Sankt-peterburgskaia fantastika Serebrianogo veka* (St. Peterburg: Renome, 2020). Among the subsequent editions, especially valuable is the handsome volume published in connection with the 150th anniversary of the New Hermitage and St. Petersburg's tricentennial by the State Hermitage Museum: L. I. Davydova, introduction, commentary, and supplementary materials, in A. P. Ivanov, *Stereoskop. Publikatsia rasskaza A. Ivanova s kommentariiami i prilozheniiami* (St. Petersburg: Izdatel'stvo Gosudarstvennogo Ermitazha, 2003). Additional useful commentary is found in S. Shargorodskii, Commentary to A. P. Ivanov, *Stereoskop. Sumerechnyi rasskaz* (Salamandra, P.V.V., 2013).

The illustrations reproduced here appeared in the original publication and were made by the writer's wife, Evgenia Alexeyevna Smirnova-Ivanova (1875/78–1970), who was a student of Nikolai Roerich. The appearance of the protagonist in these illustrations strongly resembles Alexander Ivanov. The copy of the first edition I have in my possession bears traces of special care on the part of a previous owner: there is a depiction of a live scarab glued to the book's front and, most importantly, in all illustrations that portray the protagonist inside the stereoscopic realms, his clothes are colored by hand. This is quite appropriate, as he is the only living person in the twilight world of the sepia photograph.

1 *G-ya Street.* Thinly veiled omissions in place names are frequently found in Russian classical literature (cf. the opening chapter of Dostoevsky's *Crime and Punishment*). Here it refers to Gorokhovaya Street, the central ray in the trident of streets converging on the Admiralty. The Auction Warehouse visited by the protagonist was an established business that occupied the building at Gorokhovaya, no. 47, and belonged to the Company for Storage and Pawn Shops for Bulky Movable Property. A city guide from the 1860s describes it as follows: "The purpose of the company is to accept for storage and pawn various objects, as for example: carriages, furniture, weapons, clothes and other movable items, not at all necessarily bulky. The warehouse of the company is quite spacious, but the pawn shop office is located in a relatively small chamber, constantly full of people and at times quite crowded. It is here that auctions are held for items that were not redeemed" (M. Mikhailov, "Peterburg i ego okrestnosti," *Severnoe siianie*, no. 3 (1862), 168).

2 *The impression I had the first time I looked into the lenses of a stereoscope will remain with me until the day I die. This happened very long ago, in my childhood.* Stereoscopes were widespread since the middle of the nineteenth century. For a pictorial reflection of this see Nikolai Podkliuchnikov's painting "Girl Looking into Stereoscope" (1865) in the collection of the Tropinin Museum in Moscow.

3 *an image of the Abu-Simbel Colossi.* One of the iconic monuments of Ancient Egypt, these gigantic rock-cut figures of Ramesses the Great were often photographed with a living person in the scene in order to emphasize their gigantic size. The stereoscopic photograph mentioned in the text and featuring an Arab sitting on the pharaoh's hand is perhaps the one taken by Francis Frith in the 1850s. See Kirill Kuz'michev, *Tret'e izmerenie. Rossiia Aleksandra II vo frantsuzskoi stereofotografii* (St. Petersburg: Kriga, 2018).

4 *April 21, 1877.* As is confirmed in the finale, this is the exact date on which the photograph was taken. Despite the autobiographic feel of the tale, it cannot refer to the chronology of Ivanov's own life, since he was born in 1876 and visited the Hermitage as a boy only in the 1880s. The year 1877 saw a number of important events in various spheres of life: for example, Leo Tolstoy released the final installments of *Anna Karenina*; the grand Ciniselli Circus was constructed on the Fontanka; *La Bayadère*, choreographed by Marius Petipa, premiered at St. Petersburg's Bolshoi Theatre; and, on April 12 (according to the Julian calendar), the Russo-Turkish War began. None of the specifics pertaining to this particular year or the broader period figure in the tale, however, with references to the past being quite generic. Thus, the choice of the photograph's date remains unexplained.

5 *The statue of Zeus with an eagle at his feet rose up in its expected place.* The point of entry into the world of the stereoscope is near the gigantic statue of Jupiter, which has been kept in the same hall since its arrival at the museum (it is currently hall number 107). Many other things have changed. The action takes place in the New Hermitage, built as a public museum to house the open part of the collection prior to the revolution. Subsequently, the museum spread to the adjacent buildings, including the Small Hermitage, the Old Hermitage, and the main imperial residence, the Winter Palace. Today's visitor wanders through an enormous complex with an intricate maze of halls, passages, and staircases. In Ivanov's time, it was a much smaller space with a straightforward layout. There was only one entrance—through the central portico of the New Hermitage (now closed)—with the grand staircase leading to the second floor. This contributes to the circular movement of the protagonist. On the first day, he moves along the perimeter of the New Hermitage on the ground floor: from today's hall 107, to hall 106, to halls 128, 129, 127, and further clockwise to the entrance. From there he goes up the stairs, walks around the main stairwell, and goes down the stairs, again to the lobby. For details pertaining to the Hermitage in the tale, see Lyudmila Davydova's commentary in the 2003 edition of the tale. For a map of the Hermitage, see the official site of the museum: hermitagemuseum.org > Pull down menu > Explore > Trip planner.

6 *The large window in its depths barely let in a brownish light, and through it [...] a wall of the Winter Palace was visible.* This is the only inexactitude in the otherwise immaculate descriptions of the Hermitage in Ivanov. The wall belongs to the Small Hermitage, but it could be easily confused with the palace wall, especially since both buildings were not part of the public museum. Nowadays, this window does not exist, as in the 1930s it was replaced with an opening to a gallery linking the New Hermitage, the Small Hermitage, and the Winter Palace.

7 *The Egyptian Hall faced me.* Since 1940, the Egyptian collection has been located in a different building (hall number 100, on the ground floor of the Winter Palace). In Ivanov's time, it was in the first hall to the left of the entrance to the New Hermitage (hall number 109, which today houses Venus Tauride). There, the protagonist steals the scarab and topples the old woman. Although the statue of Jupiter is only one hall away, in his terror, he runs toward the lobby and, going counter-clockwise around the ground floor, returns to the Hall of Zeus from the other side.

8 *And here I was standing on a long-gone porch, surrounded by gigantic atlantes.* The protagonist leaves the New Hermitage through its main portico, which is supported by ten colossal figures of atlantes made of gray granite. The atlantes have become one of the symbols of St. Petersburg. A song about them ("Atlantes Hold the Sky on Stone Hands," by Alexander Gorodnitsky, 1963) was recently adopted as the official anthem of the Hermitage Museum. The street going left is Millionnaya. The narrator turns right onto the Palace Square that lies in front of

the Winter Palace, with the Alexander Column in the middle. The "misty Cathedral" in the distance is St. Isaac's. "The huge needle" that "shone dully and lifelessly above the familiar white tower" is the spire of the Admiralty.

9 *The [. . .] façade of the Winter Palace stretched out in front of me, ending to the left, allowing me to freely see the distant crowds of ghostly houses across the river. This was how things used to be. Marveling, I thought that from this spot in the living square, no one will ever be able to see those buildings: the high railing of the new garden in front of the palace covers them.* The view across the Neva from the square was obstructed in 1902 by the railing of the recently created garden at the Western façade of the palace. After the October Revolution, the garden was destroyed and the railing, stripped of its double-headed eagles and royal monograms, was hauled away and re-erected in a park (located in a working-class district, it had been established to commemorate victims of the Revolution of 1905). Thus, the vista observed by the narrator in 1877 has been reopened.

10 *Then I went out onto a large, wide street, which I recognized as [. . .] Nevsky Prospect.* After the Palace Square, the protagonist turns left to Nevsky Prospect, the main avenue of the city. He passes Kazan Cathedral ("the temple with the dull colonnade") and the Alexandrinsky Theater ("the receding mass of the Theater").

11 *A lone living person was walking further and further, drowning in the depths of a vast dead city [. . .] I was reminded of an old Arabic tale about the City of Brass, which Emir Musa and Sheikh Abd-al-Samad had once entered.* This is a reference to an episode from *One Thousand and One Nights* (nights 573–77). Another important precedent is the tale of the Sleeping Beauty. The illustration by Gustave Doré reproduced here emphasizes slumbering rather than life stopped in mid-motion, but the general situation is very similar, as the hero is the only person who is fully alive in an enchanted realm.

Figure 1.10. Gustave Doré, illustration for "La Belle au bois dormant," in *Les contes de Perrault* (Paris: J. Hetzel, 1862).

12 *a large engraving depicting the head of a giant with closed eyes and earrings in his ears, two knights with swords, three ladies, and their gloomy surroundings.* The engraving is an illustration by Gustav Doré to accompany Ariosto's *Orlando Furioso* (15:88). A slight aberration of memory on the part of the narrator is involved: there are actually three knights and two ladies, although the long-haired knight in the center of the image, who is not wearing a helmet, could be mistaken for a lady. There is also an anachronism, since, according to the catalogue of the French National Library, the book was first published in 1879, and thus could not have been photographed in 1877. Ivanov could very well have seen engravings from the book in a magazine in 1883 or 1884, though, when he was the age of the boy in the tale ("seven or eight").

Figure 1.11. Gustave Doré, illustration for Ludovico Ariosto's *Roland furieux: poème héroïque* (Paris: Hachette, 1879).

13 *I [...] finally stepped onto the small, familiar bridge. The wide darkened river briefly showed through the opening of the arch, built over the dreary canal. [...] I ran up the porch with the gigantic atlantes.* The middle portion of the protagonist's foray into the city, with the visit to his childhood home, does not have specific topographical markers, but the final segment of his trajectory is spelled out. He approaches the New Hermitage from Millionnaya Street. Crossing the bridge over the Winter Canal, he sees the arch under the gallery connecting the Old Hermitage and the Hermitage Theatre. Leaving the museum, he walks to the Palace Square and then returns from the opposite side. Thus, he makes yet another circle, reiterating the circular pattern in the spatial, temporal, and thematic structure of the tale.

## Alexander Izmailov

# The Antiquarian*

---

## I

Several years ago, certain persons, who undoubtedly belonged to the St. Petersburg intelligentsia and were involved in various types of artistic endeavors, received strange letters by means of the usual postal delivery. They were written on old paper—a kind not used anymore, with obscure watermarks—in a slightly trembling and highly peculiar but perfectly distinct handwriting, with a watery, reddish ink of the kind old men write with. The letters were unsigned and were usually of an accusatory and edifying nature, but the strangest thing about them was that they contained references (sometimes quite clear and sometimes more ambiguous) to details of the life and conduct of the addressees which only they themselves could have known. The one writing them was like an embodied, walking conscience, and since the reproach was always fair, sometimes striking at things and deeds that the sinner thought would be concealed for centuries and generations, the letters always left an impression, causing confusion and awakening an anxious curiosity. The letter-writer began by advising the recipient that it was better not to tell anyone—not about the letters themselves nor their content—for his goal was solely the person's "rectification." He encouraged the person to find within himself a "cell" into which he might, at least temporarily, retreat for solitary self-examination, since even this could suffice.

As for excessive talk, it is incompatible with goodness: idle social chatter can cool and soothe a conscience that was pained through honest introspection. However, these warnings were evidently not taken to heart by everyone, and often, when for one reason or another there was talk in society about the mysterious teacher (or circle of self-appointed teachers), more than one of those present admitted that this conversation was not new to them, and that such letters had reached them as well.

I knew several people, from very different walks of life, who became objects of this mysterious tutelage. The letters were received by an old archimandrite, venerable and influential, who lived in our Nevsky Lavra; they came in the last few years before his death. People talked often of one dignitary who supposedly did not even hide his contacts with the strange correspondent, and even obeyed his advice, having received evidence on more than one occasion that he did not advise in bad faith. Letters came as well to a few writers, and to a representative of an office very close to literature but not particularly loved by writers—a man who, holding a flaming sword in one hand, paid homage to the muses with the other.[1]

Once, I went to visit him and found him in a bit of confusion.

"See," he said, "I have to go to today's meeting and argue, and fight, but something odd is happening to me, something that is confusing and almost unsettling. Between you and me: for some time I have been haunted by anonymous letters . . ."

"But who," I asked, "gets upset over anonymous letters?"

"I know how one should react to anonymous letters," he retorted, "but these are special. They would be meaningless, but they were written by a person who clearly wishes me well. And besides, it is not so much the letters themselves that baffle me, but the conclusion I must draw from them: that some kind of secret but tenacious surveillance has been established over me. Perhaps someone is just playing an April Fool's joke on me, but this feeling of bewilderment is in any case unpleasant and burdensome. Can you keep secrets?"

"This isn't the first day you've known me."

"Read then. This is today's."

He gave me a small piece of thick old paper, the kind on which books were printed in the 1810s and 1820s, and a narrow envelope, opened, with a small wax seal depicting a plain Latin cross in the center of a circle. The page said:

"You are making me grieve for you. You are scaring away your guardian angel. Was your conscience not wounded last Thursday night? Do not assume that sin is invisible. Sin is visible. I wanted to get close to you, but you moved away. You were closer to the light, and then you became more distant. Test your conscience in solitude."

"As for the context," my friend clarified, "I must add that last Thursday is indeed repulsive to me, because that day I went against justice to please the strong, and I would give dearly to change that. It is possible that this is simply a lucky guess, but most likely, it is not luck and not a guess. And most importantly, who wants to toy with me and track me—and why? This is uncanny. I have reached a mature age, and I don't provide any particular reasons to be made fun of."

"How do you explain these edifying messages?" I asked.

"It is not impossible that some late branch of Masonry or Rosicrucianism exists among us today. And it would be completely in keeping with their whimsical style and genre to elevate a person to perfection and at the same time recruit him into their lodge. They used this method often in the past. But that is rather uncharacteristic of our current cold and non-mystical times. I have come to suspect that this is not a mystical affair, but a hoax, and to carry it out, someone is spying on me."

"And you can guess who it is?"

"If it is indeed a hoax, then it is certainly the work of the one I am thinking of. It is N."

He mentioned a name—at the time, a very big literary name. This was a strange person, able to combine his deep and philosophically inclined mind and great artistic talent with the incomprehensible need to deceive: a boyish spirit whose playfulness was not always harmless.

"We were once close," my interlocutor explained. "More than once, we stole hours from the night to talk about mysticism. But then we parted ways."

## II

For me, this was the time of my first interest in the occult, of my first, as it used to be said in the olden times, "striving towards the radiant gloom of mysticism." Is there not a mystic asleep in every person until the time comes, and is not only a small jolt needed for him to awaken and raise his head, like one needs the first swell of water for the river to break the ice that has been holding on all winter?

There was something intriguing about the case of the mysterious correspondence. It was, of course, the work of human hands, and most likely a hoax, but in any case, it stepped out of the ordinary and stirred the mind, directing it to various conjectures. Was this the work of a single person, bored with life, whose yearly income allows him to do nothing, or was it the work of a whole company of eccentrics, for whom it would be quite easy to establish surveillance over someone? Or was this indeed the peculiar implementation of a plan to re-educate humanity by a late-born mystic idealist—for is this not indeed the best way to show the strong their sins, which everyone is silent about? To wound their conscience, which is perhaps already bewildered and slightly aching? Our ancestors believed in this effect of reprimanding at a distance, and it is possible that they sometimes achieved their goal.

Of course, it was impossible to conclude anything from my speculations, but I was very curious to conclude something, especially because about two or three weeks later, I found a letter from the same source with the same stamp on my own desk.

"By directing attention to the realm of practical knowledge," wrote my unknown and unexpected counselor, "this age closes the door to the luminous realm of the spirit. But the spiritual is greater than the earthly. Do not extinguish the beginnings of a love for the mysterious in your soul. When you have looked intently at your life, you shall see in the insignificant and small something significant, important, and mysteriously wise. In this lies the path to true happiness, which you now seek in vain. Happiness is in that knowledge—which itself finds those worthy of it, which is easily seen by those who love it, and which is obtained by those who seek it. Search in solitude and silence, and read what the knowledgeable ones wrote, but keep silent about the letters."

The handwriting was strangely beautiful, with a kind of archaic ornateness. To some extent the letter did indeed give the illusion of antiquity, enhanced by the writing style and even a certain characteristic spelling. Was this a skillfully stylized imitation or was there really an eccentric somewhere, still living in a past age, imbued with its views, sympathies, and idealism? Did he sit next to me somewhere in society, where conversation turned to the cryptic letters? Perhaps this mysterious "someone" did not read into my thoughts as I sat at my desk, in the solitude of evening, poring over literature of the mystics, but overheard my interest in the subject when I discussed the enigmatic messages with my friend.

For lack of anything better, I had to accept the latter explanation. But the new letter—more of a note, a dozen words into two lines—seemed to suggest otherwise. It consisted of just one famous verse:

"Before that Philip called thee, when thou wast under the fig tree, I saw thee."

This seemed like an answer to my hidden thought; it was a figurative and allegorical answer, but one that could directly and without a stretch be adapted to the question that was stirring in my soul: "No, your friend has nothing to do with this, and I have read the thoughts in your soul before." Of course, this could also have been a coincidence, but for the first time, I had to seriously think about the letter.

Inside the envelope there was another note. It turned out to be a list of Latin, German, and Russian mystic literature. There was a sense of taste and knowledge in the selection. Among the names, as far as I knew them, I did not find a single charlatan.

A new letter arrived the next week. It was very short. "Continue to be an active student," wrote the stranger. "Love, labor, solitude, and silence. You yearn for the impossibility of communication and guidance. The guide is coming to you. Do not neglect him on account of the modesty of his position. God hath chosen the foolish things of the world to confound the wise."

*Yearn.* That was not the right word. The mysterious correspondent was exaggerating. But I won't deny that a burning and anxious curiosity was already stirring in me. I still could not say anything for or against my unsolicited teacher, but it was quite clear that he did not want to leave me alone, and wouldn't. And with interest and impatience I resolved to wait for the mysterious and uninvited "guide" coming to meet me.

## III

In my free time, I like to wander around the stalls of our various antiquarians. Under the low ceilings of the Apraksin and Aleksandrovsky Markets, there is still much worthy of great attention.[2] In the past, they contained veritable treasures. Now you won't find a Rembrandt or Van Dyck for ten rubles, but one can find an Aivazovsky and stumble across splendid curiosities of old art, or a book that has survived water, fire, and even the sharp sword of the censors of the Catherine and Alexander the Blessed eras, when, after the Novikov affair and the decree closing Masonic lodges, books were burned by the thousands. Sometimes one can even find an interesting manuscript: I once managed to find Herzen's correspondence at a Moscow flea market.

In these antiquarian stalls, among all kinds of paper rubbish, it is not uncommon to run into one of our literary old men or zealous lovers of antiquity. A few years ago, one could often see the old man Leskov here, with a cane, in a fur coat and fur hat with a visor; or the late singer Stravinsky, a great bibliomaniac; or the figure of the famous bibliographer Ye., resembling an Old Believer. These were aristocrats in the art world and well-off people, but literary bohemia was also strongly drawn here.[3] For this crowd, there was to be found here a kind of noble sport, exciting not with the practical calculation of buying a ruble for three kopecks, but for satisfying the legitimate need of the beautiful, exciting not in its practical calculus—the purchase of a ruble for three kopecks—but in its satisfaction of the legitimate need of the beautiful, which the delicate soul wants to bring

Букинистъ.

Рождественскій разсказъ

А. А. Измайлова (Смоленскаго).

I.

Нѣсколько лѣтъ назадъ нѣкоторыми лицами изъ петербургской несомнѣнной и, большею частью, близкой разнымъ видамъ искусства интеллигенціи были получены обычнымъ почтовымъ порядкомъ странныя письма. Написаны они были на старинной, вышедшей изъ употребленія бумагѣ, съ неясными водя-

Figure 2.1. Pavel Shkarin, illustration for Alexander Izmailov's "Antiquarian" in *Novaia illiustratsiia*, no. 51–52 (December 1903). Lurking in the background of the elaborate H is the silhouette of a sphinx, resembling those at the Egyptian Bridge near the Aleksandrovsky market, which is a possible location of the antiquarian's shop in the story.

even to a shabby furnished room. Such a weakness, acquired in youth, is difficult to overcome even having reached a mature age and having acquired a respectable status. There is in all this some kind of link between antiquity and mystery, something alluring and intriguing, something attractive, as it were. Finally, among the antiquarians themselves one comes across a curious and peculiar type of person, with whom it is sometimes interesting and useful for a literary person to talk. It seems that a simple but continuous contact with books throws a ray of light on even a simple mind, and I was fortunate to find people of serious and multifaceted erudition and a lively natural sense here.

One fall evening of that year, I was walking down a long row of book stalls in one of our markets. It was getting dark. From the opposite side of the street, through the open window of a tavern favored by market-goers, came the sounds of a street organ, wheezing, as if it had a cold. Kerosine lamps smoked in the stalls. Buyers scurried around the gallery; clerks called to them, cajoling and teasing. The visit was turning out to be unsuccessful, and I was already prepared to go home, when I saw a light in the corner shop . . .

It was a strange shop. Tiny, and by the looks of it, quite meagerly stocked, it usually stood closed, and a weighty, rusted lock, resembling a huge bedbug from a distance, sat on the bolt of the door shutter. I could never see its owner. Even when the shop was unlocked, there was a snot-nosed little boy, shuffling from foot to foot, with a glass of muddy tea in his hands, and no matter what was requested, he always responded that such-and-such book was currently "not available" in the shop. He wouldn't let you rummage through the shelves, and, wiping his nose, would explain that the owner was not there and would not be for a long time, so either way there would be no one to discuss the price with. This happened so often and was so strange that I, being not completely inexperienced in this area, had already had the flickering thought that this shop perhaps persisted through what antiquarians call "dark" trade, which had flourished in the past and still existed in those years. The "dark merchant" of yore would interact with the occasional customer out of politeness and to avert the eye, but his main activity was to satisfy his own, regular customers, for whom he obtained "dark" books—those which are not found in libraries. Whether or not someone bought something for fifty kopecks that day did not matter to him, because he earned good money on the side, and his suppliers, obtaining the needed materials for him, knew well at what hour and in which tavern to find him.

This time, things were different. The shop was lit, the doors were open, and at the entrance stood a figure: a man with an intense gaze and a faded, narrow beard, like that of Metropolitan Isidore, which the clergy call "prelatic." When I was almost even with the shop, the man standing by the door jumped slightly to the side, evidently making way for me into his storeroom and, lightly touching his hand to his warm fur hat with a visor, but without raising it in the slightest, said:

"Welcome sir!" in such a positive and confident voice, that it was almost as if he had added: "I have been waiting for you for a long time."

## IV

A tin lamp with a tin reflector, dulled and greasy, illuminated the narrow shop and the descent into the basement, where books were strewn all over. Its light fell on the face of my new acquaintance, who was small, withered, and earthy brown in color, with deeply sunken eyes and an expression of either uneasy suspicion or concealed curiosity. He was short and lean, his figure and face of that strange sort from which it is impossible to discern an age: he could be forty, or sixty! Some kind of strange and unpleasant black spots lay on his sunken cheeks, as if dirt had settled in the pores of his skin and would not wash out. His gray mustache was trimmed and stuck out in sharp bristles, and because of this, and the arch of his thin brows, his face had the expectant expression of a weary lynx. His coat of cheap fur, with its slightly mangy collar, clung tightly to his small figure, so that he resembled a Francisco Goya painting, and from a distance, without seeing his gray beard and his face, one could mistake him for an adolescent.

Following me into the shop, the old man, with the agility of a youth, jumped onto a stool, reached his hand to the upper shelf, and took down a small bundle of books wrapped in newspaper.

"You will find these curious and useful."

This was a little presumptuous, as they could have turned out to be of no interest or use to me at that moment, but he quickly and deftly unwrapped the books and banged them on the table, placing them spines up. It was strange, but they turned out to be precisely what interested me, and all of them were in their own way remarkable and rare. Even as a neophyte I knew that all of this mystical wisdom was at one time vigorously persecuted, relentlessly confiscated during searches of booksellers and private individuals, and burned by Prozorovsky and Kurbatov under Catherine.[4] I immersed myself in these small, old books, printed in faded ink on thick, ancient paper, still under Novikov's auspices, and above my ear I heard a calm and weighty, imposing voice:

"There is little interest in this nowadays, sir. That time has passed. Few people now know this and love it, and even those who do sit in their corners and don't reveal themselves. And indeed, it's better to keep quiet. Cast not your pearls. It is hard to know the truth alone, but one needs the loneliness of truth. The truth is bitter. Don't even tell anyone that you are a mystic. For what purpose? They'll laugh about your sacred secret. Not many have the truth, and those few who do, will help the ones seeking it. You are more than welcome to visit me. I will help any way I can, and prepare something else for you . . ."

It seemed to be that even what I was looking at now, he had prepared specifically for me, and I couldn't help but smile and ask whether he had anticipated my visit.

"I had a feeling you would be here," he answered, without a smile, and even in a peculiarly serious fashion. "If you begin to carefully look at life, you will see that there is not a single chance meeting, and nothing is insignificant or pointless. Everything is important, wise, and meaningful. You had to meet me,

Figure 2.2. *"You will find these curious and useful."*Pavel Shkarin, illustration for Alexander Izmailov's "Antiquarian" in *Novaia illiustratsiia*, no. 51–52 (December 1903).

for this was necessary for both of us. And I wouldn't have shown these books to just anyone. Not everyone needs them. To just anyone, this is the nonsense of Masonic folly. It has long been rejected and condemned and ridiculed. Clever people rejected it, and who wants to contradict them? And truth be told, we too will reject and condemn much of what is here. The chaff has indeed not been winnowed from the grain. But once we winnow it away—there is so much wheat!"

He invited me to come down the stairs, promising curious material. Two basement rooms, spacious to the point where I never could have guessed it from the entrance and the booth, were dimly lit by two bulbs. It was a little terrifying in this semi-darkness, saturated with the smell of damp paper—the distinct smell of a book warehouse or library that is not heated. Everywhere there were books, books, books: moist, dampened, with torn and cracked spines, like coffins of literary thoughts, faded interests, passions lived and experienced and then sent away to the archives. Antiquity reigned, and there seemed to be a lot of rubbish among the old serials that were preserved for some reason—from *The Well Intentioned* to *Beneficial Exercises for Youth, Morning Dawns, Amphions,* and *Calliopes.* Why did the irony of fate save these stacks of ruined paper, from which no one will ever read another page, from destruction?

„Изъ угла его на меня глядѣли два большихъ, острыхъ, болѣзненно возбужденныхъ глаза"...
Оригинальный рисунокъ художника „Биржевыхъ Вѣдомостей".

Figure 2.3. *"From the corner two large, sharp, sickly, agitated eyes were looking at me."* Pavel Shkarin, illustration for Alexander Izmailov's "Antiquarian" in *Novaia illiustratsiia*, no. 51–52 (December 1903).

Distant, dead memories wafted from them, from these treasures of the book cellar; once compelling, they had lost their appeal. They resembled a graveyard, where I, a chance, latecoming, and extraneous guest, read, as if on graveyard crosses, the names of dead people and the titles of forgotten works. This damp semi-darkness of the cellar, the figure of the strange old man who remained upstairs in the bustle of the day and the atmosphere of ordinariness, his assured words—all this put me in a strange and nervous mood. I glanced into the second room of the basement and flinched. From its corner, where a dim night light burned, two large, sharp, sickly, agitated eyes were looking at me. Sitting by the night lamp was a boy, thirteen or fourteen years of age, skinny, pale, in a worn-out reddish coat and creased cap, with a cheap booklet for commoners in his hand. A small crutch leaned against his chair. The crutch, and his head, which seemed somehow wrongly placed on his shoulders, and he himself, as if immured in the dead cellar, created a peculiar impression that intensified the overall feeling of the evening, and increased my interest in the strange owners of this strange shop.

I remember it was not without pleasure that I found myself back upstairs, out of the basement. Regarding the books we quickly reached an agreement. The old man gave them up for very cheap, for a price not aimed at a high bidder, as if he was happy to share his treasures.

"I am selling them very cheap," he concluded. "And I will take them back from you anytime for the same price. Tomorrow, even."

"No, tomorrow I will come to you, not to return the books, but to look at new ones. By the way, who is that little fellow down below?"

"The little fellow? Oh! That is my little chap. He guards the lamps. From catching fire. Heaven forbid a fire."

## V

The next day I stopped by to see the antiquarian. The shop was closed. The iron bedbug sat on the door as always. His neighbor, selling ready-made clothes, replied to my inquiry that the shop had not opened today. I left with a disappointed feeling, and at home there was already a message from the unknown correspondent waiting for me. He wrote, among other things, that now the "guide was at my side," and my "desire to learn" could enter a phase of active realization. There was nothing noteworthy in this theoretical guidance, but the new letter was strange. In a confident tone it stated that I had just escaped a huge catastrophe, and that the hand of death had already been stretched over me, but the time for that had not yet come, and the incident appeared only as a sign, showing me the significant in the insignificant.

I did not have to decipher the letters: their author was entirely correct. It was on one of those very days that an accident happened to me, one of the sort that we usually forget the next day, but which could be recorded in the book of life as greatly significant. My dozing cab driver nearly collided with a speeding horse-car, and I jumped off the droshky right onto the rails, almost under the drawbar of the horses. I would have been at great risk if the car had not immediately managed to come to a full stop. As is always the case, five minutes later, sitting in that same carriage, I had already forgotten the incident. Now someone, truly smart and thoughtful, was giving me a reminder of this . . .

The next Saturday I went to see the antiquarian, deliberately choosing his day and time. Already from a distance the light in the shop was visible. The old man cordially let me in, as before.

"Please come in. I have something prepared for you again. Would you like to go down?"

We descended into the cellar. The "little chap" hobbled up past us with a crutch, grasping onto the handrail of the stairs with his tenacious, monkey-like hands. I took note of his thin, colorless yellow face, typical of people who live at night and are forced to spend their days by the light of a smoking fire instead of the warming sun. He, it seemed, was going to guard the entrance to the store. The old man wore the same clothes, only now a pair of thickly tinted smoky glasses darkened his eyes.

My mysterious "guide" was extraordinarily interesting that evening, and his shop was turning out to be surprisingly fascinating. I was acquainted well enough with the subject to see that his mystical and antique library was absolutely unique in the whole capital. Being an antiquarian seemed to be his calling, and when he carefully pulled the dull and faded volumes from the shelf by their spines, one could read on his face, in spite of his strangely disguised eyes, a real, now rarely seen, love for books.

"Kapnist's *Chicane*," he said, wiping the dust off the binding with his sleeve. "First edition. Recognizable by this engraved frontispiece. Confiscated from all shops by the highest decree. The author was sent to Siberia but was returned the same day and promoted to the next rank.[5] And here we have the curious *Cradle of the Stone of the Wise*. Written in the language of the Masons and fully in cursive. From the library of the Rosicrucian Schwartz with his notes and ex libris. *On the Incorruption and Burning of all Things by Miracles in the Realm of Nature and Grace. Chrysomander*—reveals the secret of alchemy. Burned for being harmful.

*Henochisme*. The preface was removed and burned. The bookseller Zaikin was seized with it on the street and condemned to punishment by whip, the cutting of his nostrils, and exile to hard labor. Copies with a preface are rarer than a white crow. *Divine and True Metaphysics* by John Pordage.[6] Printed in a secret Masonic printing house. Never put up for sale, was only given to the chief dignitaries of Freemasonry. The rest were burned. Madame Guyon, *On Following the Infancy of Jesus*. It was fabulously prized in the days of mysticism. And here is the sixth edition of *Dushenka*. For you and me it is of no use, but for others it is of great value. It all burned before it was released for sale, in the invasion of the Gauls. It is the sixth edition, but more valuable than the second and third, because those have omissions, but this one and the first are complete. And here are *Letters to a Friend about the Order of the Holy Cross*. Very rare. You see here the edifying vignette."

On the title page of the book there indeed was an original vignette engraving. A rainbow encircled the earth. A pig slept, its snout buried in the dirt. A donkey, with its rear turned to the rainbow and the sun, nibbled on grass. A monkey, sitting on a tree, used one hand to hold onto a branch, and the other to throw a rock at the rainbow.

"The favorite allegory of ancient mystics," explained the old man. "A most beautiful display of nature. There is no need to stare at the rainbow, for it reflects divinely in the stream. But the spectators of this are a donkey, a pig, and a monkey. One has his back turned and devours grass, the other sleeps in the dirt and sees a vile dream, and the third is bothered by the sun's undying radiance, and thoughtlessly casts a stone at it. Let us ask ourselves, are people not the same? Let's say a person was a hair away from death. Another moment, and the thread of life would have broken. The wall of eternity has fallen. But man is poor in spirit and continues to peacefully nibble on grass. The grass of worldly concerns, so to speak. And he already forgets what had happened. There is no time to think—too much to do!"

The hint at my recent accident was clear, and the company the old man put me in was not at all flattering. I intently gazed at him from the side. But nothing could be read either in his calm face or in his voice. No smile, no irony. Rather, there was a note of irritation or vexation in his words. It occurred to me suddenly to startle him with the question of why he was watching me and writing me letters, and it took a great effort to stop myself.

Fortunately, the old man started talking again, and before I knew it, an hour of conversation had flown by. It was damp in the cellar, and my legs started to feel cold. A few of the books he did not put away, but instead put aside on the table. "These are the ones I recommend." Once again, we immediately agreed on the price. He added two more books to the purchased ones, saying, "Return them after you read them," and lifting the brim of his cap. "I look forward to seeing you again. Please do stop by."

"Perhaps it would be better for me to come to your apartment, so I don't interrupt your work?"

The old man seemed to shudder.

"No, it is better for you to come here. And don't feel uncomfortable; I consider this to be my real work. I live far away . . . but I am here every Thursday and Saturday. Remember: the shop is Labzin's. Number one hundred six. And read my books; don't delay."

## VI

Labzin! What a strange coincidence![7] I was of course familiar with this name, well known in the history of Russian mysticism. A tireless worker in its propagation, publisher of *The Herald of Zion*, translator of a multitude of mystical books while hiding behind the initials "D. W." ("Disciple of Wisdom"), the opponent of Sturdza and Photius—he'd ended up exiled in Sengilei and Simbirsk, like many did in those terrible times. As I was leaving, I happened to glance at the sign outside the shop. It said "A. Labzin." This was coincidence to the point of absurdity! He had the same initials!

I was getting more and more acquainted with this branch of knowledge, which not so long ago was alien and uninteresting to me. The field promises an inexhaustible and captivating experience for a neophyte. In it are deposits of ancient wisdom and old madness, and there is indeed, as my "guide" said, a full and satiating portion of grain—of knowledge—in the piles of book chaff. There is a great deal of close observation of the "mysteries of nature," and sharp and inquisitive insights into the innermost depths of the spirit, which are now becoming the subject of calm, sympathetic attention from the experimentalist-psychologist and physician. It is almost indisputable that the Rosicrucians knew the uses of electrical energy, its wireless transmission, and so forth, long before the Edisons and Marconi. Chemistry and alchemy, astronomy and astrology, medicine and witchcraft— are they not all closely related? Indeed, is it not the point to separate the wheat from the chaff? And the old antiquarian crooned his strange mystical speeches at our every meeting.

"There is a wisdom other than the ordinary human wisdom. It is clearly described in the books of Solomon, with which the wise begin their science. There is nothing hidden from it, and the greatest of all mysteries—the human soul—is revealed before it. Everything is clear to it: the state of the world, the powers of herbs, the thoughts of men. Mind reading, in our words. From an ordinary perspective, this wisdom is temptation and madness. But to those who reach it, the whole world is but a sleepy mirage. Except it is difficult to reach this wisdom, and hard to live with. Everything dies as soon as you glance at its face—happiness, sadness—nothing will be left. Such a man needs nothing on this earth. He will love everything: the thieving sparrow and the lowest little dog. He will kiss the entire world on the lips. People usually don't have time for such wisdom, but every now and then a person will come across it. And he whom it stings will never betray it. One chance day, a person will see a miracle and tell his earthly wisdom: 'I will not get far with you alone.' And he will change . . . And miracles are clearly visible all around us, but we stand with our backs to them, like the pig to the rainbow, and are lazy and have no time to notice them . . ."

It was always quiet, damp, and dusky in the book cellar. The cheap kerosine in the lamp flickered on and off. There was something medieval in the strict and stern outlines of the niches, strewn with books. If it is true that the spiritual is layered upon the material, then how many thoughts and feelings must have stuck onto these old, musty books!

I became a frequent guest at Labzin's, and soon went from the status of a buyer to that of a subscriber. It was of course impossible to buy the entire treasure trove, and it was hardly necessary. The enigmatic old man appeared to me as a profound mystic, sincere and fanatical. Occasionally, though, I would catch a certain expression, strange and suspicious, slithering across his features like a snake. The old mystic shrouded himself in a deliberate fog, and as a private individual he remained as unknown to me as he was on the day I first met him. I did not know who he was or how he lived, whom he spent his time with, or what he did all week apart from the two days I saw him. In an obviously deliberate fashion he would deflect every question about himself that I ventured to ask. I talked to the booksellers I knew, his neighbors at the market. "A smart old man!" they all said. But some were not acquainted with him at all, while others maintained a merely casual acquaintance and could not do anything to supplement my information. "A marvelous old man . . . Perhaps a little crazy . . . Lives alone . . . Does not make acquaintances . . . Does not go to the pub . . . Buys old books from them, always pays generously, not like an antiquarian, but like a collector . . . A great expert in his field . . . Accurately guesses both the place and year of a book's publication not only by the font, but by the beetle[i] . . . However, appears to be a bad merchant . . . He seems to cater more to established customers."

---

i "Beetles," in the language of booksellers, are the four copper or wooden buttons which were in the past usually attached to the back board of a bound book, so that the leather would not wear down when the book was moved [Author's comment].

I have to admit, this secrecy was starting to become quite irksome to me, especially since I myself lived as if under a glass dome before the old man. I still could not say for certain that the letters I received, albeit less frequently, were written by him. Perhaps they were too refined for him. But there was no longer any doubt in my mind about his complete knowledge of them. If he was not the one writing them, he was in direct contact with their author. He would make references to the letters left and right, and the letters sometimes contained allusions to his speeches.

Further, the allusions to my personal life were becoming at times obtrusive and tiresome. Someone was undoubtedly watching me, but watching me with a normal human eye, and more than once I had to smile at some of my tutor's conjectures. They were exactly what an intelligent person observing me from the side would assume, but they were not always in tune with my real psychology. I asked our caretaker, an old and faithful man, whether anyone had inquired about me. Someone had indeed made inquiries, and recently, but I could not guess who this unknown spy was from the description.

"And also, some boy with a crutch befriended your Mishutka . . . He'll come to the courtyard and ask about you . . . If you're home . . ."

This was telling evidence, and in spite of myself, I was becoming suspicious. Mishutka, an eighteen-year-old lad, had been faithfully serving me for half a year. But it was necessary to test him. I purposefully placed some papers on my desk, took notice of their position, and held them down with a small water level, setting the air bubble in the center. A water level can be useful not merely on the desk of an engineer or a technician: would he touch it or would he not? There was no doubt that Mishutka succumbed to the temptation: the level was facing the same direction, but the bubble had moved, and the corners of the papers did not line up.

Once, at twilight, leaving the house for the entire evening, I noticed, about twenty steps away, a small figure darting into the neighboring gate. I walked forward and glanced into the courtyard. The gate was ajar, and sitting on the pedestal in the courtyard was the antiquarian's "chap." His crutch stood propped up next to him. Evidently not expecting my attention, he sat with his back to me, waiting for me to move away but not seeing me. I turned the corner without looking back, and, stopping there, invisible to him, looked around and began to wait. The figure with the crutch slipped out of the gate, looked around, and darted into my courtyard.

That evening, I returned home after only half an hour. The servant was sure I would return later at night. It was because of this that a little surprise occurred. Walking up to the house, I saw a light in my study on the first floor of the building. Mishutka was standing in front of the open drawer of my desk and was reading some kind of paper. I could not see his face through the gap in the blinds—only his hands, the paper, and his vest with a silver chain.

He did not answer my call for a long time, then he opened the door, yawning artificially, and explained that he had already fallen asleep. But in his voice, I heard not the languor of slumber, but a shiver of nervousness. "Forgot my cigarettes," I explained, not entirely truthful in my turn.

I left again after five minutes. Only this time, not only all of my drawers, but my study and the room in front of the study were locked. My cabby overtook the small youth with the crutch. The freak's sharp eyes stared at me inquisitively.

I won't deny, I would have liked to get off the cab and beat him about the ears.

## VII

Mishutka was, of course, very surprised when the next morning I gave him a swift dismissal and a statement that curiosity was a good trait, but not everyone in my position would hold back and not slap him across the cheeks in a case like this. Poor thing—he had let down his guard overnight.

The old man I could not visit until two days later. He, of course, knew everything. I did not notice any confusion or nervousness in him. Those damn bulging glasses, giving him a completely stone face!

But he was hardly awaiting me that day. If he had been, then he would likely have troubled to remove the letter with its familiar stamp, lying on his desk, the address facing down. As I walked in, he took it and put it in his bosom. I caught his shrewd sidelong glance at me. "Did he see?" he asked himself, answering himself: "He did."

The old man was taciturn and gloomy. He watched and waited, hiding behind his usual mystical talk. And it was of course unexpected for him when I suddenly stopped him and said: "Let us leave this, and tell me rather, what's the point of you following me and writing me letters?"

He did not shudder, did not change, but also did not turn his face to me.

"I am following you? Writing you letters?"

"Yes, there is one of them, which you have just prepared and hidden, and which I will receive today or tomorrow."

"You are mistaken. This letter is not to you, but to me," he answered calmly.

„Мишутка стоялъ предъ открытымъ ящикомъ и читалъ какой-то листокъ"..
Оригинальный рисунокъ художника „Биржевыхъ Вѣдомостей".

Figure 2.4. *"Mishutka was standing in front of the open drawer and was reading some kind of paper."* Pavel Shkarin, illustration for Alexander Izmailov's "Antiquarian" in *Novaia illiustratsiia*, no. 51–52 (December 1903).

"Why send the limping boy, strike a deal with my servant, watch my entrances and exits! I'm sick of it," I said, raising my voice. "It's getting on my nerves."

"You'll laugh at this accusation later," he said with the same composure. "This all has nothing to do with me. The letter is from my 'guide.' I am not responsible for the lad. You have received letters even before knowing me . . . I did not come to you; you came to me. I was only fulfilling someone else's will . . ."

"Just show me the address of this letter. If it is not written to my name, I will believe everything you said."

"The letter is not written for you, but I will not show it to you. You must overcome idle curiosity . . . And I will not bother you with myself anymore. Forgive me, I have to lock up the shop . . ."

The old man told the truth. He did not bother me "with himself" ever again. I did not meet him anywhere else, though I walked past his shop dozens of times. It was usually locked. If there was light in it, the same boy as before, with the cup of tea, would be hanging around the table, but I never saw the limping "lad" in it. Perhaps he was still sitting there, in the lifeless book cellar, by the smoking lamp, but he never showed himself when I was there. Once, when the shop was closed, I asked its neighbor, a merchant of ready-made clothes, where the old man had gone.

"He told me to say that he had gone to the village and died there," he answered, and smirked stupidly. There was obviously collusion between them, and any questioning was in vain. Another time, I asked an antiquarian acquaintance about him.

"He stops by occasionally," he said, "only quite rarely recently. And we hardly ever see him. A strange gentleman."

"How so?"

"No reason . . ."

The letters did not stop after our parting. On the contrary, they were especially frequent at first. I was given energetic reproaches that I had deprived myself of my "guide," and that it would be a long wait for another one. Then I had to leave St. Petersburg for a month on personal business. Not a single letter came to me during the time of my absence. Evidently, the one watching me was fully aware of my departure. The correspondence did not renew afterwards.

And one day, after a lengthy intermission, I went into the market and saw that in place of the antiquarian, there was a wretched seller of frames and cheap paintings. Only the sign reading "A. Labzin" was still hanging above the entrance. I went into the tradesman's as a customer and asked him two or three questions. It turned out that he had opened there about two weeks ago. The old antiquarian, whom he had never met, had died, according to him. The sign was left just so. "And the antiquarian's surname was not Labzin, but something else," added the frame-seller. "But anyway, God knows . . ."

I inquired at the address bureau about the place of residence of A. Labzin. Indeed, there was now not a single person in St. Petersburg with that surname.

## Notes

* **Alexander Izmailov, "The Antiquarian."** This was first published with the subtitle "A Christmas Story" in December 1903. It appeared in *Novaiia illliustratsia* (*The New Illustration*), a literary and artistic supplement to the popular newspaper *Birzhevye vedomosti* (*The Bourse Gazette*), where Izmailov for many years headed the department of literary criticism: A. A. Izmailov (Smolenskii), "Bukinist. Rozhdestvenskii rasskaz," *Novaia illiustratsiia*, no. 51–52 (1903), 410–416. In subsequent reprints, the subtitle was changed to the more appropriate "From the Book of Mystical Stories"; see A. A. Izmailov (Smolenskii), *Oseni mertvoi tsvety zapozdalye* (St. Petersburg: Energiia, 1906), 113–142. The illustrations, which are reprinted here, appear in the first publication of the story and are designated as "original drawings of the artist of *Birzhevye vedomosti.*" They were made by Pavel Mikhailovich Shkarin, who was also the editor of the newspaper. He drew the protagonist to resemble Izmailov.

1 *a representative of an office very close to literature but not particularly loved by writers—a man who, holding a flaming sword in one hand, paid homage to the muses with the other.* This is a literary censor.

2 *Apraksin and Aleksandrovsky Markets.* Apraksin Dvor (colloquially, Aprashka) has been a major market in the center of St. Petersburg from the eighteenth century to the present day, gaining especial notoriety during the post-Soviet years. It incorporated the adjacent Schchukin Dvor, where the action of Gogol's "The Portrait" begins. When Apraksin Dvor was devastated by fire in the 1860s, the Novo-Aleksandrovsky Market was built further down Sadovaya Street, at the intersection with Voznesensky Prospect. This was demolished in the 1930s.

3 *the old man Leskov.* Nikolai Semyonovich Leskov (1831–1895) was a prominent writer, known outside of Russia mostly through Dmitry Shostakovich's opera *Lady Macbeth of Mtsensk* (1934), based on one of Leskov's tales.

*the late singer Stravinsky.* This is Fyodor Ignatievich Stravinsky (1843–1902), a famous bass, a soloist of the Mariinsky Theatre, and the father of the composer Igor Stravinsky.

*the famous bibliographer Ye., resembling an Old Believer.* Pyotr Alexandrovich Yefremov (1830–1907), a prominent historian of Russian literature, bibliographer, editor, and publisher, combined indefatigable scholarly pursuits with a distinguished career in government and finance (for many years, he was the Director of the State Bank of the Russian Empire). Because of his long beard he could indeed resemble an Old Believer, a follower of those groups that refused to accept the mid-seventeenth century church reforms and remained faithful to the old Russian ways in ecclesiastical matters, lifestyle, and appearance.

4 *I knew that all of this mystical wisdom was at one time vigorously persecuted.* The antiquarian offers books by European and Russian mystics printed in the late eighteenth and early nineteenth centuries, which was the golden age of freemasonry in Russia. On two occasions, the imperial authorities, alarmed by the proliferation of secret societies, tried to suppress masonic organizations: under Catherine II, in 1791–92, and under Alexander I, in 1822. Freemasonry in Russia experienced a revival in the early twentieth century after liberalization following the 1905 revolution. This involved mystical teachings, including Rosicrucian varieties due to the influence of Rudolf Steiner (a reflection of this is seen in the very title of Blok's play *The Rose and the Cross*, 1912). There was also a veritable mushrooming of political freemasonry, so much so that practically all major figures involved in the overthrowing of Nicholas II were masons. "The Antiquarian" was written in 1903, before the beginning of the actual return of freemasonry.

5 *The author was sent to Siberia but was returned the same day and promoted to the next rank.* This is one of many historical anecdotes about the impulsive character of Paul I. A century after the emperor's murder, a collection of anecdotes and historical sources pertaining to his reign appeared in print: *Pavel I. Sobranie anekdotov, otzyvov, kharakteristik, ukazov i proch.*, compiled by A. Geno and Tomich (St. Petersburg: Sinodal'naya tipografiia, 1901). It provided ample

material for historical fiction, including Merezhkovsky's play *Paul I* (1908) and Auslender's story "Nelidova's Shoe," a part of his *Petersburg Apocrypha*. The anecdote about Kapnist served as a basis for the poem "The Magical Power of Art" (1984) by Yuly Kim, who subsequently turned it into a play called *Kapnist: There and Back*. The most famous literary use of anecdotes about Paul is Tynyanov's novella *Lieutenant Kizhe* (1928). The musical score by Sergei Prokofiev for the 1934 Soviet film based on the novella was expanded into the suite *Lieutenant Kijé*, which remains among the most popular works of the composer.

6 *"Divine and True Metaphysics" by John Pordage.* Of the numerous works mentioned by the antiquarian, the writings of the English mystic John Pordage (1607–1681) are especially intriguing because of his teachings about Sophia, the feminine incarnation of Divine Wisdom. Sophiology became extremely prominent in Russia in the late nineteenth and early twentieth century in philosophical, artistic, and even theological circles, so much so that in 1935 both branches of the Russian Orthodox Church condemned it, the émigré church even labeling it a heresy.

7 *Labzin! What a strange coincidence! I was of course familiar with this name, well known in the history of Russian mysticism.* Alexander Fyodorovich Labzin (1766–1825) was a writer, translator, editor, and statesman. Influenced as a student at Moscow University by Johann Schwartz and Nikolai Novikov, he became one of the leading Russian masons and mystical authors. In 1822, Labzin was exiled to a provincial town on the Volga.

Ночной принцъ

романтическая повѣсть

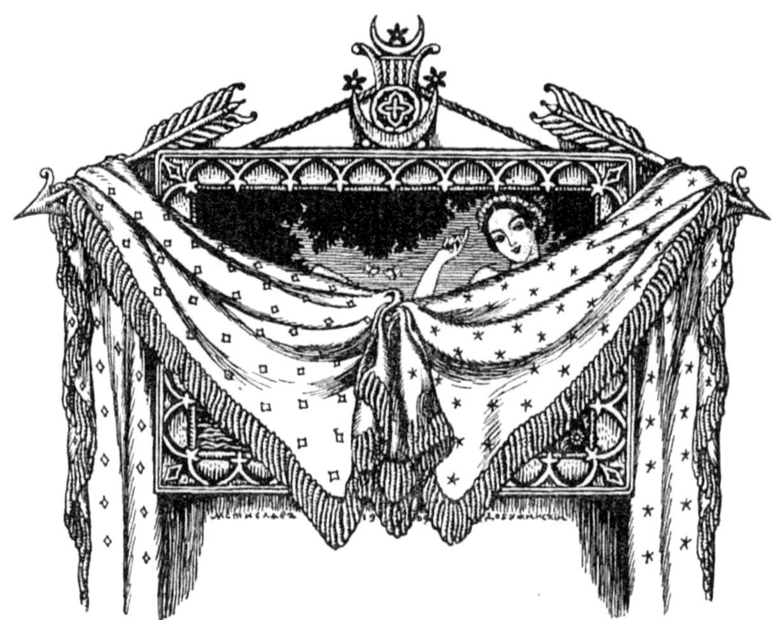

С. Ауслендеръ

Figure 3.1. Mstislav Dobuzhinsky, illustration for Sergei Auslender's "Night Prince" in *Apollon*, no. 1 (October 1909).

Sergei Auslender

# The Night Prince

(A Romantic Tale)*

## CHAPTER ONE

which tells of the strange reveries of Misha Trubnikov, of a bathing girl, of a broken plate, and of a yellow lady.

*The aforementioned items bear depictions of personages.*
From auction listings

Your Lordship,
Every action should have its reasons. How do you intend to excuse your behavior of yesterday? The dinner service, from which you broke the fish set, cost me 500 rubles in banknotes, but you know that it was not the loss that outraged me. Nadenka and I are anxiously awaiting your explanation, for we would rather see your fit as a momentary lapse of reason, rather than impertinence.
I remain your faithful servant,
Prince Grigory[1]

The late morning of a dull, snowy St. Petersburg day and a letter on thick gray paper, inscribed in fine and stern handwriting—"To His Lordship Mikhail Ivanovich Trubnikov in the red house opposite the Ascension, into his own hands"—awakened a young man in a big square room that combined a certain pretension to luxury with the neglect of an almost uninhabited space.[2]

He looked to be about fifteen. His delicate features were not wanting in amiability, though they were somewhat spoiled by his short and unevenly cut hair and the pallor of his face.

Embarrassed, he crumpled up the letter and shoved it under his pillow, almost without reading it. A heavy confusion came over him. The restless gleam of his eyes told of some secret, agonizing anxieties. His nightly visions had not yet fully passed, the same ones he had every night in that room, and the letter, with a vexing vitality, reminded him of all of yesterday's events, and with them a long chain of other miserable and burdensome days. Everything was blending together and it all wearied him: the dull, didactic voice of Prince Grigory; and the pink little face of Nadenka, with whom he had only recently thought himself to be in love; and the veiled bathing girl on the wall of his uncle's study; and the burdensome, tempting conversations with Pakhotin; and the evening in the restaurant; and she, who with her smile overfilled the cup of all his torments and doubts, a seductive delusion, a sly enchantress, of whom only broken pieces of pottery remained after yesterday's dinner, but who through some strange spell was now eternally alive in restless dreams, in twilight visions, a sorceress in yellow silks, with the secret message of three beauty spots, she who bore a sumptuous and fatal name—Marquise de Pompadour.

"And you, sir, should be getting up," Kuzma finally said with suppressed disapproval, for Misha, pulling a blanket over his head, was making a desperate effort to avert the unbearable moment of getting up, which the old servant rightly found improper.

As if caught at the scene of a crime, Misha began to dress himself with obedient haste, not even daring to rebuke Kuzma for the uncleaned boots and the school uniform that hadn't been smoothed out. The respectful insolence of the pampered lackey depressed and irritated him, which he strove to conceal by indifferently asking questions about the weather and the state of his uncle's uncomplicated household, over which he had been made the temporary master.

Misha hastily finished his simple toilet, not even smoothing out the ridiculously protruding bushels of his hair, disfigured by the careless hand of the Lyceum's barber, Efimych.[3] Kuzma served him a miserable breakfast on a scratched tray, swept a feather duster over the sofas and the table, and, thus completing the ritual of cleaning the rooms, retired to the servants' quarters, mumbling something about the disorder of the house.

The fried potatoes with herring and yesterday's meat, dried to a sponge, discouraged the appetite. There was an unpleasant taste in his mouth, and the lethargy after a heavy sleep was not going away. Out of habit, Misha began to wander through the rooms—there were five of them, each one resembling the other with their strange furnishings. It was as if their owner, after a successful raid on the palace of the Sultan of Bakhchisaray, did not know where to put the looted riches, and filled all of his rooms with ottomans, soft rugs, brocade curtains decorated with half-moons and harps, colorful lanterns, gilded sabers and daggers, in short, with all the trappings of the "Oriental" style. Intricate screens with fiery birds and golden dragons thoroughly concealed every accessory of home life—the dinner table, the bed, the washbasin—so that not one of these pedestrian objects would reveal that this was the peaceful abode of an honorable (though unmarried) official of the fifth rank, and not a frivolous refuge for the immodest pleasures of a young rake. Such was the fantasy of Misha's uncle, Dimitry Mikhailovich Trubnikov, in whose quarters he was spending his lonely Christmas break, haunted by strange, often incomprehensible, thoughts, dreams, and even visions.

Quietly moving apart the curtains hanging above every door, Misha went from room to room, stopping by the frozen windows, behind which the snow was falling thickly; the rare passerby hurriedly ran across the deserted street, his bundled-up silhouette attesting to the frost outside, and Misha was already seized by the sweet, familiar languor of the early twilight and the empty rooms.

The bells of the Ascension rang out from time to time. After stopping once more by a window, Misha quietly, as if sneaking along the soft rugs, went through all the rooms, lingered by the last door, looked around, and entered.

This was a large room with four sofas along the walls, called a study for whatever reason. With a feigned carelessness Misha wandered around the room, touched the intricate tobacco pipes displayed in an orderly row on a bronze stand, warmed his hands by the well-heated stove, and only after collapsing onto the silk pillows of the sofa did he finally lift his eyes.

On the opposite wall hung a veiled picture of a bathing girl.

His uncle, when preparing to depart, had pinned the two ends of the curtains around her and said, with a chuckle, "You are too young for this." Only her half-turned head crowned with a blue wreath and the tip of her bare shoulder were visible against the greenish sky.

At first, Misha did not give in to the power of those gentle eyes, even whistling something indifferently, thoroughly convincing himself that all of this was rubbish and nonsense . . . but, imperceptibly to himself, he soon could not tear his eyes from the pert and slightly surprised face of the bathing girl. His whole body became dry, as in a fever, and only the silk of the pillows gently and pleasantly cooled him. So he lay on the low sofa until dark. The outlines of the furniture were almost blending together, and the pink shoulder and pert (though simultaneously doleful and tense) face were dimly visible.

Suddenly, it seemed to him that the portrait had moved.

The corners of its mouth had moved ever so slightly, and Misha recognized from the day before the smile of the yellow lady, who had glanced at him just at the moment he was shamefacedly poking his fish cutlet with a knife.

Mortification colored his cheeks. "Just you wait, you cursed witch," he whispered with spiteful bitterness, remembering yesterday's disgrace and the broken plate.

He jumped up, and with a trembling hand, ripped down the curtain.

A thick tunic covered her entire body, except for the tip of her shoulder, and he could make out her mocking smile even more clearly. Quickly, holding back his steps so as not to run, Misha left the study. A gentle laugh, like the tinkling of a thousand silver bells, followed him from the darkness of the rooms. Kuzma was snoring in the entryway. Pulling on his overcoat, Misha rushed outside.

"Well, well! Where are you going?" Smiling, covered in snow, Pakhotin stood in the entrance. "Last night I . . ." And clapping his hands together, he was already spurting out some story, not paying the slightest attention to the bewildered appearance of his companion.

## CHAPTER TWO

which tells of a fateful encounter, Misha's awkwardness, of ballet, and many other things.

The second act of *The Triumph of Clectomis or the Lazy Seducer* had ended. Finishing her final pirouette, Istomina flew into the pink wings. The corps de ballet girls each smiled to her own admirer.

Pakhotin was ecstatic. Leaping up from his seat in the thirteenth row, he ran up to the orchestra, unceremoniously pushing past several old men in civilian clothes, and applauded, hanging over the barrier, until a chubby Cupid from the cheerful crowd of pupils slyly threatened him with a gilded arrow. Then he returned to his seat, sweaty and triumphant, not caring much about the mocking smiles of the dandies from the Imperial Guard, or about the ladies who pointed their sarcastic lorgnettes at him from the mezzanine floor.

"My little letter had a great effect. I have procured an exceptional favor for myself. Have you noticed her figure? She has not turned sixteen yet, but Prince Vasily claims . . ."

Pakhotin spoke loudly and boastfully. Misha listened, admiring and envying him. He blushed with shame that curious neighbors were listening to their conversation, growing pale from excitement when his friend's words became too immodest and captivating.

"Enough, enough, that will do," he muttered, embarrassed, both afraid and wishing for the continuation of the alluring conversation.

"Oh, big deal. Just wait 'till you see what I'll show you! Come eat dinner with us tonight. I have a carriage ready, we'll go straight from here," Pakhotin urged his friend, and bent down to whisper the final details, so that the old man sitting in front of them could not help but grunt loudly and turn his ear in their direction.

Misha remembered that he had in his pocket six rubles, which were supposed to last him until the end of the holidays, and he firmly refused. Pakhotin was displeased and left to go smoke.

The opulent hall with its elegant audience, its gold and lights, wearied Misha. Pakhotin's stories, the nymphs and cupids in semi-transparent garments, showing their pink leotards that deceptively lured the imagination, the fashionable ladies in boxes, with their necks and arms open to hungry gazes, the air itself, sweet and warm and filled with temptation—everything merged together into one languid desire.

"I thank you," said a damsel in a lilac dress with a prim smile, when Misha picked up her dropped playbill, and, all crimson, blocked her way for a few seconds. She looked him straight in the eye in amazement, not understanding his embarrassment.

"I thank you," she said again, and slightly moved his elbow, which was blocking her way. Misha stood stock still for a long time, though he hadn't even made out if she was beautiful or not. His neighbors glanced at him scornfully—he had trampled over their feet, doing the lady the awkward favor.

"Oh, the things I'll show you. Come on, come on," Pakhotin pestered him again, pulling him by the arm out of the hall, though the musicians were already preparing to begin the prelude, and the ushers were extinguishing the candles.

In the narrow corridor, people were walking, jostling each other, and dawdling. It was especially crowded near the third box on the left side. Several uhlans and civilians loitered around the columns. Ladies, passing by, looked back with disdain. Through the heads, Misha could already make out a high toque of gray fur with white feathers.

Pakhotin nimbly pushed him forward. On the steps of the box there stood a lady. She was wearing a dress of dark-pink velvet. Her exquisite necklace was blinding, hindering the viewer from taking a closer look at the stones, while her earrings—large pearls in golden half-moons—hung down almost to her shoulders. Her black, slightly wavy hair and the gentle swarthiness of her face suggested a southern origin. Her powder, her brightly made-up lips and eyes, thinly lined with blue, gave her face an inexpressible allure with their deliberate artificiality. She was well proportioned and slim, like a boy. She seemed not to pay any attention to the gawking public. Her dark, gray eyes were doleful and indifferent. Like a queen, she descended the steps, gathering up her heavy train, covered in golden stars. The crowd parted before her, whispering. She slowly walked down the corridor and disappeared into the ladies' room.

"Who is that?" discussed the men in a group. No one knew for certain.

"A Spaniard. Count N. brought her," someone said uncertainly.

"No, that one was fat."

"She lost weight."

"Why would she lose weight?"

Everyone was laughing excitedly. No one even looked at the passing beauties. And indeed, all women after her seemed coarse, unattractive, and dressed poorly and tastelessly.

When Misha entered the half-dark hall, gloomy and agitated, Istomina was already dancing on stage, untwisting a yellow veil, rising on her toes, twirling, languid and beckoning; the lazy Guliam was lying on a lonely bed; and nine muses, quarreling on the sidelines, were preparing the victory of their favorite.

During the performance, Misha many times furtively glanced over to the third box on the left.

The lady was sitting completely alone, leaning in a careless pose on the barrier. Her opened fan covered the bottom half of her face, and only her eyes, as if completing a tiresome job, indifferently observed the commotion taking place onstage.

By this time, Clectomis had seduced the lazy Guliam who, as he rose, expressed his fiery passion in a rapid dance. Clectomis danced her joy, and all participants (the nine muses, cupids, nymphs, peasants and peasant girls, Turks, and Aurora), circling in a *grande valse finale,* expressed their common satisfaction. Finally, the cavalier dropped to one knee, and giving his hand to the ballerina, helped her fly up onto his shoulder. Everyone froze in picturesque poses.

The curtain slowly fell, hiding the bliss of the triumphant Clectomis and her indecisive lover.

Misha lost Pakhotin in the corridor. He did not remember where he had left his overcoat, and mechanically turned left. A lackey had already helped a lady into her dark-blue coat lined with sable, and making way for her, pushed Misha quite rudely. Misha looked around angrily and met the lady face to face. For a second, she paused under his almost insane gaze. It seemed to him that she smiled, just slightly, at the corners of her lips. It was that same damned smile. Misha took a step back, trampled on someone's hem, and stumbled, flying three steps down headfirst. When he stood up, the lady was already gone. Two lackeys, doubling over with laughter, were pointing their fingers at him. Confused, rubbing his bruised spot, Misha hurried to hide in the crowd and find his overcoat.

Imperial Guardsmen in heavy beaver coats were loudly discussing where to go. Ladies, their feet in golden slippers peeking from under their coats, twittered pretentiously. Two gendarmes with torches pranced around at the entrance. Caretakers ran around and announced carriages.

"Ivan from Galernaya," someone shouted piercingly.

"Tomorrow, my dear, tomorrow."

People were being helped into carriages, hands were being kissed, a note fell out of the quickly slammed door of a carriage, and an officer deftly caught it on the fly.

Misha made his way through the joyous crowd, lonely and gloomy. He barely made it over the snowdrifts that had piled up during the evening on the square. Fighting off the advancing cabbies, he went out onto Nevsky Prospect.

"Make way, make way!" resounded a fierce cry, and Misha barely had time to jump out from under the carriage and into the snow.

By the dim streetlight, in the window that flickered by, he clearly made out two shadows joined in a kiss.[4]

## CHAPTER THREE

which contains the dull, but necessary discussions on the bridge.

Misha walked, his face buried in his collar, hands shoved in his pockets. Gripped by a heavy excitement, he did not notice the cold, or the snow that seemed intent on covering the entire city up to the very roofs, or the streets, which he quickly passed one after the other, turning corners, going back,

Figure 3.2. Mstislav Dobuzhinsky, illustration for Sergei Auslender's "Night Prince" in *Apollon*, no. 1 (October 1909).

walking straight again, as if surrendering to some external force, benevolent and wise.

At last, he stopped on a high bridge above a canal.

The snow enveloped the houses in a thick web, and it seemed that all around was a desolate square, on which figures were running, twirling, intertwining, at once threatening or malicious and beckoning, even tender. Leaning against the parapet, Misha listened to their whimsical game. The snow had covered almost the entire bridge with its tall statues, and gently fell on Misha's head, shoulders, and hands.

Thus he stood, gazing into the blizzard, until he felt a sharp pain in his freezing fingers.

Then Misha jumped up and down in the middle of the bridge, and hiding from the wind, turned to the opposite side. The second floor of the corner building on the embankment shone through the snow. Dancing couples passed one after the other across the illuminated windows.

Spellbound, Misha could not tear himself from the festive sight. The gliding, curtseying, and whirling couples looked like ghosts to him behind the half-frozen windowpanes. Their flowing movements conveyed inaudible music, gentle smiles and languid sighs, and everyone seemed to him happy, elegant, and in love.

"The cavaliers are trying hard, but the ladies are already looking at us too often. Don't you find such behavior somewhat inappropriate?"

A tall stranger in a fur cap, who had appeared out of nowhere, was standing quite close to Misha, likewise intently gazing into the windows, and speaking in a tone as if they had just a minute ago interrupted a long conversation, which he was restarting with this cue.

"Do you think they are noticing us?" Misha asked, turning towards him.

"Are they noticing us? What innocence! For whom, then, in your opinion, is all this pomp?" the other exclaimed with a merry laugh, which Misha disliked for some reason.

For several minutes they were silent. The stranger spoke first, softly touching Misha's shoulder.

"My dear prince, I know that your melancholic moods are not simply a boyish caprice, but are there really no remedies for your sorrows? Am I, whose loyalty I hope you do not doubt, really not able to help you in any way?"

Misha interrupted him quite impatiently.

"First of all, sir, you are clearly confused, calling me a prince for some reason; and secondly, let me say that I have never even had the occasion to meet you before, let alone give you the right to ask questions, which seem more than strange to me."

Turning around briskly, he was about to leave his disrespectful interlocutor.

"A penalty, a penalty," yelled out the latter, with such simple-hearted cheerfulness that Misha unwillingly stopped, intrigued by his speech. "I pay the penalty. I have violated your disguise. I have violated the wise rule of not noticing other people's annoyance. Of course, sir, we have never met before, and even your name is unknown to me, just as mine is unknown to you. It is only for this reason that I gave you the first title that came to my mind. Only for this reason. But such a meaningless slip of the tongue should not hinder us from spending this night together, as neither I, nor you, it seems, have the slightest inclination yet to return to our hovels."

And he suddenly laughed again, so piercingly that Misha made another impatient gesture, which immediately calmed the strange joker, and he continued, though not without a chuckle.

"And so, we shall spend this night, sighing dolefully about our sorry condition. We will wistfully observe from the bridge, through dull windows, the merriment of others. There, by the house of the Jewish banker, on the embankment, a poor poet, leaning against a pillar, and lifting his eyes to the two windows of the second floor, will tearfully tell me the touching tale of the beautiful Jessica and the cruel Jew. Isn't that right?"

"What Jew are you talking about?" muttered Misha, both confused and interested by the incoherent chatter, the meaning of which completely evaded him.

"Oh, all wandering, sorrowful poets like us have been in love with the beautiful Jessica since the blessed time of Mr. Shakespeare. But I am not insisting at all. Perhaps the subject of today's improvisations will be the mysterious Spanish woman, or even the eternally charming Marquise de Pompadour, who often keeps the imagination of certain young people awake."

"How do you know about that?" Misha cried out in angry terror.

"Now you've given yourself away, my friend," he laughed, touching Misha's overcoat. "However, there is nothing surprising about this. Poets love to dream about the impossible."

"About the impossible," Misha repeated with a heavy sigh.

"But, my dear prince—" The stranger spoke with unexpected seriousness. "The impossible is just what you wanted. Our agreement was precisely to spend this night dreaming of the impossible." Then he yelled, waving his arms in the direction of the illuminated windows: "Oh, be quiet! I'm sick of it. Shush."

And suddenly, as if following an agreed-upon sign, the lights all went out simultaneously, and the snow covered all—the dancers, the hall itself, the embankment, and everything that had been illuminated by the bright lights of the hall—in its dim shroud.

Misha was silent, stunned. The stranger gently continued his speech.

"And should one even wish for anything other than the impossible? Should one even waste time saying, 'I want the possible, the earthly, the simple'? No, my dear prince, that is the fatal mistake—to regret that the charming bather will never come down to you. That is what closes the confining and bleak circle, leaving no room for our dreams. Madame de Pompadour, in all likelihood, would have gladly fulfilled your desires, but you yourself destroyed her as soon as she tried to incarnate herself and come out of her faience. Although I will not remind you of this incident, which for some reason is unpleasant to you." The stranger hastened to finish on a conciliatory note, sensing again his interlocutor's displeasure.

Misha remained stubbornly silent. The stranger spoke again with enthusiasm, not bothered much by this impoliteness.

"You can't even imagine what a boring mess it would be if all our dreams came true. The noble profession of poets would be abolished. All the ardent lovers, pale from languor, would be united, and the merry nights of sighs, of woeful meetings through windows, of timid tearful vows, of serenades, disguises, chases, of somber separations, all of which the poets sing and which in essence is only a constant dream of the impossible, would cease. Frown, weep, dear prince, but do not betray our professional duties. We are poets; we must not be too cheerful. Although it seems that my advice is completely useless to you. You are as virtuous in this respect as ten poets, all are preparing to pour out elegies, stanzas, or even strike up a tempestuous ballad."

But at last even he exhausted his reserve of loquacity, and they were both silent—Misha hopelessly and resentfully, the stranger mockingly and expectantly.

The blizzard was dying down: only occasionally now did orderly rows of countless snowy sparks, raised by the wind, fly like soft waves and calm down again, falling. The snow, however, fell in steady, heavy, even flakes, and the few streetlamps were only vaguely visible.

"Ah, and here is the baron," exclaimed the stranger, who had been anxious for awhile, as if awaiting someone.

And indeed, at that very moment, another person, of a shorter than average height, in a top hat and fashionable fur coat, stepped onto the bridge. He bowed courteously to Misha, who had turned dourly upon hearing the exclamation, then attempted to make an obeisance according to ballroom regulations, almost slipped and fell, and was caught by the first stranger, who cheerfully introduced him.

"Mister baron, I ask you to love and favor him. A great philosopher, patron of the arts, and a man of rather good judgment. I hope that with his help I will be able to convince you sooner of your calling to be content with the noble profession of a sorrowful poet, dreaming the nights away about the charms of the shattered marquise, and not wishing to become a smug scamp delighting in finite and crude pleasures with some wench."

"Buffoon," the baron interrupted him, though in a rather approving tone.

"So you say, but I remind you of our deal," the other retorted, as if chafed, and quite disrespectfully smacked his interlocutor's top hat, pushing it right down onto the baron's nose—at which his grace only laughed merrily, exclaiming "Buffoon" once again.

"We will continue our conversation later, my friend," the stranger interrupted significantly, turning to Misha, and resumed speaking with the same liveliness as before.

"Before we begin a joyful night of sorrowful adventures, I think it wouldn't be a bad idea to grab a bite to eat. Besides, 'The Pink Swan' is not much of a detour. What do you think, baron?"

"Buffoon," shouted the baron almost spitefully, but as if missing the disparaging word, the stranger grabbed both of his companions by the arms and dragged them, without interrupting his chatter, from the bridge to a snowdrifted alley.

## CHAPTER FOUR

which describes everything that occurred in The Pink Swan, as well as the appearance of the Night Prince.

It was bright, warm, and lively in The Pink Swan, because although the shutters were already closed, the visitors had no intention of leaving yet. It was especially noisy in one corner, where a group of students was feasting, their uniforms cast off; they had struck up a Latin song that was heard even two houses down the street and could have been mistaken for the distant howl of a wolf pack. As our travelers were nearing the restaurant, they heard not only the student song, but also the intense din of a fight, for at that very moment the waiters, trying to maintain their polite demeanors, were escorting out an unruly visitor. Two students had stepped in for him and brought out their swords from under the table; others were restraining them and singing their song; the owner, trying to calm everyone, was yelling the loudest; and the orchestra, consisting of a guitar, two violins, a drum, and a harp, was playing to the fullest.

The stranger, entering the cellar, somehow immediately interfered in the scandal and stopped the noise in a moment. Only the drunkard who had been thrown out was still yelling, from a snowdrift outside the door.

"Just you wait. You're going to get it. I also know something about your tricks, and you can't surprise me with a winking jack. Come on out, Mister Zillerich, come on out."

As if taking the man's drunken chatter seriously, the stranger quickly ran up the stairs and closed the door behind him, standing outside for several

Figure 3.3. Mstislav Dobuzhinsky, illustration for Sergei Auslender's "Night Prince" in *Apollon*, no. 1 (October 1909).

seconds—and then nothing else disturbed decorum, if one does not count the orchestra occasionally, at the signal of the owner, furiously playing the polka from *Le Postillon de Lonjumeau* and the students striking up their couplets, cutting them off at the second line.

In the light, Misha could finally take a good look at his companions.

The "baron" turned out to be quite a young man, very pink, very well-fed, and very blond. His hair was carefully brushed and curled at the temples. His clothing was refined: a pink silken vest, delicate lace, fashionable buttons, and an ivory lorgnette peeking out from under his foppish coat, which was trimmed with gray fur.

The other also was not old, though one could not call him young either. His thin, sneering mouth seemed youthfully fresh and his eyes glistened merrily from beneath his heavy lids. But his yellow forehead, all covered in wrinkles, merging with his low bald spot; the sparse hairs on his temples, colored and already faded; his knotty hands: all this gave him the appearance of senile squalor. His modest, worn but neat clothing was inconspicuous. On his pointed head, under the hat, he wore a small green velvet skullcap.

"So," he began, taking a seat and slapping his hand on the table. "So, honorable gentlemen. We can finally get to know each other better. How do you find our baron, young man? And in general, you do not seem very happy with our company, eh?"

"It's not that at all, trully," Misha protested, unable to maintain his rudeness in the light. "Of course, you must agree, our acquaintance happened quite strangely and unexpectedly. But I am very glad, very glad. My name is Trubnikov."

"You are still being stubborn? Well, have it your way."

"What would you like me to call myself?" Misha asked, timidly, as if he himself was not quite sure of his name.

"Your Highness," began the baron, gracefully bending down. "I greatly appreciate your ploy. I am delighted, but Zillerich is crude and worldly. He knows the tricks of a street charlatan and deems himself almighty. Put your trust in me. I know how to appreciate subtle feelings."

"Bravo, bravo, baron. You are an excellent diplomat, though I do not recommend you quarrel with me."

"If you do not shut up, I will throw you out like a dog. My authority—" the baron yelled piercingly.

"I don't give a damn about your authority. My find—" interrupted the old man, and made a grasping move, as if trying to drag Misha over to his side.

"Honorable gentlemen, quiet down. There has not been such a racket in my establishment for ten years. Don't quarrel, for God's sake," said the stout, out-of-breath owner, heading toward their raised voices. "You can sort out your quarrels at home. Drink wine. Stepanida will now sing "Sure Signs," the latest romance. Do not quarrel, honorable gentlemen."

The musicians squeezed together on their platform, and two Gypsies, bowing low and amicably nodding to their acquaintances, ran out clinking their silver shoe taps. An older Gypsy, unusually portly, in a white caftan with braids, was not even really dancing, but simply standing in one spot, moving his shoulders, turning his hat in his hands, occasionally tapping and stomping one foot.[5] Yet it turned out wonderful, nimble, lively, and tasteful.

Stepanida began, wailing and gesturing with her hands:

Oh why, lieutenant,
Are you under arrest,
In bitter imprisonment,
A swordless convict.

Zillerich seemed keenly interested. He sang along with the Gypsy, banging his hand on the table to the beat, and only occasionally glancing over to Misha, to whom the baron was whispering, leaning over the table:

"One word, Your Highness, one word, and everything will be fulfilled. We are not only united by the highest wisdom, but also by a constant readiness to help a hungering brother in everything, without sparing our lives. Put your trust in me. Reveal your desires."

Misha was examining the baron's white hand with its filed nails and noticed a black ring on his left pinky.

"Are you and your friends freemasons?" he asked, instead of responding.

"In appearance, only in appearance," the other replied, bending down even further from Zillerich, "Isn't it all the same, Peter to Truth, Vladimir to Order?[6] All of this is only an outer shell. We look for a Night Prince, find him, and serve him. The final truth lies in the fulfillment of his wishes. The chosen one should not resist."

The face of the baron did not change: pink, with blond curls.

The Gypsy finished, waved her red shawl, jumped off the platform, and went around the audience with her plate. Laughing, she fought off the students whenever one of them tried too hard to hold her back by grabbing her waist. Approaching the table in response to Zillerich's signs, she started talking, showing her white teeth in a smile.

"Generous sir, you are lucky. Give me your hand, I'll tell your fortune."

Misha stupidly and intently stared at the woman. Black braids had fallen out from under her shawl. Her swarthy face with painted lips leaned down to him.

"Why are you staring, handsome? Give me your hand. I'll tell you the whole truth."

"He's a shy one," laughed Zillerich.

"Young sir, my handsome, why are you afraid of me? I won't eat you. Treat me, and I'll tell your fortune," the Gypsy persisted. "May I sit next to you?"

"Please, please," Misha said hastily, moving awkwardly to sit by the baron, who was watching the Gypsy's pestering (which was greatly pleasing the old man) with a disgusted grimace.

"I won't bother you; I won't bother you," Stepanida smiled, and sitting down right next to him, hugged Misha, pressing his head to hers with one hand and taking Misha's hand in her other, and, swaying, began her habitual divination.

"You will be happy, my sweet; you will love me, and I will cater to your every whim."

"Comedians," Misha heard the baron say. He was hot and ashamed, feeling that it would be foolish to fight off the pretty Gypsy.

"Oh Stepanida," was heard around the room, and a great number of people with mugs and pipes gathered around their table, laughing, listening to Stepanida, who was usually stingy with her fortune-telling.

"And I will tell you one last word, my dove," she finished and suddenly pressed her pinky on the tip of Misha's nose. "There is no double line, do you know what that means?" she whispered in his ear. "You do not know love yet, but you think hard about it day and night."

Pretending to whisper something else, she brushed her lips below his ear.

"Leave me alone." Misha stood up, feeling a strange new resoluteness.

"Prince," the Baron cried out in an alarmed voice. "Look, look!"

Misha turned and saw in a small oval mirror a youth, almost a boy, with a stern blazing face, in a crown and dalmatic like the ones in portraits of Emperor Paul. At first, he did not recognize the miraculously changed features of his own face. Then, recognizing them, he almost fainted, and turning away from the mirror, staggered into the arms of the baron and Zillerich.

## CHAPTER FIVE

which tells of the coronation of Misha Trubnikov, and everything that preceded it.

Misha came to in a snowdrift. He was lying as if dead, pale, with his eyes closed, on the fur of his coat, like a very young boy. The baron was rubbing snow on his temples. The alley was quiet and starlit. The noise and stuffiness of the restaurant seemed like a dream.

"There we go, there we go, it's all over now," the baron said simply and gently. Zillerich was no longer there.

Misha stood up. He felt weak and empty as if he'd been poisoned by toxic fumes. He was very sleepy and hungry.

The baron took him by the arm. They slowly walked down the alley with its dark windows, taking a barely trodden path between the snowdrifts.

"I'm not used to it," Misha said, as if apologizing. "Forgive me for troubling you. Where will we go?"

"Please don't worry. I think it would be good for you to rest and warm yourself. All the inns are already closed, unless you agree to stop by my friend's house. His house is right around the corner. They don't sleep all night there, and no one will disturb us. We can make ourselves at home."

"Alright," Misha agreed, experiencing a sweet will-lessness.

They entered the house without knocking, for the baron unlocked the door with his own key. A servant was sleeping on fur coats in the entryway. Blue candles were burning in low candleholders, and incense wafted towards them as they entered.

Leading Misha through the halls, the Baron brought him to a large room, evidently the library, fully lined with shelves. In its depths stood a small table with a candle, set for two people. Wood burned in the fireplace.

"You see, we were expected," the Baron said, gesturing for Misha to take a seat in the armchair by the table.

Spicy dishes, unfamiliar to his taste, were quickly brought in and then taken away by a servant who entered and exited in silence.

Figure 3.4. Mstislav Dobuzhinsky, illustration for Sergei Auslender's "Night Prince" in *Apollon*, no. 1 (October 1909).

Misha's face burned from the wine and the proximity of the fire in the hearth. The baron was a simple and pleasant interlocutor, with not a single gesture or word reminiscent of those strange and frightening minutes. During their conversation he seemed to avoid addressing Misha by any name in particular. They spoke of outside subjects. Misha told of his pranks at the Lyceum with an unusual liveliness. The baron listened, smiling, and prodding the dying logs in the fireplace.

"Well, then, how should we decide?" the baron said suddenly. He had not changed his tone, but he spoke in such a way that Misha understood what he was asking about. And yet, he timidly asked: "What do you want to decide?"

"The three holy amulets. The red ruby for love, the green emerald for high power, the cloudy opal for wisdom. The hour has come to choose, Your Highness, to choose."

"Alright," Misha replied, quietly and pensively, not surprised, staring into the fiery flowers among the coals. "Alright; the ruby, the emerald, the opal." Even quieter, he answered: "The ruby."

The baron stood up, and Misha followed suit.

"I am ready, Your Highness. Would you please follow me." He unlocked an inconspicuous door, painted the color of the wall, between two bookcases. A hall opened before them. Two old men, conversing on a couch in the corner, did not pay them any attention. The chandeliers and candelabra were all lit and sparkling and reflecting in the mirrors.

"One moment, Your Highness," the Baron whispered, and smoothly gliding over the parquet he withdrew, leaving Misha in the middle of the brightly lit empty hall with columns and pink cupids on the walls. Misha did not know what to do. He glanced over at the old men. They were whispering as before, nodding to each other with their gray, pomaded heads.

A moment later the sound of quick footsteps was heard from the adjacent room. The door swung open. A tall, slightly plump lady with an old man at her side came straight towards Misha. A multitude of guests followed them.

"My dear Prince, at last you have come to us. I am so delighted," the lady said, looking at Misha. "I am extremely delighted."

Lowering his eyes in embarrassment, Misha nonetheless caught a glimpse of her smiling lips and the curls of her high coiffure.

"Why are you silent, Your Highness?" Misha heard a voice, reminding him of Zillerich's. The guests surrounded him in a tight circle.

"You don't even want to greet me."

"My lady," said Misha, blushing. "My lady." Bending over, he kissed the outstretched hand, not lifting his eyes to her. Misha remembered from his quick glance the delicate, beautiful hands, both of which the lady had held out to him, yet when he touched his lips to this hand, he felt cold, flabby skin that filled him with an unbearable disgust.

Lifting his eyes, Misha saw Zillerich standing in front of him, with his green skullcap. Misha was holding his hand, having just kissed it, while the lady had stepped back in embarrassment.

Misha stayed the way he was, not letting go of Zillerich's hand, as the other smiled maliciously.

"There's been a little mistake, Your Highness."

Everyone started talking, trying to move on from the uncomfortable situation, and the lady, gently taking Misha's arm, walked into other rooms, showing him to everyone and saying, "What a wonderful Prince we have." But Misha could not forget or calm down; he felt disgusting, his head was spinning, and he wanted to run, but couldn't.

Big rooms, small rooms, halls, the living rooms, couch rooms, all were lit as if for a celebration, but there was no music, and loud conversations were only wherever Misha and the lady were passing, while in the adjacent rooms it was silent, so that it was strange to find a full room of guests after opening a door. Anxiety gripped Misha, though nothing signaled danger. The lady gently squeezed his elbow, all the guests bowed politely and tried to take on a look of merriment whenever the prince came near. Once or twice the face of Zillerich flashed in the crowd. Misha wanted to yell something at him, to throw himself at him, but as if guessing these intentions, he always quickly vanished. The baron also appeared occasionally and tried to cheer Misha up with a smile. The lady rarely addressed Misha with words, which allowed him to remain silent as well.

"Do you not enjoy our celebration, where you are the master?" she asked. "All desires, all desires must be fulfilled today. Tell me: what do you want?"

"I want to leave here," Misha said sluggishly.

"But why, but why?" the lady became nervous, squeezing his elbow ever tighter. "What happened? What is pushing you away? If you do not want festivities, there will be silence and prayers. Would you like that?"

"I want to leave here," Misha repeated, not making any movement to do so.

"That is impossible," the lady said, and with the same gentle demeanor she led Misha further, repeating her words over again to everyone: "What a wonderful prince we have here today."

The guests bowed and smiled, greeting the prince as one usually does at court, while he walked past them with a proud and doleful expression. At last, the lady said loudly: "But why is there no music playing and nobody dancing?"

As if hearing an agreed-upon signal, everyone started to exit the halls into the corridor, the men to one side, the women to the other. The baron came up to Misha and, taking him by the arm, led him away from the lady. Walking down the corridor, Misha said:

"I want to leave here."

"One moment, Your Highness," he answered.

In a small room in front of a mirror lay a crown, a mantle, and a chain of precious stones. The baron placed them onto Misha.

"Now everything has been fulfilled. You are crowned. Nothing is prohibited for you."

Misha felt himself losing consciousness. He wanted to look in the mirror again to see that blazing and beautiful youth in the dalmatic one more time, but suddenly it was as if a cold wind restored his willpower, and he firmly said:

"I know everything now. And now I will leave alone. That is how it must be and how it will be."

The baron looked at Misha with some surprise, as if not recognizing him, but he bowed obediently and rushed to pick up the mantle, which Misha had carelessly thrown to his feet.

Misha went out to the entryway. The servant awoke.

"Are you leaving, sir?" he asked, and found Misha's overcoat among the heap of other military, civilian, and women's coats.

## CHAPTER SIX

which describes the final adventure of that night.

Having thus left his companions, Misha started slowly walking up the street. The bonfire, by which Zillerich had only recently entertained everyone with his jokes, had gone out. The policeman, who had scared Misha, was sleeping on a guard stone, and looked like a bear again.

A carriage, creaking in the snow, passed Misha, and stopped in front of a doorway.

Slowing his steps, he could clearly see a lady in a blue coat as she alighted. He recognized the gray toque, and then the lackey who had pushed him in the vestibule of the theater. This encounter seemed to Misha the most striking event of that night. Leaning against the wall, he waited for the carriage to leave and then walked up to the house. There was no light in the doorman's round window. The step was so covered in snow that Misha was already doubting whether it was this door he had seen open just a minute ago.

"Your doings, damn it," he muttered, spitting in annoyance, and was getting ready to leave when he saw a yellow rose, like the ones in the lady's hair, in the snowdrift. Misha picked up the flower and, afraid of changing his mind, walked quickly up the steps and knocked loudly on the door.

"There are no barriers for the Night Prince." He recalled Zillerich's words with bated breath.

A tall young servant immediately opened the door, as if expecting a visitor. Blocking the light with his hand, he examined Trubnikov for several seconds. "Wait," he said. He put the candleholder on the floor and went up the dark stairs in long strides, skipping steps.

Misha almost passed out from the fear he felt in the damp spacious vestibule, which was lit by one melted candle.

"Run, run," were his thoughts, but the door was already closed. Like a prisoner, he accepted his fate and sat down on a bench, dropping his head to his knees.

"If you please." The servant, lighting the way, stood before him.

Along the way, Misha noticed many doors, and could hear voices coming from behind one of them. One was male:

"Louisa, Louisa."

The other was female:

"It is not true, I can't anymore."

"Would you like to undress, sir?" asked the servant, placing the candle on a table with leftovers from dinner, in a large room almost free from furniture.

Misha threw his overcoat onto the arm of a chair. The servant used the edge of his livery to brush the snow off Misha's boots.

A Moorish girl, in an immodest red dress, came out from behind the curtain separating the adjoining room, and said something hoarsely and merrily. The servant laughed, but, restraining himself, said:

"This is the lady's maid. She will be the one escorting you. She's always up to something," and, with another burst of laughter, he quickly left, taking the light.

The Moorish girl came up to Misha in the darkness, staggering, as if drunk, and said, in an inhuman, parrot-like voice: "You sweet." Laughing, she took his hand, and led him, muttering something. The scent coming from her, mixed with wine and sweet resin, made Misha's head spin.

Behind a low door there was an unexpectedly large room, also empty. A huge bed stood in the center. A magnificent dressing table with a light blue armchair stood on a dais, illuminated by two candles in silver candleholders. For a moment Misha thought the chamber was empty. He did not immediately see the reflection of a woman in the mirror of the dresser. She was sitting deep in the armchair, her ring-covered hands drooping helplessly to the floor. Not moving, not opening her eyes, which were thinly lined in a light blue color, the lady asked something in an incomprehensible language. The maid responded in a hoarse bark and reluctantly left.

Plucking at the yellow rose, Misha stood, his head lowered, but his embarrassment was only partially real.

At last, the lady stood up and started talking. The words of her sweet, drawn-out language were gentle and sad. He understood a slight motion of her hand as permission to come closer. He walked up and kneeled on the steps of the dais. He felt light, triumphant, and curious.

He seemed to understand her slow speech. She seemed to be saying: "It is good that you came to me. I have been awaiting you for a long time. You will love me."

"Yes, yes, I will love you," he answered, smiling with a joy he did not fully comprehend. She also smiled, and her smile no longer scared Misha. His words came together easily. He spoke.

"I have searched for you all night. Not just one night. I have known you for a long time. Did you know?"

"I knew, my dear," she said, and continued the conversation, which perhaps was understood differently by each of them.

Nothing embarrassed Misha anymore, and he no longer marveled at the empty room in the strange house, at the lady in the pink gown with flowers, slender and languorous, leaning down to him from her dais, at his own free and tender words.

Without interrupting her own gentle words, the lady continued her toilet, took off her rings, let down her coiffure, hid her hair under a round bonnet with a wide ribbon, fleetingly but intently looked at herself in the mirror, sprinkled her arms and dress with perfume, and, extinguishing one candle and holding the other up high in her hand, walked through the room. Sitting down on the bed, she took off her purple stockings and said something, tenderly.

A certain disparity between the lady's actions and her words and smile baffled Misha, and he did not know how to respond to her. Seeing his indecisiveness, she ran up to him and sat next to him on the steps, her bare legs tucked up. She put one arm around his neck and coaxed him affectionately, undid the buttons of his stiff uniform, and, putting her fingers behind the collar of Misha's shirt, laughed shortly and innocently. The unexpected mischievousness of the sorrowful lady

Figure 3.5. Mstislav Dobuzhinsky, illustration for Sergei Auslender's "Night Prince" in *Apollon*, no. 1 (October 1909).

bewildered Misha, and the dark, heavy desires of the past few days did not even come to mind.

"I am not ticklish," he said, boyishly shaking his head.

An unprecedented and wild joy gripped Trubnikov, who had always been modest and quiet, even as a little boy.

Strange games began in the empty room. They were chasing each other, wrestling, pushing, laughing, like mischievous children.

Out of breath, the lady fell onto the bed. Misha leaned over her with sparkling eyes. Laughingly, she beckoned him to her, and laughingly he dared to kiss her for the first time.

The Moorish girl, entering quietly, extinguished the flickering candle.

## CHAPTER SEVEN

in which everything that occurred on the morning after that night is described.

Misha woke up late. The sun shone on the red screens in fiery spots. Opening his eyes, Misha jumped up as if under attack. Barefoot, in his nightgown, he jumped into the center of the bedroom, not knowing why. The familiar vacancy of the familiar rooms, the sun directly in the window making the snowy rooftops across the way glitter, the silence, his uncle's large bed, from which he had just gotten up, his own scattered clothes—everything seemed extraordinary.

Vexed and afraid, Misha could not recall where his dreamy visions parted from actual events. Seeing his own frightened, pale face and tangled hair in the mirror, he did not recognize himself. The entrance of Kuzma forced him to adopt a calm expression. Misha dressed unusually slowly. Kuzma, lighting the stove, began his respectful grumblings.

"The prince sent a letter yesterday and today again. I was told to say they are awaiting a reply. What do you want me to say? You came back late yesterday."

"Oh, shut up already, you old geezer. Get out. Right away," Misha shouted, not recognizing his own ringing voice, astounded and delighted by his own anger, as if his face had been struck with a whip. Turning toward the mirror, for a moment he saw a yellow brocade and the almost unfamiliar features of a thin, blazing face, with a radiance around him like a crown. For a moment, this vague vision continued, sweetly reminding him of yesterday's evening.

"Dear God, what is this? What is this?" he muttered, choking with delight and terror again, like the night before.

But the sunlit room, the messy bed, Kuzma crouching in front of the stove with his mouth agape, all this brought him back to his senses. Hesitantly glancing at the mirror, he saw himself ordinary, slightly flushed, smiling with embarrassment, in a high collar and yellow flower-patterned suspenders. Suppressing his shivers of rage and sudden delight, Misha combed his hair more diligently than ever. In a newly strict way, he told Kuzma:

"Go on then, serve breakfast. And it better be neat in here, or I will write to my uncle today."

The astonished Kuzma served quickly and respectfully.

Feeling slim and somehow especially handsome, Misha finally fully recovered in front of the mirror, took a clean handkerchief and gloves from the servant, and with joyful, exaggeratedly slow steps he walked to the entrance hall through the brightly lit rooms that glistened festively with sparkling clean floors.

Trubnikov quickly walked along the canal, delighting not only in the frosty sun, the wintry sky, the soldiers returning on Gorokhovaya street from a parade, but also in something vague and slightly frightening, something secret and solemn. He graciously smiled at passersby, and it seemed to him that everyone was thinking, and even speaking about him: "What a wonderful young man. Who could he be?" Almost reaching Nevsky Prospect, Misha stopped at a corner across the bridge. The entire street was filled with wagons, blocking the way.

Waiting for them to pass, Misha lifted his eyes and suddenly recognized the intersection where he had met Mister Zillerich the day before. The statues on the bridge, the slanted guard stones, and thousands of other details suddenly reminded him of yesterday's events. Not without nervousness Misha found the house in whose illuminated windows he had seen the ball yesterday, serving as a sort of beginning to the marvelous adventures of the past night.

"Hey, watch out, master," shouted a cabman at the distracted Misha, who, avoiding the horse, ran onto the high bridge. Across from him stood a long, shabby house, once painted green, but now turning gray. The ragged shutters, the broken drainpipe, and the dirty entrance gave it a slovenly appearance. Coming up closer, Misha made out a broad white sign with the inscription:

**"Hamburg Restaurant,**

For honored guests the room is available for weddings, dinners, and family evenings at an agreed price."

"What nonsense," Misha exclaimed after reading. "What nonsense," and he laughed so loudly, that passersby stopped and turned to watch him.

Calling a cabman, he still could not contain his laughter and was barely able to utter, "To Liteyny."

"A cheerful master," the cabman smirked, covering him with a blanket. Misha grew breathless from the fast ride and the frost. Carriages and officers in sleighs flashed past on Nevsky Prospect. By Frenzel's Pakhotin called out to him, but Misha only waved his hand, covering his face with his sleeve from laughter and the cold. It was amusing and freeing to gallop like this in the loose snow. All heavy and somber thoughts melted away somewhere. The entire way he was happy, smiling to himself for no reason. All Trubnikov thought was: "What a good cabman I got; I'll have to give him a half ruble."

At the dark blue house on Liteyny, into which he had since childhood always entered nervously and with conflicting feelings, he merrily and thoughtlessly jumped from the sleigh, threw his coat to the porter, and ran to the landing of the second floor.

The lackey stood up from his chair and said, somehow with more respect than usual, "Happy Holiday, Mikhail Ivanovich." Then, after receiving an unexpected ruble as a tip, he stood to attention and, in a completely astonished voice, reported: "His Excellency is expecting you and has asked you to wait in the living rooms. The princess is there."

Quickly and indifferently, Misha entered the white and gold hall. The cold order of the room—the strict row of chairs along the wall, the chandeliers draped with covers, the Venetian mirrors in the piers—was broken by a richly decorated Christmas tree in the center.[7] The room was filled with its sweet and invigorating festive scent.

Nadenka was coming towards him through a long gallery. Without a trace of his former embarrassment, Misha responded to her cheerful smile with a smile of his own, and squeezed her hand so tightly, kissing it, that the princess lowered her eyes for a moment, surprised and even embarrassed.

"Where have you been, cousin?" She spoke, not fully rolling her r's. "We were so worried by your fit."

"Yes, but now all of that has passed."

"What has passed? What happened? Don't torment me, Mishenka," the princess exclaimed, flushing with curiosity.

With a smile, Misha examined the quivering mouche on her rosy cheek, which meant "consent," and felt that no more smiles, no more inappropriate words, could now embarrass him.

Looking at her pink face, playful and curious under a light hairstyle à la Grecque, at her festive, green dress with ribbons of the color *une plainte étouffée*, revealing her elbows, he felt even more cheerful and free in front of this girl who had lately teased him, who was the recent object of his secret sighs.[8]

"Strange encounters can occur, my little cousin. I can entertain you with a marvelous tale in the style you love so much." Half-jokingly and hinting, with suppressed pride, that there was much he would have to skip, Misha began his tale by the large window where a thin pink moon could be seen in the winter sky against a blazing sunset.

"Oh, how wonderful that is," the princess sighed, infatuated.

"Yes, an amusing case, but I did not really submit to their tricks."

"And so, you are a Prince. It is true, true. Today, as soon as you walked in, I noticed that you had changed."

"But I am only the Prince of one night," Misha objected mockingly, to hide his excitement.

"No, now you are forever a Prince to me. I envy you, Mishenka," she ended in a whisper, timid and delighted.

"But you know, it is in your power to become Her Highness too," Misha responded in a whisper. And leaning down, with an unprecedented boldness, taking even himself by surprise, he kissed the princess's rosy cheek.

Prince Grigory, who, because of some convoluted calculations, had long wished for such a turn of affairs, paused in the neighboring drawing-room and, coughing once, went out into the hall, giving his face as affectionate a look as possible.

"I am very pleased, very pleased," he began, moved, embracing Misha in a hug.

## EPILOGUE

in which all the misfortunes and wonderful adventures of Misha Trubnikov appear only as distant memories.

During holidays and birthdays, when Prince Grigory ordered the table to be set with the blue earthenware, the butler always made sure that the fish plate, with the Madame de Pompadour who had suffered a lot from gluing together, would be put before none else than Emilia Vasilievna, the former governess of the princess, who was sitting at the very edge, as the person lowest in rank among those allowed at the prince's table.

Misha did not fulfill the prince's expectations and did not marry the princess, which caused a considerable scandal, and fed the malicious talk of society for at least two weeks.

Upon receiving the inheritance that only Prince Grigory had foreseen, Trubnikov joined the Imperial Guards without finishing the Lyceum. Even in an officer's uniform, he did not deem it necessary to abandon the languid look of a bashful boy, though he was widely rumored to be the perpetrator of many reckless and immodest pranks. Bragging to his comrades, he would say that the decisive blow in his attacks on ladies who were favorably disposed to him was the touching story of Mr. Zillerich crowning him the Night Prince.

November, 1908.
St. Petersburg.

Эпилогъ,

въ которомъ всѣ невзгоды и чудесныя приключенія Миши Трубникова являются только смутными воспоминаніями.

Въ праздничные и именинные дни, когда князь Григорій приказывалъ сервировать столъ голубымъ фаянсомъ, рыбную тарелку, съ много отъ склейки пострадавшей госпожей Помпадуръ, дворецкій всякій разъ зорко наблюдалъ, чтобы ставили никому другому, какъ сидѣвшей на самомъ краю Эмиліи Васильевнѣ, бывшей боннѣ княжны, особѣ, по положенію самой низкой изъ допускаемыхъ къ княжескому столу.

Миша же надежды князя не оправдалъ и на княжнѣ не женился, что вызвало большой скандалъ и служило пищей свѣтскому злорѣчію не менѣе двухъ недѣль.

Получивъ наслѣдство, котораго для него ожидалъ только князь Григорій, Трубниковъ вышелъ въ гвардію, лицея не кончивъ. Томный видъ застѣнчиваго мальчика нашелъ онъ нужнымъ не оставить и въ офицерскомъ мундирѣ, хотя общая молва указываетъ на него какъ на затѣйника многихъ отчаянныхъ и нескромныхъ шалостей. Рѣшительнымъ ударомъ въ атакѣ на благосклонныхъ къ нему дамъ, хвастаясь товарищамъ, называлъ онъ трогательный разсказъ о посвященіи его господиномъ Цилерихомъ въ ночные принцы.

Figure 3.6. Mstislav Dobuzhinsky, illustration for Sergei Auslender's "Night Prince" in *Apollon*, no. 1 (October 1909).

# Notes

* **Sergei Auslender, "The Night Prince. A Romantic Tale."** Originally published as Sergei Auslender, "Nochnoi prints. Romanticheskaia povest'," *Apollon* 1 (October 1909), Literaturnyi al'manakh, 33–69. Included as part of the section "Peterburgskie apokrify" ("Petersburg Apocrypha") in the second collection of Auslender's stories: Sergei Auslender, *Rasskazy. Kniga II* (St. Petersburg: Apollon, 1912), 11–45. The story appeared in print again in 1988 in a collection of historical tales: *Russkaia istoricheskaia povest'*, in 2 volumes, compiled by Iu. Beliaev, vol. 2 (Moscow: Khudozhestvennaia literatura, 1988), 707–732.

The illustrations reproduced here were made by Mstislav Valerianovich Dobuzhinsky (1875–1957) especially for *Apollon*. Sergei Makovsky, an art critic and the founder of *Apollon*, in an essay written during emigration, described these illustrations as follows: "Dobuzhinsky's 'The Night Prince' [. . .] is a typical Petersburg *blanc et noir*, pen drawings with precise and stubborn contours, in places touched up with gouache [. . .] with a vivid counterbalance of black and white spots. The composition is free, not following any older model, rather a two-dimensional stylization, with an inclination toward the grotesque. It is definitely 'retrospective,' in the spirit of Auslender's entire story, and the font and the vignettes of the title page evoke *Biedermeier* from the epoch of Nicholas I. Most typical for Dobuzhinsky is the Russian gothic, more than Empire or any other style, although he stylized masterfully in any style" (S. K. Makovskii, *Siluety russkikh khudozhnikov* [Moscow: Respublika, 1999], 321). One of Dobuzhinsky's drawings (depicting Misha's conversation with Zillerich on the bridge during a snowstorm) brings to mind the passage from the memoirs of Vladimir Nabokov, who writes about himself and his adolescent sweetheart strolling through Petrograd in the winter of 1915-16: "And then out again into the cold, into some lane of great gates and green lions with rings in their jaws, into the stylized snowscape of the 'Art World,' *Mir Iskusstva*—Dobuzhinski, Alexandre Benois—so dear to me in those days" (Vladimir Nabokov, *Speak Memory. An Autobiography Revisited* [NY: Alfred A. Knopf, 1999], 184).

1 *Prince.* There can be confusion concerning the title *prince*, which is rendered in two ways in Russian. *Kniaz'*, the designation for rulers in old Rus, subsequently became an aristocratic title, albeit the highest one, alongside count and baron. The form of address to a bearer of such title was "Your Excellency" (*Vashe Siiatel'stvo*). This is the title of Prince (*kniaz'*) Grigory and his daughter, Princess (*kniazhna*) Nadenka. The protagonist, Misha Trubnikov, belongs to the same circle of aristocratic families, though he does not bear a title. *Prints* is the Russian equivalent of a Western European prince: a member of a royal family, possibly the son of a king and heir to the throne. The form of address to a bearer of such title was "Your Highness" (*Vashe Vysochestvo*). This is the title conferred on Misha during the night.

2 *in the red house opposite the Ascension.* The Church of the Ascension, located at the corner of Voznesensky (Ascension) Prospect and the Catherine Canal (present-day Voznesensky Prospect no. 34), was demolished in the mid-1930s as part of the anti-religious campaign. Much of the subsequent action happens on the embankments of the Catherine Canal, including the Bank Bridge, where Misha is approached by Zillerich.

3 *the Lyceum's barber.* Misha is a student at the Imperial Lyceum in Tsarskoye Selo, an elite educational establishment that opened in 1811. Among those who graduated with its inaugural class (in 1817) were Alexander Pushkin and Prince Alexander Gorchakov, who became the foreign minister of Russia. In Pushkin's time, students were supposed to stay in the Lyceum through their term of study. Beginning in the 1820s, they were allowed to leave for vacations; thus Misha is in St. Petersburg on Christmas break. Although the school is not in session, he wears, as he should, the student uniform. However, he violates the Lyceum rules on multiple other counts. When on leave, students could attend theaters only accompanied by a chaperone. They were supposed to sit in private boxes and were not allowed to enter the stalls, the parterre, the balcony, or the gallery. They were strictly forbidden to attend balls and masquerades.

See *Istoricheskii ocherk Imperatorskogo byvshago Tsarskosel'skogo nyne Aleksandrovskogo litseia za pervoe ego piatidesiatiletie, s 1811 po 1861 g*, compiled by I. Seleznev (St. Petersburg: V tip. V. Bezobrazova, 1861), 382.

4 *in the window that flickered by, he clearly made out two shadows joined in a kiss.* Also, further in the beginning of Chapter 3: *whirling couples looked like ghosts to him behind the half-frozen windowpanes.* Silhouette images, fashionable in the late eighteenth and early nineteenth centuries, contribute to the overall sense of stylization in the story and are also very much in tune with the aesthetics of *Mir Iskusstva* (cf. Dobuzhinsky's illustrations for the tale reproduced here).

5 *Stepanida will now sing "Sure Signs," the latest romance [. . .] An older gypsy, unusually portly, in a white caftan with braids, was not even really dancing . . .* Stepanida/Stesha Soldatova (1784–1822) was a celebrated Gypsy singer. The descriptions of Stepanida, the romance, and the dancer are taken from the famous diary by Stepan Zhikharev, *Notes of a Contemporary*, which provided vivid details for many subsequent works about the epoch, including Leo Tolstoy's *War and Peace*. This particular episode dates back to 1805 and is connected with Count Alexey Orlov, who had introduced the fashion for Gypsy music by bringing its performers from Moldavia. In 1910, Boris Sadovskoi, another author in the genre of historical stylizations, used the same passages in his story "The Petersburg Fortune Teller" (Peterburgskaia vorozheiia), where it is likewise anachronistic, since the action takes place in 1818.

6 *Peter to Truth, Vladimir to Order.* These are names of masonic lodges.

7 *a richly decorated Christmas tree in the center.* Christmas trees were still rare in Russia in the early decades of the nineteenth century. They were widely adopted only in its second half, becoming a must for middle- and upper-class urban households in Auslender's time. See E. Dushechkina, *Russkaia elka. Istoriia, mifologiia, literatura* (Moscow: Novoe literaturnoe obozrenie, 2024). Unlike some other anachronisms in the tale, this one is perhaps inadvertent.

8 *mouche meaning "consent" [. . .] light hairstyle à la Grecque [. . .] ribbons of the color une plainte étouffée.* Here Auslender seems to deliberately mix fashion features from different periods. The language of mouches (beauty patches) is associated with the period before the French Revolution, a Greek hairdo is a marker of the Empire style, and the sentimental designation of the color dates back to the early 1790s, being a conflation of two color names from a fashion magazine: *plainte indiscrète* (indiscreet complaint) and *soupir étouffée* (a muffled sigh). See M. I. Pyliaev, "Mody i modnitsy starogo vremeni," in his *Staroe zhit'e* (St. Petersburg: Tip. A.S. Suvorina, 1892), 102. A French label of this nature, but with an Empire style twist, is found in the opening episode of *War and Peace*, where Prince Hippolyte wears breeches of a color he calls *cuisse de nymphe effrayée* (thigh of a frightened nymph).

Figure 4.1. *Spring fashions of 1912*. An illustration from the issue of the magazine in which Alexey Tolstoy's "The Satyr" was published. *Solntse Rossii*, no. 17 (116) (April 1912).

Alexey Tolstoy

# The Satyr*

## I

In September, in the middle of a clear Indian summer, a fog suddenly descended over St. Petersburg.

The fog moved from the harbor, drifted over the rooftops, and crawled along the streets, where the lanterns, lit since noon, were shining like phosphorescent eggs. It was both dark and not dark, but the houses were no longer visible. Footsteps tapped on the dry sidewalks; horseshoes clinked occasionally on the cobblestones. A horse's muzzle in a shaft-bow would appear in front of the very nose of a startled passerby, then the rest of it, then it would immediately disappear, driving on.

On Vasilyevskiy Island, in the fog, when a row of houses appears to be a forest, and a tree behind a gate appears to be a policeman who has put a whole load of brooms on his head, at this hour, somewhere near the Seventeenth Line, it is quite empty.

In the fog, on an empty street, it is not difficult to run into some drunk or offender, which is why Lyubochka Molina, who was quickly tapping along in her heels, suddenly stopped, hearing footsteps behind her; she frowned and started backing into a fence (there are still many of them in those places). It was here that she first met the person about whom all of St. Petersburg suddenly started talking the next day, gripped by curiosity, and all the ladies who had arrived for the season were tormented by worry that they would be unable to get this extraordinary person into their salon.

Lyubochka had just barely moved to the fence when a person of average height jumped out of the fog in front of her. Still lively from his brisk walk, he turned abruptly and, stretching out his sturdy neck, started to eat her up with his eyes.

The person's head was astonishing—it too was sturdy, with a protuberant forehead, like that of a ram (his bowler hat was perched only on the crown of his head); his nose was upturned; the skin on his face was pink; his beard was light-brown, curly, and shaped like a hammer, with a mustache half-covering very beautiful lips; and his long eyes were such that it seemed if the passerby opened them a bit wider, one would drown in their blue moisture.

Lyubochka took all this in at a glance, angrily lowered her eyelids, and jerking her narrow shoulder, turned to go by. The passerby jumped back, pulled his head into his shoulders, and snorted, like a cat.

And he had good reason to snort: Lyubochka Molina was known all over the Island as a beauty. She was small and black-haired, sporting a fashionable coiffure—twisted into buns over the ears. Her lower lip went over the upper one, as if she was fussy, and her dark eyes were bright and fiery.

She was so good at playing with cavaliers that no small number of clerks went on drinking binges and, in the morning, wrote down all sorts of nonsense in their account books. Salesmen from the Andreevsky market told each other unpleasantries, and there was even a duel, but one does not know whether it was fought with fists or pistols.

But Lyubochka Molina was not dreaming of clerks—it was not for nothing that she had fussy lips. During sleepless nights she imagined an automobile, and articles in the Gazette, and her portrait on Nevsky Prospect at Mrozovskaya's.[1] At the moment, though, she was not even too fussy for starving students, and was currently hurrying to an agreed-upon place to meet a new admirer—except now the passerby was following her.

Jerking her shoulder, Lyubochka ran across the street in little steps and entered a postcard store. But when she left it, holding a card in her hand (the card depicted a zeppelin with roses hanging from the boat), the passerby was waiting by the door and started chasing again, one step behind her . . .

Lyubochka liked this slight fear of a chase, when a man crazed with lust is running behind you and your back seems to tingle with electricity, and your heart either begins to thump or stands still, waiting (you could after all be groped any minute). But today Lyubochka was not in the mood for all of this:

she was almost an hour late, and, when crossing Bolshoy Prospect, the passerby ran ahead, blocking the way, Lyubochka pushed him, got in a cab, and shouted: "Go, go, you fool!"

In haste, the coachman drove fast at first, but soon he dropped the reins, sat sideways on the coachbox, and dragged along, grumbling something about the fog . . .

Lyubochka was crumpling the card in her hands . . . Suddenly, she felt a hot breath on her cheek, and fearfully turned around: behind her, hanging onto the cab body, was the passerby. His mouth was spread with its corners turned up and his cheeks had become like apples; with one hand he seized Lyubochka, buried her lips in his mouth, and, breathlessly, kissed her . . .

Lyubochka raised her hands, wanted to scream but couldn't, and the passerby broke away from her, jumped off the coachbox, and disappeared in the fog . . .

Lyubochka shouted after all. Then she took out her handkerchief, covered her mouth and gave a sudden, sly laugh.

## II

Lyubochka Molina returned home after five o'clock and, in climbing to the very top of the multistory building, became so tired and languid that she sat down between floors.

The pockets of her sealskin coat were full of candy, in her muff lay warm oranges, and she could still feel the smell of tobacco, wine, and mustache on her lips.

Sitting in the corner of the platform before the seventh floor, Lyubochka was gazing into the colored window, dim from the twilight, and her soul was empty and just as rumpled as her dress, her body, and her underclothes. All she wanted to do was lie down and listen to the ringing in her ears—this ringing is heard during twilight, when a street organ is playing at the bottom of the deep courtyard, and everything is so dreary it feels good.

Suddenly, quick footsteps were heard on the stairs, and jumping over three steps, the passerby from earlier rushed past. Lyubochka quickly covered herself with her muff.

The passerby rang upstairs, but it was unclear where—there were four doors on that landing.

"He is plain crazy," thought Lyubochka, and heard the passerby ask in a clear and hurried voice into the opened door:

"Forgive me, I forgot the phone number; you see, I am in a big hurry . . . a lady is waiting downstairs . . . thank you, I will remember it . . ."

And a minute later he was already running downstairs past Lyubochka even more briskly, in his unbuttoned plaid coat. Then he stopped suddenly, grabbed the railings, turned around, glanced at her, and disappeared . . .

## III

Lyubochka finally entered her room, a low one, papered in a patterned pink, with a single window to the courtyard. She took the candies out of her pocket, took off her coat and then her haphazardly buttoned wool dress, stretched in her corset and, lighting the lamp, threw on a flannel bonnet and lay down on the couch, glancing at the tips of her shoes.

"I do wonder whom he asked about the phone number," she thought. She took several candies in a row from the round table, squinted with pleasure, opened a book of decadent poems, and rested her small, animal-like head on her hand, thinking, "What could be more pleasant?"

At that moment her mother entered—as to be expected, she was a plump, scruffy clerk's widow, not understanding any arts.

"You've been hanging around with your fancy man again, you tramp!" her mother said in disgust, sitting down in a chair by the door.

"Until you discard your philistine expressions, I do not intend to answer you," Lyubochka calmly objected, turning the page.

"Where'd you get such noble blood, you trash!" her mother continued, anticipating a lively exchange with pleasure.

But Lyubochka continued to read.

"You know the Shamshevs have been saying to me: 'You should look after your daughter, the people are laughing, and grooms nowadays are oh so picky.' Well, who'd take such a pest? You're still reading, you reader!" her mother yelled, unable to stand it any longer.

"You'll ruin my career with your talk," Lyubochka said.

"What do you mean?" The mother was taken aback and, staring at her daughter, fell silent. "Have you seen the new tenant?" she then asked. "He seems to have money, but he is sheer turpentine, running back and forth: this morning he ran into me in the hallway and groped me all of a sudden, ooh . . ."

"What turpentine? What are you on about, mother, I didn't see any of your tenants; look, the phone is ringing . . ."

The phone was indeed ringing in the entryway (the ad for the room even specified that it came with a phone). Lyubochka swiftly ran out and, shutting her mother in her room, picked up the phone.

"Hello," said Lyubochka, "Who is speaking? I don't know you. What do you mean, it doesn't matter? Listen, I will hang up. What?.. Well, alright then, I will wait, but keep in mind. My voice is wrong? Whom were you calling? No, my number is different, you mixed them up. Ah, it doesn't matter to you. You are so frivolous! My appearance? What a question... Well, alright... Yes, very beautiful: very slim... My eyes? Big. But why do you need the nose? My nose is also beautiful, with flared nostrils. Listen, you promised, I'll get angry. You are so funny. What am I doing? I am lying in my big, oriental room, on silken pillows. I am surrounded by tuberoses.[2] They are intoxicating: I love it when I get dizzy. Yes, the windows are draped in velvet portières, crimson ones. The carpet on the floor is so soft that it muffles footsteps. How am I dressed? I suppose I'll tell you: it is half dark in the room after all . . . I can't . . . I am not dressed at all, there is nothing on me except for my luxurious ginger hair. What?.. You want to come in? You are too audacious . . . Ah, only to imagine it . . . Alright, so you've come in. Sit down, no, not next to me . . . Don't you dare look at me like that: I do not like crude people . . . You are gentle?.. Yes, I am all pink, and my legs are small, I crossed them. Ah, you're not allowed to touch . . . What was that? I can't hear you . . . No, not allowed . . . Well, I suppose you can kiss me . . ."

But at that moment the door swung open, and her enraged mother stood on the threshold. Lyubochka turned her agitated face to her, her cheeks and mouth flaming.

"Stop it!" her mother shouted, and Lyubochka immediately covered the receiver with her hand. "Are you a wench or my daughter? The servants are dying of laughter in the kitchen, and the girls at the exchange are all probably listening open-mouthed. They'll end up putting you in the paper. How embarrassing . . ."

"I'd give anything to have my name in the paper, you old philistine!" replied Lyubochka, hanging up the phone with a clang.

## IV

After the o'clock it rang at the front door and when the maid returned, Lyubochka asked her who had come.

"Oh, the new tenant," the maid answered. "Some kind of idiot: I'm taking off his coat and he paws me. 'At least you pity me,' he says. 'The whole day I haven't been able to get any sense out of anyone.' But what sense he needs, I do not know."

"I see," said Lyubochka and, walking up to her closed side door, started listening . . . The tenant's room was adjacent. Lyubochka could make out footsteps behind the door, grunts, then the squeak of the bed . . .

The tenant let out sighs for a long time, probably lying down, then fell silent. And Lyubochka was suddenly terribly curious to know who this tenant was . . . Could he be a rich landowner? Her mother had hinted at it. Maybe he was even an American. Suddenly Lyubochka's ears made out strange sounds, then words. The tenant, it turned out, was singing:

Darkness, darkness, dense the woods,
In them flows a stream.
You can sleep, or you can sing
Songs of distant lands.
Lie in grass, look at the spring,
Blow on singing reeds—
Sing: "Come here, I yearn for you."
A nymph's white hands
Sprinkle herself
With water from a brook.
Nymph, nymph, daughter of streams,
Comes out, blushing gently;
Behind the woods the sun is setting . . .
You watch out—she is no one's.

"My God, it's a poet," Lyubochka whispered. "What an opportunity! He should dedicate this poem to me. I'll be the talk of the town! Should I go to him? I don't have the courage. Or? Mother is sleeping . . . I'll only knock and ask whether he has a poetry book, to read for the night. There is nothing reprehensible about that. We'll talk, and then . . .

Lyubochka hastily sprayed herself with perfume, patted her hair with her palms and, tiptoeing to the tenant's door, knocked softly.

"Who is it? A woman?" the tenant asked in a hurried whisper and immediately opened the door.

In front of Lyubochka stood, terribly shaggy, without a coat, the stranger from earlier. His shirt was unbuttoned and underneath it his broad chest was covered in thick hair, like that of a ram . . .

Lyubochka gasped, wanted to run, but was scared to make noise, and it was too late anyway: the tenant pulled her into the room by the hand, closed the door, quickly sat on the floor at Lyubochka's feet, tightly grasped her knees and, throwing back his head, begging, gazed into her eyes.

"You've lost your mind! What are you doing—listen here!" Lyubochka whispered, pushing against his shoulders.

"I have dreamed of you, I came for you," the tenant said in a voice so gentle and clear that Lyubochka's fear vanished at once, and only fierce curiosity remained. "Do not be afraid of me. It was I that kissed you this morning. Darling! I ran after others too, the whole day, but they all rejected me. I do not understand what they—what you—need? You are women, are you not? Well, you are afraid for a bit, you struggle a little, and then you give in . . . Only one almost agreed to love me, and it was over the phone . . . But at least she was a princess, and she said such things to me, that I felt a little guilty. If only I could meet her . . ."

"But that was me talking to you. Did you like it?"

"You, a princess . . ." began the tenant.

"And are you not a poet?" Lyubochka hastily interrupted. "Recite me poems. You are very strange, but I am not afraid of you. I will sit with you: you won't touch me, will you? And you can't either, everyone will hear, and oh how I'll shriek . . . Well, well, well, now you're upset . . ."

"I do not understand what you are saying this for. What do you want?" the tenant said in despair.

Lyubochka laughed, freed her legs from his weakened arms, walked over to an armchair, and sat, propping up her cheek.

"Naïve man," she said slyly. "What does a girl want? Girls like to walk at the edge of danger, you have to love and caress them, but not become too enamored . . . no, no, my dear poet!"

"I am not a poet," the tenant said, even more despairingly. He got up from the floor and sat down on the bed, bending his head like a ram. "Poets are wise men; they understand all your confusions. But I am just a beast. An ordinary satyr."

"What do you mean—a satyr?" Lyubochka asked, jumping up.

"Well, yes, the most ordinary satyr. I even have the horns, and the hooves, and everything you'd expect. Forests have been cut down; the nymphs have scattered . . . where are we supposed to live? We go to the cities . . . And it's even worse here . . ."

Listening, Lyubochka got up from the chair and stood by the bed.

"My dear, I will do everything for you. Just show me a hoof," she begged.

"Everything?" The tenant cheered up.

"But of course, you silly. Oh, my head has even started spinning." Lyubochka sat down on the bed and, stroking the stranger's head, felt little horns.

"Ah!" she yelled. "Listen, we will have fame and fortune . . ."

And, frightfully agitated, Lyubochka felt the shaggy legs, and the hooves of the stranger, and breathlessly, her eyes glistening, began to explain that they should get married immediately, then call the newspaper to send a photographer, and take pictures of them naked in a fantastical setting. The next day, their portraits would be in every paper, then there would be a tour around Europe, and an engagement to America for one hundred thousand dollars, Lyubochka dancing in the costume of Ida Rubinstein, and he—naked, showing his legs.[3]

While Lyubochka was thus persuading and fantasizing, the satyr was becoming more and more upset, timid, and shrunken . . . Then, thinking of something, he got dressed and, not lifting his eyes, went to the door . . .

"Where are you going?" Lyubochka asked, glancing worriedly at the suitcases of the tenant and at the silver necessaire by the washbasin.

"I'll be back right away, right away," the satyr responded in a high voice as he walked sideways out the door.

"Look, don't come back late! You hear? I'll be waiting," Lyubochka yelled strictly.

The satyr, slowly descending the stairs, went out onto the sidewalk, stopped by a streetlight shrouded in fog, looked both ways, where the same lanterns hung in the fog like matte eggs, raised his head to the sky (it was not visible), blinked, waved his hand, and disappeared into the darkness.

## Notes

* **Alexey Tolstoy, "The Satyr."** The story was published in a weekly magazine: A. N. Tolstoi, "Satir," *Solntse Rossii*, no. 17 (April 1912), 2–4. A reworked version entitled "The Faun" ("Favn") appeared in the third volume of Tolstoy's collected works in 1913.

1 *articles in the Gazette.* In the original, this is *Birzhevka*, the colloquial term for the *Birzhevye vedomosti* (*The Bourse Gazette*), a popular newspaper published in St. Petersburg.

*her portrait on Nevsky Prospect at Mrozovskaya's.* Elena Mrozovskaya (Hélène de Mrosovsky) was a famous photographer, whose clients included members of high society and all kinds of celebrities. Her atelier was located at Nevsky Prospect no. 20. Igor Severyanin, the founder of Ego-Futurism and "the king of poets," recalls Mrozovskaya long after the revolution in his novel in verse *Leander's Piano* (*Roial' Leandra*) composed in the mid-1920s and published in Bucharest in 1935. Chapter 2 of this novel contains an extensive panorama of St. Petersburg of the Silver Age. Among other things, Severyanin mentions his own portrait supposedly displayed at Mrozovskaya's studio.

2 *I am surrounded by tuberoses.*The tuberose is a marked flower in the poetry of the Silver Age, appearing in Mira Lokhvitskaya, Innokenty Annensky, Konstantin Balmont, and Marina Tsvetaeva. Tolstoy's Lyubochka would have certainly appreciated the opening lines of the poem "Feasts" ("Piry," 1913) by young Boris Pasternak: "I'm drinking the bitterness of tuberoses, the bitterness of autumnal skies, and in them the burning stream of your infidelities."

3 *Lyubochka dancing in the costume of Ida Rubinstein, and he—naked, showing his legs.* Ida Rubinstein, the decadent diva of the Russian ballet, donned many costumes. In the famous portrait by Valentin Serov (1910) she is shown naked, with only a long green scarf at her feet. Coincidentally, Vaslav Nijinsky's legendary *Afternoon of a Faun* was premiered by Ballets Russes in Paris on May 29, 1912—practically simultaneously with the publication of Tolstoy's story.

## A. Bezhetsky (Alexey Maslov)

# The Wax Museum*

## I

"It seems the curtain has risen," said a beautiful, slender lady to a middle-aged gentleman, who was sitting pensively on the small couch in the antechamber. "You are sitting so quietly that I thought you had already left, without saying goodbye . . . Come, let us finish watching *Coppelia*."[1]

"Let me sit here a little longer," answered Boromlev, "I'll come a bit later; after all, you have Mikhail Ivanovich with you, and I must confess, I do not particularly like the third act of this ballet: it is no longer in the genre of Hoffman . . . The fairytale and fantasy end in the second act . . . And besides, I have a bit of a headache . . ."

He was alone . . . The elegant melodies of Delibes dimly reached him through the closed door. Fragments of various thoughts and scenes from the ballet—automatons, the music-box melodies of the second act—all this was getting muddled in his head and melting like the smoke of a cigar in the open air. In a box near theirs sat a very attractive young woman with a swarthy face and a mysterious and magnetic gaze. The originality of her dress made one think she was a foreigner. She was alone in her box: Boromlev had seen her several times, and she was always alone. At the beginning of the performance, she had thrown him a meaningful look, and going out into the antechamber during the intermission, she glanced at him every time as if inviting him to come over . . .

Boromlev quietly left his box, stood outside the door to the box adjacent for a few seconds, and then resolutely entered.

She was sitting in the antechamber. She too was not watching the third act.

"You've finally decided to come here," she said. "You won't believe how triumphant I feel. You, who call all women dolls, could not resist, have forgotten all decency, and directly came to confess your love to me . . . Oh, I am certain that you are in love with me! I immediately noticed how your conceited and cold heart softened at my very first glance . . ."

"But excuse me!.. How do you know that I . . ."

"I know everything . . . I know, that from our very first meeting only the thought of me lives in your head, and everything else has flown away . . . You are completely entranced by my charm. Everywhere you see only me, and not only with your eyes, but with your soul, too! It does not even interest you where I am from, or what I am . . . Perhaps I am . . . a witch. But you don't care, isn't that right? Ha-ha!"

"Excuse me, madame, but . . ."

"Ha, ha! But alright, we cannot speak long here . . . I am setting up a date for you . . . Come to the wax museum tomorrow evening at seven. You call women dolls, and so I am inviting you into the company of my kind."

***

The next day Boromlev ate a hurried lunch and hastened outside to get a breath of fresh air and to calm his nerves in the noisy crowd before his date with the mysterious beauty. Only about twenty minutes remained until the appointed hour when he started off with hurried steps to the most well-known wax museum in the city.[2] Approaching it, he was unpleasantly surprised, as he saw the sign was not illuminated, and the small ticket booth was closed. "She probably knew this," Boromlev said to himself, "and purposefully set up the date for me here, to make fun of me? And who even is she?.. It's strange, I can't remember—what language did she speak to me? It must have been a hoax!"

His excitement instantly subsided, and his heart was gripped by the melancholy feeling of unrequited love. He was already heading in the opposite direction, thinking how he might kill the evening, but he had barely taken a few steps before a clean-shaven old man with faded eyes and red eyelids walked up to him and said: "Monsieur, would you like to see the museum? It has been moved to a different corner, on the occasion of the expansion and growth of the exhibitions . . . Oh, it is now a veritable showplace!.. A huge variety for the eyes!.. Novelties and incredibly rare specimens . . . A mobile automaton, playing

Rams and winding up his own golden watch . . . A priestess of Pythia on a tripod . . . The mummy of Pharaoh Psamtik I . . . A magic rifleman, always hitting the mark . . . In addition, we have the rarest apparatuses: Paracelsus' clock of life and Nostradamus' horoscope apparatus, made by his own hand—that same astrologist who predicted the future of Catherine de' Medici. We also have a rare performance: The Visions of a Severed Head," designed after the painting of the famous Belgian painter, Wiertz . . . This way, it is not far . . ."

Boromlev obediently followed the old man, who tottered along ahead of him.

"It is a pity, monsieur, that you did not see our little dwarfs. They are a highly curious natural phenomenon, but to make up for it, instead of them, we are showing an astonishing living *fin de siècle* nymph, swimming dry in wet water; but what is truly marvelous is the magician from India. For that we charge extra . . ."

This strange chatter, and the old man himself with his uncertain face, somehow matched Boromlev's mood, which was also uncertain and languid. Not saying a word in response, he followed. The old man turned from Nevsky Prospect into one of its perpendicular streets and, leading him to the entrance, coughed meaningfully into his hand and said, "Today entrance is one ruble," then disappeared somewhere . . .

Purchasing a ticket on the ground floor, Boromlev began to climb the stairs, not wanting to be late. The staircase was narrow, without a carpet, and dim lighting gave it a somber atmosphere. The entrance door was also narrow, and dirty, not promising anything good, but upon entering, Boromlev changed his mind for the better. There turned out to be a spacious double-height hall, newly done. Along the middle section were long sofas, upholstered in dark crimson velvet. Here and there, according to the fancy of the organizer, wide corridors and large niches went out from the hall to the sides. Near the ceiling, on both sides, there were long balconies on metal columns with windows; their stained-glass panes, lit from within, rendered the ceiling multicolored. To the left of the entrance, a mirror was so cleverly installed in the wall that Boromlev was surprised to suddenly see himself. Such mirrors were placed in various locations. In several niches there stood a variety of tropical plants and flowers, very artfully made, and between them were concave and convex mirrors, drastically altering both a person's face and entire figure. The wax figures, for the most part life-sized, were so skillfully placed around the hall that not only from a distance, but even quite close-up, they could fool you and make you think that the museum had quite a lot of visitors. There were both women and men, some dressed very richly, others in simple domestic clothes, but all in modern fashions, and because only their heads and hands were waxen, and everything else, from the hats to the boots and shoes, was exactly like those on living people, they resembled the living. Some were sitting, others were standing in the most natural poses, nothing separating them from the passing living visitors—as if they were only frozen, paralyzed in their immobility, as if an infernal cold had swept over them, or a wave of a thin and very strong poison had instantly disrupted their existence. For the melancholic visitor, this place provided the benefit that he could quietly sit down on one of the couches, upholstered in crimson velvet, next to some waxen Jules Favre, Edison, or Sarah Bernhardt, and, as if listening in on the conversations of these celebrities, quietly pass away from cardiac arrest.

## II

At the entrance to the exhibition, a guard in black livery lined with silver galloons shoved a catalogue into Boromlev's hand. Boromlev asked him whether there were a lot of visitors, and whether a beautiful young lady with a swarthy face and large sparkling eyes had not passed by. The guard responded that he did not remember, but he believed she did. After absent-mindedly looking at some famous dancer in front of a mirror, sectioned off behind a silk ribbon, Boromlev hurriedly walked through the entire hall, peering at every woman, a good three-quarters of which ended up being dolls, leaving him with an unpleasant impression. She was not there . . . He walked through all the adjacent rooms, but she was not there either . . . Then he turned back, remembering that people who are looking for each other often walk in the same direction, and therefore cannot meet each other. During this quest, in a dark passageway dimly lit with greenish light, he thought he heard someone calling his name. A familiar female shape flitted behind a column. He quickened his steps, but she was not there. A dancer in a Spanish costume stood nearby, holding a fan in her motionless hand. In the distance, heading towards the exit, walked a soldier leading a plump, elderly lady by her arm. The illusion repeated several times. Boromlev thought he saw his mysterious lady on one side or the other, and every time, coming closer, saw that he was mistaken. The mirrors only confused him further. The futile rushing from side to side agitated and tired him. Evidently, she had not come . . . People kept leaving, and there were few new visitors, although there were still over two hours before the museum closed. Boromlev decided to arm himself with patience and wait.

He sat down in a corner on one of the couches and sank into thoughtfulness. Two steps away from him, on that same couch, sat a waxen gentleman, with a frozen smile on his wax face. On his knees lay an open book, which the gentleman was pressing to his knee with his wax hand. Although Boromlev had the catalogue in his pocket, he did not care to check who this celebrity was. Out of boredom he started to look at the motionless pupils of the wax person, but after about a minute a chill ran down his spine. He quickly shifted his gaze to another gentleman, in a light-colored coat, gracefully leaning on a thick cane and merrily looking in his direction. Boromlev first mistook him for an acquaintance, but the fixed smile soon revealed his error—that was also a "figure." He felt even more uncomfortable and terrified. Luckily, right across from him on an Empire style couch, sat a very beautiful lady with a lorgnette in her hand; she regarded Boromlev curiously, taking him, it seemed, for a "figure." He coughed loudly in indignation, to let her know of her mistake, but the lady continued to impudently look at him . . . "Oh, damn it, that is a doll too!" he thought. Happily finding one of the attendants with his eyes, standing not far from the side door, he beckoned him over with his hand. The attendant did not move. "Come here, dear fellow!.." said Boromlev, but the attendant was also waxen and continued to stand in his spot, as if nothing had happened. Close by there was not a single living soul, and steps were audible only in the distance, growing softer and softer . . .

When the remote noise died down, Boromlev suddenly heard some kind of rustling next to him. He stared at his neighbor, and it began to appear to him that blood was pumping slowly and hesitantly under the waxy skin of this face, and that some kind of sparks were flickering in his brown eyes. Then those eyes seemed to come alive, as if a sepulchral flame was lighting up in the pupils, and under the frock coat, in the place where a real person has a heart, something was slowly beginning to move. The motionless wrinkles of the face started to smooth out, and suddenly the bottom lip lowered slightly. Horrified, Boromlev wanted to turn away, but all his limbs were frozen, and he sat as if rooted to the spot. At that moment the swarthy lady, whom he had been awaiting so long, finally appeared on the threshold of the inner staircase, and nodded to Boromlev. He wanted to stand up but couldn't. His neighbor, though, suddenly jumped up, quickly, almost at a run, made his way to her, gave her his hand and they both disappeared. He made another attempt to stand up, but it was impossible; even his breath had stopped. Hours seemed to pass, yet he could not move a finger. His eyes clouded over from fear. Finally, a small bell rang somewhere far off, and another answered it close by, then several bells rang all at once, and every doll immediately moved from its spot and ran upstairs along the inner staircase. Boromlev cried out fearfully and awoke. A guard approached him and said: "The museum is closing soon, sir, and that lady, whom you were asking about, has gone upstairs, to the Indian magician." He jumped up. The wax gentleman next to him was no longer there. There was only a numeral on the back of the sofa.

"But where is Number 132?" he asked.

"It broke while still abroad," answered the porter, "and has not been replaced yet."

"And is it not in the catalogue?"

"No, it is not in the catalogue, and we do not know who it is . . ."

The remaining figures were still in their spots. Afraid he was now too late, Boromlev started to quickly climb up the inner staircase. The sounds of music came to him from up there, up above.

Next to the wide doors leading to the upper hall hung a large banner, on which was written, in fiery letters: "Ball of the automatons. Visitors are asked to drop a silver ruble in the mug upon entering." By the doors stood a large black man merrily flashing his white teeth. Boromlev dropped in a ruble; the door opened and immediately slammed closed behind him. The ball, it seemed, was in full swing. Invisible music (it must have been a very good organ) played a noisy Parisian waltz, and several couples twirled neatly and smoothly around the hall. A shepherdess was dancing with some general in a cuirassier's uniform, a marquise with Mephistopheles, a very old man with disheveled hair energetically twirled a prima ballerina in short gauze skirts and a pink leotard. In one of the illuminated corners a beautiful plump lady was fanning herself; two cavaliers, leaning down to her, were telling her something, all the while laughing to the beat of the waltz, and everywhere stood groups of guests in the most varied poses, and they were all stirring and trying to be as loud as possible.

Little black boys were carrying mirrored trays with refreshing drinks, and these drinks were reflected in the trays. They deftly maneuvered between the dancing couples, and not once did someone run into them, and no one took anything. Apparently, everyone was so pleased with the dances, discussions, and laughter, that no one felt any thirst. Boromlev noticed a respectable middle-aged gentleman next to him, wearing a tailcoat with a ribbon in the buttonhole, who was watching the dancers with great enjoyment, bowing to some of them, tapping his foot to the beat, and unabashedly puffing out his cheeks as he sang along with the melody of the waltz in a hoarse baritone. As it could be concluded from this behavior that this gentleman in a tailcoat knew everything that was going on here, Boromlev asked: "Excuse me, but where are the automatons here?" However, the gentleman, merrily nodding his head, did not respond and continued to puff out his cheeks. Then Boromlev started to make his way along the wall to another gentleman, who was sitting on a chair, and he accidentally knocked into one of the black boys. The glasses rang out and one of them fell to the floor, but nothing spilled from it. The black boy stopped and stared at the wall, perplexed. It was then that Boromlev realized that these were all automatons, and the gentleman whom he had questioned was also an artificial human. He became unimaginably frightened, even more frightened than in the hall of motionless figures, because around him was not real life, but only the artificial imitation of life, devoid of any feelings. The mysterious and invisible hand of the master had set these dolls into motion, forced them to talk and smile, dance to the music, and pretend that it was terribly fun, while the materials from which they were made could not care less about what was happening around them. In anguish and horror, he started to look around, his eyes searching for even a single living face and firmly deciding not to give in to the illusion, to find a truly real person.

To do that, he first needed to get out of there. There were two exits, and as if on purpose, he had forgotten which one he'd used to enter. Choosing the closest door at random, he resolutely headed towards it, avoiding the twirling dummies in disgust, scared to even touch them. He grabbed the door handle and pulled. Someone was stopping him from the other side. Then he gathered all his strength and pulled again. There was a noise and a metallic clanging, as if a large spiral spring had snapped. The automatons all suddenly stopped—and the door opened. There, in a small room, near a large curtain from behind which light streamed in, stood the Indian magician: a tall, thin, and swarthy person with long black hair and a dull gaze. He was wearing a long, dark, sleeveless shirt, tied at the waist with a shawl, and pointed-toe shoes. With an imperious gesture he stopped Boromlev across from the curtain and waved his black cane. The curtain opened, and he saw his mysterious beauty, tied at the hands and feet . . . She was frightfully pale and looked at him in despair . . . But Boromlev could not move a muscle: the gaze of the magician had rooted him to the spot.

"Now the most interesting act will be presented!" someone yelled in a nasal voice. "The Visions of a Severed Head! Welcome, gentlemen, welcome!!"

All the automatons that had danced before him in the hall scurried into the room, and waited with soulless curiosity to see how the head of a living woman would be cut. The Indian waved his hand again. Everything quieted down. He went up the steps to the bound woman and, grabbing her hair, in a dull voice, slowly and deliberately counted in English: "One, two, three . . ." The blade of the knife flashed, blood spurted out and the head separated from the body. With terror-stricken eyes she looked at Boromlev, and her lips clearly uttered: "I swear, I am alive. Save me!"

"The head is severed and now the visions will begin; the most interesting part!" the voice rang out.

Boromlev rushed to the stage and awoke again . . . this time in the theater antechamber.

"What's the matter with you?" asked his lady, leaving the box. "You shouldn't get lost in thought so. You missed a very interesting act. What a charming ballet, *Coppelia!* Isn't it?.. But I see you are thinking of something else . . . At least order my coat to be fetched and bring me home. The show is over . . ."

## Notes

* **A. Bezhetsky (Alexey Maslov), "The Wax Museum."** The story first appeared as A. Bezhetskii, "Muzei voskovykh figur," in his *Nevedomoe . . . Fantasticheskie rasskazy* (St. Petersburg: Tip. A. S. Suvorina, 1914). According to the catalogue of the Russian National Library, the collection went through three editions in one year.

1 *Come, let us finish watching Coppélia.* The action takes place at the Mariinsky Theatre, where the protagonist attends Léo Delibes's ballet *Coppélia* (which is loosely based on E. T. A. Hoffmann's *The Sandman*).

2 *the most well-known wax museum in the city.* Such a museum was located at 86 Nevsky Prospect. The entrance for an adult visitor was twenty-five kopecks, so the fee of one ruble paid by Boromlev was an increase that could be justified only by some kind of special programming.

Отдѣльные нумера въ Петроградѣ ШЕСТЬДЕСЯТЪ ПЯТЬ (65) коп., въ провинціи СЕМЬДЕСЯТЪ (70) коп., на станц. жел. дор. 75 коп.

ОГОНЕКЪ

№ 1 – 1918 г.

МИРЪ ИЛИ НОВАЯ ВОЙНА?

На Невскомъ въ смутные и тревожные дни въ концѣ февраля.

Рисунокъ съ натуры для журнала «Огонекъ» худ. И. ВЛАДИМІРОВА.

Figure 6.1. ***Peace or a New War?***
*On Nevsky Prospect during the chaotic and troubled days of late February.*
*Life drawing for the "Ogonyok" magazine by I. Vladimirov.*

The front cover of the magazine in which Alexander Grin's "Club Sponger" appeared (*Ogonek*, no. 1, 1918). The drawing depicts crowds of soldiers and civilians on Nevsky Prospect, with the City Duma Tower on the left and the spire of the Admiralty in the background.

Alexander Grin

# The Club Sponger*

## I

A certain Jung, having sold his house in Kazan, moved to Petrograd. He was a bachelor. Bored without acquaintances in the big city, Jung frequented theaters at first, and then, signing up as a member of the gambling club The Society of Elderly Martyrs, he developed a passion for card games, returning to his hotel room no earlier than seven in the morning every day.

Never before had gambling flourished so in Petrograd. By fall of the year 1917, more than fifty gambling dens had been formed in the city, bearing euphonious, proper names: The Gathering of Pensive Musicians, The Society of Cultured Laborers, The Leisure of the Proplyuisky District, and so on.[1] Nothing was done in these dens except for playing cards. Anyone who wanted to could come in from the street and receive a membership card for 10–15 rubles. The crowd was a most varied one: officials, students, profiteers, skilled workers, merchants, cardsharps, professional card players, and an extraordinary number of soldiers, at times in possession of quite large sums of money of unclear origin.

When Jung started playing, he had around forty thousand rubles left over after paying off his mortgage. Extremely excitable and hungry for sensations, he devoted himself to the game with all his being, diving not only into the titillating sharpness of dealt or beaten cards, but into the whole structure of the gambling nightlife. He became so intimately familiar with it, that he did not separate it from the game; its immediacy and his reflections on it somehow greased the dry fervor of gambling and often smoothed the agony of losing, entertaining with its fraudulent, lively nature. If this backdrop to gambling did not exist, if Jung played in an old-fashioned club, a prim one, where the "shock factor" does not go past an unpaid debt, a bullet to the forehead, or—the worst misfortune—the exposure of an elegant cardsharp who committed a blunder, Jung, perhaps, would soon have stopped playing. If he remained a stranger to the club's public and concentrated only on the game with its hypocritical ceremonialism, reining in passions for the sake of propriety, he would have quickly tired, becoming fed up with the monotonous bouncing of points of the cards in play. But in the Society of Elderly Martyrs, he was infected with excitement and riveted by the thick, strong smell of a greedy immorality and a bestial attitude towards money, which gave it a weighty, lifelike taste, whetting the appetite and making it as desirable as a meal to a hungry man.

In all of Petrograd's clubs, the game played was mainly Macao, an ancient Portuguese game somewhat modified with the passage of time.

In a week, Jung had come to understand the way of life of the Elderly Martyrs. Cardsharps, in the direct artistic meaning of the term, did not exist there. This was partially because, for dealing, cards were put into a special machine that hindered substitution or "loading" (using, for one game or many, a set of extra cards hidden in one's sleeve), but mostly because the sheer multitude of clubs offered a wide selection of arenas in which to display cheating prowess. Furthermore, wealthy gambling dens, with the goal of advancing their game, would snatch up famous touring cardsharps from each other, in order to have everyone talking about a large win or loss that occurred in such-and-such a place. For the sake of publicity, they did not even shy away from fronting large sums of money specifically for "handouts," which was the word for the persistent "bad luck" of the banker.

The Elderly Martyrs was filled with all manner of people. Here one could see the frock coat of a littérateur, the thick and tasteless watch chain of a butcher or mercer, the galloons of a sailor, the leather jacket or kosovorotka of a workman, an officer's epaulets, and a soldier's uniform (without shoulder strips, according to the latest fashion). The amount of money the soldiers and workmen had was astonishing. These, in terms of their fervor and their money, were perhaps the most prominent patrons of the venerable establishment.

As it has been said, there was no direct cheating. But there was "sponging": something between begging and swindling. More on this later, however.

## II

Jung was winning, at first. The phrase "beginner's luck" is apt, perhaps, because a beginner instinctively adapts to the only law of the game—chance—and so he bets *wherever* and *however* he can. In addition, a beginner usually worms his way into a club by chance. Thus, the combination of three chance events increases the odds of winning (just as the execution of three intentions at once rarely results in success). Later, after observing how others play, and imagining that he has learned to calculate how and where to bet (a ridiculous notion), the player closes his eyes to the fact that he is now fighting against the law of chance, to his detriment, because the inevitable exhaustion of nerves leads to confusion and the loss of will power. There is no telling how the cards lie in the deck. You think you have guessed which tableaus you should now bet on and in what order—meaning you think you know. But cards mock conceit. There is, of course, a small number of people with an especially finely developed intuition when it comes to guessing, but these people are hindered from winning by their own distrust of intuition. Often second-guessing their inner voice, they bet on a different tableau than they initially thought, and, thinking they have tricked fate, they burn their fingers.

While Jung was still getting away with only the occasional heart-stopping moment, betting wherever, dealing cards without taking face cards and nines into account, he was lucky. Every evening, he left with hundreds or thousands of rubles in winnings. It should be noted that leaving with winnings is a rather difficult thing to do. The winner has likely assigned himself an amount with which, upon reaching it, he intends to leave. But if his luck is holding, then he, out of greed, starts to dream of a higher threshold—and, naturally, not reaching the limitless limit, he begins to lose money. His wishes begin to narrow, becoming ever tighter and more like a supplication. Now the player is wishing to reach the high point of the disappearing amount again. Now he says: "I'll lose no more than this much, then leave." Now he has lost all his winnings, and, pale, with a dulled gaze, bets all his money again. No luck! Hastening to get to paradise, he bets large sums, doubles them, and is left at the end with petty cash for a tram or cabby; often deprived of even this, he borrows a ruble from the porter.

Jung was lucky, and for about a month, happily keeping the bank, dealing, or punting, he bathed in tens of thousands of rubles, getting accustomed to viewing them, when he played, not even as money, but as gambling tokens, a kind of technical unit for transactions. However, luck finally turned its back on him. Losing five thousand one day, he came back the next day with fifteen, and by the time the club closed he had completely squandered it. The blow was palpable. He began to mistrust his own bets, and, wishing to recoup his loss, Jung started giving his money to the bank or to other players, whose boldness and experience seemed to him a sufficient guarantee of success. These persons, playing for him, but more so (if they were decidedly unlucky) for their numerous friends, who in such cases would bet very aggressively, rid him of three quarters of his money in less than a week. Sometimes they would stealthily pay more for bets than was necessary and would then split the resulting difference among themselves. Sometimes, after the cards were already opened on the tableau where the winning points shone, a large banknote would be deftly slipped in there to claim a share of winnings. Sometimes the banker, as if he had inadvertently mixed Jung's money with his own, would then divide the money, not without profit for himself, and swear that he had done everything right. With the help of such uncomplicated tricks, which were common among the visitors to The Society of Elderly Martyrs, the card swindlers brought Jung into a state of utter dismay and indecision. Left with a small sum, he would either bet little when luck seemed to be on his side, or bet a lot when card after card was definitively being beaten, and soon, reaching the point of coming up with unbeatable "systems" (the worst thing that can befall a player), he would end up with twenty or thirty rubles, get drunk, and show up at the club again five days later, depressed, worn out, and without any concrete plans, with only one desire: to play, to play no matter what, to be in the hell of that eternal thirst, waiting for an opportunity, jostling around and trembling, counting blind points.

The transition from temperance to drunken gambling, and from that to sponging, occurs imperceptibly, just like in everything else where passion is the main character. Having lost everything and left with no more income of his own, the player usually begins collecting debts: this one owes him, that one and that one does. These sums last for a while, but gambling has become a passion for such a person, its itch firmly stuck in the soul, like the irritation of the gums when one constantly chews tar or nibbles on sunflower seeds. But then, all loans outstanding have been demanded, begged for, and lost. There might have been moments of relative luck during this time—all the worse. The player already sees it as someone else's, as gifted money. His frayed nerves require numbing. He drinks, indulges in debauchery, gambles without comprehending the stakes in proportion to his cash, and soon begins to borrow himself. At first people lend to him—then shy away, bringing up their own losses, then they curse and mock his whining, discouraging any inclination to ask for money. All regular visitors know him and his habits, even the unofficial circle of "spongers," to whom he already belongs, but for the most part, no one knows his life, his name, or surname. Such is the strangeness of all-consuming activities! Present is only the perceptible shape of a person, which means less to such society than cards without a point value.

When the so-called moral fortitude has been sufficiently dulled, when gambling has filled and sucked out every aspect of life, and the control centers cease to pay attention to such trifles as humiliation and resentment—then, the sponger is ripe. He is composed entirely of begging, the ability to catch the right moment, buffoonery, persistence, and petty fraud. Having learned to quickly make calculations on the complexity and accounting of bets, he, like a true croupier, for ten percent helps anyone who wants to punt but is slow with numbers. He heroically handles other people's money; he grabs it from the hands of the banker or from under his nose; he shouts: "You're off!" . . . "The non-trumps are gone!" . . . "Wings in full!" . . . "What is your word?!" (the bent corner of a banknote, denoting a smaller bet than the banknote itself) . . . "A set!" . . . "The bank pays!" . . . "Place your bets!" . . . and everything else of that kind: the stock expressions of winning, loss, and expectation. He is an intermediary in pawning watches or rings to another gambler or porter. He procures the vodka. He gives a ruble to the bank "for luck" and in the case of a win is unusually clingy. He slips extra money to the victorious tableau. He brings in rich and drunk players. He tries to snatch money from under the elbow of a player and, if this is noticed, he says he just wanted to fix it, that it was about to fall on the floor. In such clubs, detected attempts to steal or cheat are readily overlooked. Those instances never cause a scandal. In the worst case there is a brief quarrel, in the best, a stern look and wag of the finger.

Those who play constantly must always be losing. The arithmetic here is as follows: the club collects an average of two thousand a day with the membership fees, banking fees, and fines (for playing after hours). The total amount of money put in the game (according to the correlating percentage between punting and the bank) is one hundred thousand. After a month and twenty days, that hundred thousand goes entirely into the club coffers.

Jung had become a sponger.

## III

He was out of luck. When he stepped away from the table, there was no money at all.

Shaking, fumbling in his pockets, and blinking often, as if blinded by a cloud of dust, Jung tried to recall the order in which his misfortunes had occurred, but felt only helplessness and anguish. A deep loathing towards himself, towards gambling, and towards life took hold of him. At a loss for what to do next, he stood by a table where forty rubles were being played and yelled out like a madman, in despair, "I'll cover the bank!" The bank won.

"I'll owe this," Jung said dully.

There was a sickening uproar. One of the winners, after carefully scrutinizing Jung, put in forty rubles.

"The bank has eighty!" said the placated banker. "Taking the first!"

## IV

Jung made his way into the reading room, picked up an issue of a statistical journal, flipped through it, tossed it aside, and sat down in a chair. The dull depression of despair held him outside of space and time.

"What should I do?" he said to himself. "I'm done for. There is only one solution left: to throw myself off a bridge into the water." He had constructed the phrase, but as he repeated it again, he fully grasped the meaning of what he had said, and he realized that to throw himself off a bridge into the water was . . . to die. The resolve to commit suicide comes on suddenly—even to those with the most melancholic disposition. One can contemplate it at twenty years old and still live to see one's grandchildren. On the contrary, it is possible to never seriously think about suicide and, suddenly feeling that life is intolerably repulsive, rush towards death, as if towards rest. Such an ill-considered but already wistfully attractive decision suddenly revived Jung. In a new, unaccustomed state of nameless agitation he rose from his chair, but in that moment his gaze by chance fell upon one of the stereoscopic pictures scattered on the table. The image depicted a woman at a lakeshore, sitting on the end of a log that protruded from the water.

Jung picked up the picture. The morbid desire to see water before his end, the same water that would soon close over him, made him insert the image into the stereoscope and bring the device up to his eyes. At first the electrically illuminated image remained flat, but soon, yielding to his strained gaze, it little by little revealed the perspective and vitality of three dimensions. Jung saw a large forest lake, the log's shadow in it, and the barefoot (bared to the knee), strong legs of the woman, strained by the discomfort of their position. Her face surprised him. Outside of the device it was frozen, with that unnatural expression characteristic of a person being photographed, but now it was smiling. A heavy feeling, an anticipation of something extraordinary, akin to the heaviness before a fit or in expectation of dismal news, took possession of him. He quickly lowered the device, but shuddered as he did so, as if from a sudden blast of cold, having noticed, as his eyes were leaving the image, that the woman had swung her leg, as if she intended to leave the log and descend onto the ground.

"Nonsense," he said to himself, wincing and placing a hand on his palpitating heart. "Is this madness, or perhaps the beginning of it?" His anxiety did not pass, but swelled, like an approaching drumbeat. He glanced around and experienced a strange, electrifying sensation, as if every object in the room came to life, left its spot, then instantly returned to its previous position, all with the rapidity of splashing drops of mercury.

Across from him, in the previously empty armchair, sat a swarthy young woman, the same one Jung had been watching in the stereoscope. Her black brows, straight like laces, were set high above her bold, large eyes, shining with the sort of eerie spirituality that is characteristic of old portraits, with their fluctuating and unsteady lighting. An utter destruction of reality emanated from her dress and figure. What Jung felt during this remarkable encounter cannot be called fear. The elements of the supernatural are inherent in us: revealed by secret forces and against all expectations of the staggering bewilderment of fear, they lead only into the familiar realm of belief in facts, albeit accompanied by great excitement. To understand this, one need only imagine the feeling of a person coming under gunfire for the first time, or experiencing a train wreck. The contrast between such a fact with the ordinariness of facing the fact is striking, and yet, whatever logically minded people may say, it is not fear that accompanies these facts. Dazed excitement is a more accurate characterization of the experience. Being shot at, if it has never happened to you, is just as hard to believe as the appearance of a demon.

"What is this?" Jung asked, breathing heavily.

Except for him and the mysterious lady, there was no one in the reading room.

"Listen carefully," the woman said, leaning across the table towards Jung. "Today is the twenty-third, the day on which I come out from the fog. You will not see me again. I am offering you a new game, with marvelous results—one which, with good luck, will increase all happiness a thousand-fold . . . and with bad luck, magically strengthen misfortune. It is a game for time. Take a look at the deck. Take it. We call it Sheyes-Magor, which means *life lost and gained*."

Jung took the deck. In it, like in an ordinary deck, were fifty-two sheets, but square in shape and made from an unknown material that was black and hard like iron, thin like cambric, silky to the touch, slightly transparent, and light. The face cards were extremely strange, colored by hand (as were all the cards) with red and white paint. Spades were depicted as short arrows, clubs as shamrocks, diamonds as red quadrangular flowers, hearts as a heart being squeezed by a hand. The heavy, grotesque decorativeness of the figures concealed something idolic, ancient, and other-worldly.

"Play against whomever you want," continued his benefactress after Jung had lifted his eyes, fully in the power of the abyss opening before him. "In any gambling game, you may bet any number of years, months, days, hours, and even minutes. A loss will transport you as far into the future as you have bet, a win will send you to the past."

The last words of the woman sounded muffled and distant. She finished talking and disappeared: she didn't dissipate or melt, but precisely disappeared, like in a cinematic scene change. Jung jumped up, dropped his newspaper, and, still shaking with excitement, bent over and picked up the cards. Without lifting his head, he saw that next to his hands, mirroring his movements, was another pair of hands. Their fingers were covered in large gold rings.

Jung looked up. Crouching in front of him, helping him gather the cards (and visibly surprised by their unusual appearance), was the famous gambler Bronstein, a complex version of Jack Hamlin in Russian conditions.[2] Round, with a small belly, perhaps not always cheerful, but invariably lively, this person said:

"Turkish cards?"

"No," Jung answered automatically.

"Greek?"

"No . . ."

"I'm seeing such cards for the first time. Where did you get them?"

Jung regained his composure. He smoothly lied:

"These are cards of an unknown origin. They were passed down to me from my father, who brought them out from Dagestan. Listen, Yakov Adolfovich. I have a superstition—" The cards were collected, and both had already sat down at the table. "If I play one no-stakes game with someone, before a real game, with this deck—I should have luck at any table."

"Alright," said Bronstein. "All us gamblers are eccentrics. Place your bets. For starters I am betting the sun and . . . let's say, the moon . . ."

With the fast, flying movements of a habitual gambler, he dealt, as one always does in Macao, into four tableaus, then slightly lifted his cards with a bored look.

"Nine," he said, with the pleasure that never leaves a gambler, even in a no-stakes game.

Jung barely managed to glance at his cards—the ones that covered the supposed first tableau. He'd lost. He had a three.

## V

While inviting Bronstein to play for no stakes, Jung had mentally determined his bet to be five years and two months, with the expectation that, having won, he would return to his most cherished days in the past: the time when he first dated Olga Nevzorova, the girl who was meant to become his wife, and who was taken from the earth by typhus. A loss, on the other hand, would carry him into the unknown, possibly towards death. The latter did not worry Jung. The fantastical club life, where every defeated bet seemed, on a small and meager scale, a type of death, and which delivered countless such individual shocks, had long since numbed his instinct of self-preservation. And besides, as we have seen, Jung was wishing for a suicidal end.

The backs of the cards had no pattern. When three of them lay face down, fanned out in front of him, there appeared several quietly shimmering dots in the glossy blackness, which reflected the light of the chandelier like the waters of a deep abyss. With a special, deep, and instinctive knowledge, Jung understood that these dots were the years he had bet. Bronstein's nine caused the first lump of spasm in his throat. Strange semblances of grimaces of thoughts accompanied the movement of his hand when he revealed his three cards.

Jung turned onto his side. His whole body was aching unbearably, as if asking for the elimination of the irritating touch of the blanket and straw mattress. A lamp screwed to a round table burned with a sickly light. A nurse, full-faced and pockmarked, was asleep in an armchair. Her head had drooped down low onto her chest, giving the impression that she was examining her own glasses.

As he was turning, Jung's elbow brushed against a vial of medicine: it knocked loudly against a glass, waking the slumbering woman.

"Nonsense . . . there is nowhere to go, Sir . . ." she muttered, half asleep, then woke up. "What do you need? To drink? Are you uncomfortable, perhaps?" she asked in her habitually caring voice. "You have slept well just now; it seems that you will recover."

"Yes. I woke up in the middle of the night," Jung said vexedly, not noticing her embarrassment. "Death is coming . . . I am unwell."

"Sick people are all hypochondriac," said the sister. "I have seen worse cases recover."

"Oh, stop it," Jung whispered in despair and closed his eyes.

The night before, with the subtlety of intuition peculiar to the gravely ill, he had seen from the tense face of the doctor that the situation was not good. Various memories ran through his melancholic mind with a haphazard vividness. Among other things, he remembered how five years ago he had been a club sponger, remembered the details of several evenings, but beyond that the strength of his recollections faded, leaving a significant stretch of vague fogginess, as is often the case for people with a weak or scattered memory. The so-called "lapse" lay between the current moment and the time when he had decided to drown himself.

Suddenly, Jung remembered the cards. They were lying under his pillow. His consciousness went no further than the possibility of finding himself, with their help, in either non-existence or in new (old?) conditions. It could not go further than this: the magical game made reality seem so upended, so much a mirror version of itself, so ruled by the extraordinary, that Jung's face contorted in helpless despair. He wanted to be with Olga Nevzorova, or to not be at all.

"Yulia Petrovna," he said in a weak voice, "could you please move the table towards me."

"What do you have in mind now? Lie down, lie down, sir."

"Oh, come on; move it, please."

She argued a bit more, but finally fulfilled his wish. Jung struggled to raise himself on his elbow, placing the deck in front of him. Due to his weakness, and additionally to avoid questions and curious looks from the sister of mercy, in case she started scrutinizing the cards, Jung came up with a simplified version of stacks. In this game—if two people are playing—the deck is split, cards facing down, into two equal or unequal halves. Each player chooses which half he wants, and the person whose bottom card is higher than the bottom card of the opponent's stack wins.

The glasses of Julia Petrovna observed his actions anxiously, and with astonishment. Jung slowly started to lift the stack lying closest to him. "Ten years . . . ten years and four months," he mentally repeated.

"Ah!" he yelled out wildly, seeing at that very moment his ten of spades against the king of the second stack.

It was all over.

Figure 6.2. ***Petrograd These Days***
*Drawing for the "Ogonyok" magazine by M. Roshkovsky.*
***Bread and Circuses.***
*The posters in the drawing are approximately 1/6 scale and the meager 1/8 pound of bread—the portion of a daily ration—is life-sized.*

The back cover of the magazine in which Alexander Grin's "Club Sponger" appeared (*Ogonek*, no. 1, 1918). The silhouettes in the background depict St. Isaac's Cathedral and a sphinx, which seems to be a conflation of two famous sculptures of this type in the city. Its location (across from St. Isaac's) and headgear suggest that this is one of the genuine Egyptian sphinxes on the University Embankment, near the Academy of Arts. However, the feminine outline of the figure is similar to the Neoclassical sphinxes on the Egyptian Bridge.

## Notes

* **Alexander Grin, "The Club Sponger."** First published as A. Grin, "Klubnyi arap," *Ogonek*, no. 1 (1918), 12, 14–18. The issue contains numerous drawings and photographs, some of them quite ghastly, reflecting the turmoil and violence of the revolution. Reproduced here are the front and back covers of the magazine.

1 *Never before had gambling flourished so in Petrograd. By fall of the year 1917, more than fifty gambling dens had been formed in Petrograd bearing euphonious, proper names. . . .* This passage is repeated almost verbatim in a tale about the revolution by Mikhail Kozakov (1897–1954), published posthumously in the anniversary issue of *Novyi mir:* Mikhail Kozakov, "Petrogradskie dni," *Novyi mir,* no. 11 (November 1957), 129. Kozakov apparently treats Grin's story as a historical source.

*The Proplyuisky District* is a comical name concocted by Grin, meaning something like "Spit-Covered District." It does not exactly accord with the aura of a grand capital city and would be more appropriate for a small and dirty provincial place—something like another invented toponym, the proverbial Mukhosransk (from "fly" and "feces").

2 *a complex version of Jack Hamlin in Russian conditions.* Jack Hamlin is the hero of many gambling stories by Bret Harte from the 1870s–90s. Among other English-language writers who influenced Grin, commentators name Daniel Defoe, James Fenimore Cooper, Edgar Allan Poe, Thomas Mayne Reid, Rider Haggard, and Robert Louis Stevenson.

## Ivan Lukash

# Hermann's Card*

The Executive Committee of the People's Will wanted to incite revolt in the whole of Russia in 1881, but does anyone really know what this Executive Committee was?

And yet, its agents were being caught all over the country; incendiary flyers were posted even on Nevsky Prospect; in the factories, pale long-haired men began to walk among the workers; the Winter Palace was shaken by a great explosion, where innocent soldiers of the Finnish Life Guards Regiment died.[1]

It was a terrible time. No one knew the Executive Committee, but it was known that the Committee wanted to raise up all of Russia, and a manifesto had already been issued for peasants to take up axes and slaughter their masters in all provinces, to set fires everywhere, to hang officials and judges, and for soldiers to turn their weapons against generals, and to kill the sovereign himself, and for everything to become like under Emelyan Pugachev: unbridled freedom, rebellion, and revelry for convicts.

And the main agent in that Committee was Sophia Perovskaya.

She was gentle, noble, of aristocratic blood. Her face was thin and sad, but with a harsh crease above her eyebrows. Looking at her, her whole face shone like a pale snowflake.

When the tsar was killed, Sophia Perovskaya, along with the other regicides, was brought to the exercise ground of the Semyonovsky Regiment for execution.

She was taken in a tall, black carriage, with her back to the coachman, and above her head, a gray plaque listing all her crimes against the state was nailed to a pole.

They were all hung at dawn. Sophia Perovskaya, as she ascended the scaffold, suddenly waved a white handkerchief. Then the drums beat, and the Guards' cordons struck the crowd with rifle butts—and so she hung without a word in a canvas sack under a trembling pole. Everyone in the sacks was hanging and twitching; she, who was half-bent over when she dropped from the gallows, froze like a strangled kitten . . . Only the old people say that she was not strangled at all. Similarly, back in 1775, in a ravelin of the Peter and Paul Fortress, the Princess of All-Russia, Princess of Vladimir, Elizabeth Tarakanova, allegedly drowned in the flood, but the old people say that she did not drown at all, but walks around St. Petersburg . . .

And about Perovskaya, too, whether she is alive or not, they say her ghost appears . . .

In the month of March, St. Petersburg is dark; wind from the seaside beats on rooftops with a roar, wet snow falls in heavy flakes, blinding the eyes, and the dim lanterns are extinguished by the wind following the snow. It is empty on the streets; only blizzards whirl . . . It is on such nights, on the Catherine Canal, on the steep bridge, that Sophia Perovskaya appears.[2] She stands on that very bridge from whence she waved her handkerchief—giving the signal to throw the bomb under the black sleigh of the emperor . . . A small shadow, bent, like a strangled kitten, with her white hair swept up by the wind, and her small face glowing dreadfully with a cold and dim light . . .

Whatever the case, in the Aleksandrovsky market, in the glass-covered aisle, from which one can take a back door into the flea-market, in that very aisle, where there is an image of two angels in blue robes carrying on clouds the Icon of the Mother of God of Smolensk, one antique dealer, an eccentric and philosopher called Sapunkov, was showing me a bronze dancing harlequin on a green malachite stand. And Sapunkov, Ilya Fyodorovich, was assuring me that the bronze harlequin escapes from his shop at night for the whole of Shrovetide and dances at masquerades . . . It may be so: under a mask, how can one recognize who is waltzing through the dim halls?

And at the Academy of Arts, on Vasilyevsky Island along the embankment, where two sphinxes on stone pedestals lie in a mocking slumber, their clawed paws gripping the granite, on days of flooding, at night, supposedly one can hear knocking on the main gates facing the Neva.[3]

One night, the doorman apparently pressed his face to the wrought metal lock and called out:

"Who is knocking, who?"

And whether it was the rumble of the wind or the noise of the Neva's waters, someone's voice answered:

"I am knocking. I am the sculptor Kozlovsky from the Smolensky cemetery. I got all wet and icy in the grave . . . Open up!"

The doorman crossed himself and ran away from the lock, because knocking was the very Kozlovsky who had died fifty years ago, and whose granite tombstone bears this inscription:

> Under this stone
> Rests an emulator of Phidias
> And the Russian Bonaparte . . .[4]

It can happen, of course . . . And whether such things happen or not, it certainly did happen that in the third hour of a white night, the famous card player Sokolovsky was walking along the English Embankment.

Every person has his profession. One builds stone houses; another scribbles poems; a third spends his whole life turning some metal pointer, some shiny lever on a foreign machine; a fourth hangs people through a court sentence; a fifth slaughters people through his own will . . .

Sokolovsky did not have any real profession: he was a card player and lived by cards.

Because of cards, he had to resign his commission as captain of the Chevalier Guard Regiment. Because of cards, he sold two estates, one in Kharkov and the other in Samara province, to merchants for timber. Because of cards, back in his youth, he lost his young and gentle wife, Zinaida Sergeevna, who faded away with tuberculosis, awaiting his return from the clubs in agonizing and sleepless nights.

Cards were his art, his beauty, his delight. He lived grandly, but by himself. His sumptuous, slightly gloomy apartment on Ofitserskaya Street was known to all the Guards' youth, though only until a certain hour, when the affably cold, reserved host would say as he stood up:

"Gentlemen, should we not head now to Cubat or Donon . . ."

The cut of his jackets was imitated, and it was from him that the manner was adopted of wearing a widely open, starched shirtfront, and white gaiters, and a monocle on a black silk ribbon.

Who in St. Petersburg does not know or remember Sokolovsky? He was at all exhibition openings, theater premieres, horse races. Always somewhat pale, he would appear in his impeccable black jackets. He also had the habit of pensively biting the golden handle of his walking stick. With his lion-like appearance and quiet mannerisms he looked like a great artist.

And he was an artist. He always played fair. During long, dark nights he would not sleep a wink, putting together countless combinations of *chemin de ferre* and Macao in a feverish frenzy. He was slowly burning out, but the dark fire eating away at him was noticeable only in the hot glare of his perpetually sad eyes and the slight, barely perceptible tremor in the edges of his coldly closed lips.

Sokolovsky was a famous gambler. Many a fortune was lost in his pale, narrow hands. Sometimes people shot themselves because of him. Sometimes they crawled and begged at his feet. And it was his silent and ominous shadow that loomed behind the case of insurance companies whose deposits were squandered by the director at the card table.

As a gambler, Sokolovsky was merciless. He had long since understood the alluring mystery of card decks rustling on green cloth; of languid jacks and pale queens, with white, strange flowers in their coy fingers; and dusky kings; and strange aces; and flickering red and black tens, twos, eights . . .

At the card table, in the dim haze of the candlelight, when the players' voices became hoarse and their fingers bent like tenacious claws, and their eyes wandered over the piles of gold and stacks of banknotes, Sokolovsky, throwing a card with a graceful and silent gesture, sometimes caught himself thinking:

"Maybe I am throwing away someone's life right now . . . Maybe we are playing not with cards, but with souls . . . In the infinite randomness of combinations, millions of lives and millions of deaths may be created and destroyed by us, the players . . . Maybe the gods, too—like us, the players—are playing with us and the entire universe, in the dark, blindly . . ."

It must be said that Sokolovsky had traced around three thousand combinations of *chemain de ferre*, but luck suddenly turned its back on him. First it was a ruddy, mustache-less officer of the Horse Guards Regiment, who for three nights, until dawn, beat all his cards. Then it was a flabby comedian from the Alexandrinsky Theater, in appearance a complaisant and kindly man, but in reality a wicked, cunning, and greedy person. The comedian, not losing a single card, was swallowing his saliva and sniffing, touching his gold five-ruble pieces with the stumps of his short fingers. Then a racehorse breeder, then a bank clerk on a spree—half-drunk, sweaty and cowardly, insolent . . .

It was becoming too much. Last week, in a club on Nevsky, someone shoved him away from the table with his shoulder and did not even apologize. He started to notice disdainful and mocking glances. He was no longer playing. Yesterday, some student in a blue frock coat with a flabby, eyebrow-less, womanly face said—behind his back, but he heard it clearly—

"A waned star. This is the one who used to be Sokolovsky . . ."

"I still am, still am," Sokolovsky said to himself, tapping the slabs of the embankment with his stick. "I'll show who I am; I'll take my revenge . . ."

His anger seared him. He took off his top hat. He walked aimlessly along the embankment, but felt with bitterness that he would again come to the gambling house and would again stand with pursed lips at the table like a lackey, and he would be carelessly elbowed away, and he would not sit down to play; he would be afraid to sit, because all of his money, down to the last three-ruble banknote, was lost . . .

It was a white night.

On such nights, in the mirror-like windows of the low palaces along the English Embankment, the dim flames of dawn shine for a long time, burning like a crimson and misty fire in the pale sky.

On such nights, St. Petersburg silently softens in the ghostly, silvery haze of that half-light, half-darkness; the sad eyes of women of the night are so melancholic and so inviting behind the dark web of a veil; and in the zoological garden, skinny white bears walk, gently swaying in their cages, deceived by the soundless twilight.

During white nights, St. Petersburg softly glimmers from within, like a pale icon lamp. During white nights, everything is smoke, a reflection, half-sound, half-ghost, a silvery vision, and sadness. During white nights, everything ripples gently, everything floats vaguely and lightly in a pale stream of deadly silent houses, palaces, colonnades, prospects, railings. In the silvery glimmering darkness, St. Petersburg leaves its place, St. Petersburg silently moves. During white nights, St. Petersburg dies, quietly and gently, without a quiver or a sound, like a burnt-out pale icon lamp.

The wrathful emperor dies, raising his horse over the pale abyss. The dark sphinxes die, their stone lips curved in an eternal and mysterious grin. The cast-iron angels die, holding their enormous, extinguished torches over St. Isaac's . . .

During white nights, St. Petersburg dies, dies, sweetly and painlessly . . .

Sokolovsky walked along the embankment as if in the depths of a mirror: without a shadow, in a dull silvery glimmer.

He stood above the pale Neva, resting his hand on the granite. The rough stone was covered in cold dew.

Near Millionnaya Street, he crossed the moist wooden pavement blocks to the Swan Canal. And when he was entering under the tall and dark archway, biting the end of his stick, the shadow of a passerby appeared across from him.[5]

Sokolovsky looked at it absent-mindedly. The strange passerby was moving towards him from the dim mirrors. His black cloak was falling off one shoulder and dragging along the slabs. His dark eyes flashed strangely and menacingly from under his hat. Sokolovsky noticed the silver tassels of a lavish aiguillette under the cloak and thought: "Strange tassels, ancient ones; such things aren't worn nowadays. And strange attire. As if at a masquerade."

The passerby was moving towards him, his arms crossed over his chest . . .

"Wait, Sokolovsky: you are searching for a lucky card?"

At the muffled and cold sound of the voice, the calm gambler trembled, but quickly recovered and asked scornfully, putting on his top hat:

"How do you know what I am looking for? And why are you addressing me informally, like a mask at a masquerade . . . Who are you?"

"I find it strange that you did not recognize me. I am indeed a mask, an eternal mask, because I am a gambler like yourself . . . I am Hermann."

"Hermann?.. Hold on—Hermann?.. I do not remember such a name. That is something from olden times. It never happened. I don't remember. I did not meet you at the card table."

"And I have not met you, but I am always with you, because you are a gambler. And have you forgotten that I know the three lucky cards?"

"You seem to be laughing . . . But anyway, tell me what they are. I am curious," Sokolovsky asked, and his mouth suddenly went dry.

"Three, seven, ace."

"Three, seven, ace . . . Ah, ah . . . Three cards . . . All right, I will remember them. I thank you; I will test them; I lost my money and I will win it back; I will go play, thank you . . ."

"Do not thank me. I will come with you. I will also be playing."

In the silvery, pale glimmer, they hurriedly walked across the empty Field of Mars, like phantoms in a strange masquerade, like shadows sliding through silent mirrors: an elegant gentleman in a black jacket and top hat, and a short officer in an ancient black cloak and black hat . . .

In the Concordia club on Nevsky Prospect, in the backyard of a huge house on the corner of Mikhailovskaya Street, the electric chandeliers shone dimly, because all the curtains were down. The gambling hall was drowning in a haze of tobacco smoke. The pale faces of the players were bent over the long green table, the light of the chandelier reflecting dully in their hair . . .

The game was intense, noiseless: a gray-haired and noble-looking trustee of orphanages, wearing a fully buttoned black frock coat, was losing over two hundred thousand to a famous lawyer, who looked like an actor, with his puffy and yellowish face, with his crumpled starched shirt in the wide cut of a black tailcoat . . .

Sokolovsky, placing his top hat and stick on the pier table in the entryway, cast a sidelong glance at the mirror. Seeing his pale and morose face lit by the dull glow of the chandeliers, he did not recognize himself for a moment, then he fixed his hair and thought:

"But where is my companion?"

He looked around. His dark companion was standing by the heavy portiere with his back turned, the black cloak draped over his forearm. Sokolovsky took a step, and his companion took a step ahead of him into the smoky hall . . .

"I bet twenty thousand," said Sokolovsky, sinking heavily into the chair opposite the lawyer. Sokolovsky paused briefly, clenched his teeth, and with a wandering glance, searched for the black shadow of his companion. The trustee of orphanages handed him the deck, and Sokolovsky, looking at his black, fully buttoned frock coat, whispered:

"Are you here, Hermann?.. Look, I am playing."

"Your three wins." The lawyer squinted at Sokolovsky carelessly and sleepily, chewed his plump lips, and held out a stack of banknotes and gold coins across the table to him.

"I bet forty," Sokolovsky muttered through his clenched teeth, pushing the winnings away from him. One gold coin rolled across the green fabric and fell to the parquet with a clear, sad ringing sound. Sokolovsky flinched.

"Your seven wins." The lawyer opened his swollen eyes, somewhat surprised. His wrinkled, yellowish face frowned angrily.

Chairs were being moved around the table. Some people stood up, peering over. People crowded behind Sokolovsky.

"I bet everything," he exhaled hoarsely, his mouth dry.

The game went on in a strained silence of utter tension, when the gambling hall went quiet, with a silence perhaps more terrible than the last moments of an execution, the last thrill of a murder. Someone whispered: "What a terrifying game."

"I have an ace!" Sokolovsky yelled, standing up. "I won . . ."

"No, you lost," said the lawyer, mockingly raising his voice as well. "You don't have an ace, but a queen."

"A queen? What queen?.. Ah yes—the Queen of Spades . . . I forgot, I forgot . . . It's the Queen of Spades, it's the damned murdered old woman who took the last bet . . . I forgot, I forgot . . ."[6]

He rose up from his chair, looking around. He glanced at the shaved lawyer with a horrified look, as if it was not him he saw, but the ugly, dead old woman, heavily painted, with a yellowish, flabby face—death itself, squinting at him mockingly with one eye.

"Masks, masks!" Sokolovsky shouted madly.

He covered his face with his hands, and laughed . . . Or maybe it was not him, but someone else who laughed then in that smoky hall?..

. . . Do you remember that the eternal Petersburgian tale, "The Queen of Spades," is cut short in this way:

## Conclusion

"Hermann lost his mind. He is in room number seventeen at the Obukhov Hospital, not responding to any questions and muttering unusually fast: 'Three, seven, ace! Three, seven, queen!'"

The cardplayer Sokolovsky is likewise confined to a psychiatric ward.

Berlin, September 22, 1922

## Notes

* **Ivan Lukash, "Hermann's Card."** First published as Ivan Lukash, "Karta Germanna," in his *Chort na gauptvakhte. Tri peterburgskikh istorii* (Berlin: Izd. E. A. Gutnova, 1922), 79–98.

The title of the story refers to Hermann, the protagonist of the most famous gambling tale in Russian literature and a Petersburg mystical classic, "The Queen of Spades" (1833) by Alexander Pushkin. Echoes from the tale are prominent in Dostoevsky's *Crime and Punishment* (1866). In his *Raw Youth* (1875), Dostoevsky calls Hermann a colossal character and a quintessential Petersburgian type. The popularity of "The Queen of Spades" was further enhanced by the eponymous opera by Tchaikovsky (1890), which has become a staple of the Russian opera repertoire. There, the protagonist's name is spelled with one "n" (Herman), as in Pushkin's drafts. Tchaikovsky shifts the action from the 1830s to the time of Catherine the Great and introduces significant changes to the plot, transforming Pushkin's terse and tantalizingly enigmatic masterpiece into a full-blown melodrama. And yet, Tchaikovsky's opera is a great work of art in its own right. Despite all predictable operatic clichés and conventions, the eerie beauty of its haunting melodies perfectly resonates with the somber mystical spirit of Pushkin's original.

1 *the Winter Palace was shaken by a great explosion, where innocent soldiers of the Finnish Life Guards Regiment died.* In 1880, a member of the People's Will attempted to assassinate Alexander II by detonating a powerful explosive beneath the emperor's dining room. Perhaps Lukash includes this episode because of a connection to his own family history. His father was a retired corporal of the Finnish regiment and a veteran of the Russo-Turkish War of 1877–78, so it is likely that among those killed in the incident were his comrades-in-arms.

2 *And about Perovskaya, too, whether she is alive or not, they say her ghost appears [. . .] on the Catherine Canal, on the steep bridge.* The succession of alleged supernatural occurrences described after Sophia Perovskaya's execution has parallels in Gogol's "Overcoat" (the talk about attacks of the dead clerk) and Merezhkovsky's *Peter and Alexis* (rumors in the crowd witnessing the bizarre funeral procession for Peter's favorite dwarf at the end of Book 7). Something similar is also found in the opening chapter of Alexey Tolstoy's *The Road to Calvary*, published in émigré periodicals in 1920, which describes the decadent and apocalyptic atmosphere of the capital on the eve of WWI.

After the revolution, the streets around the area where the successful attempt on the emperor's life took place received the names of the assassins. Malaya Konyushennaya Street was renamed for Sophia Perovskaya, Bolshaya Konyushennaya for Andrei Zhelyabov, and a bridge across the canal for Sergei Grinevitsky. Millionaya Street, leading to the Winter Palace, was renamed in honor of Stepan Khalturin, the organizer of the 1880 explosion. In 1991, these streets were again renamed, and the ghosts of Perovskaya and her comrades exorcised in a way. The enduring monument to the tragic events of March 1, 1881, is the Church of the Resurrection (Savior on the Spilled Blood) constructed by the Romanovs on the site of the assassination.

3 *the Academy of Arts, on Vasilyevsky Island.* This is another location with a strong family connection for Lukash, since both his father and mother were employed at the Academy.

4 *the Russian Bonaparte . . .* This is an obvious technical mistake repeated in all subsequent publications of the story. The actual epitaph calls Kozlovsky, who was a prominent sculptor, the Russian *Buonarroti*—that is, Michelangelo.

5 *Near Millionnaya Street, he crossed [. . .] to the Swan Canal. And when he was entering under the tall and dark archway [. . .] the shadow of a passerby appeared across from him.* Lukash confuses two canals: there is no arch by the Swan Canal, so Sokolovsky must be turning from the Neva embankment into the arch of the Winter Canal. The arch is a clear marker. Besides, the Winter Canal is the right place for an encounter involving *The Queen of Spades* by Tchaikovsky. It is here that in the opera the last meeting between the hero and the heroine occurs. The inconsolable

Liza drowns herself, and the deranged Herman leaves for the gambling house, and for his ruin. It is easy to confuse the two canals: both are relatively close to one another, situated on the opposite ends of Millionnaya Street; both are between the Moika and the Neva; both have a diminutive in their name (*kanavka*); both are beautiful and very Petersburgian.

6 *"A queen? What queen?.. Ah yes—the Queen of Spades . . . I forgot, I forgot . . . It's the Queen of Spades, it's the damned murdered old woman who took the last bet . . . I forgot, I forgot . . . ."* "The Queen of Spades" revolves around the secret of the three cards supposedly known to the old countess. These cards (three, seven, and ace) played in sequence prove to be a winning combination indeed, but during the final game the ace is inexplicably replaced with the Queen of Spades, an "avatar" of the dead countess, and Hermann loses everything. While Sokolovsky, except for the three cards episode, is a true gambler, Hermann is not, as he is unwilling to take genuine risks and wants to cheat Fate. Hence his punishment. Sokolovsky, one might conclude, is punished for being oblivious to Russian classical literature, and more specifically, to the great tradition of mystical tales from St. Petersburg.

# Contemporary Reactions to “The Stereoscope”

## Valery Bryusov, Review of “The Stereoscope”

A. Ivanov, *The Stereoscope. A Twilight Tale.* Drawings by E. Smirnova-Ivanova. St. Petersburg, 1909; Price: 90 kopecks.

The hero of the story buys a stereoscope with one image permanently inserted into it: a view of a hall in the Hermitage. In his room, in the evening, examining this old photograph, he suddenly feels himself being transported into that hall, standing inside it. His wanderings in the world of the past begin, in that world, a part of which is captured on the photograph inserted into the stereoscope. Thus, Mr. Ivanov’s piece belongs to those stories which are colloquially called “fantastical”—and moreover, to a specific type of them. Taking one imagined situation (the ability to be transported into a stereoscopic world) as his starting point, the author develops everything else from it with an irresistible logic, with extreme realism. This is the same method used by Gogol in “The Nose;” Edgar Allen Poe in “A Descent into the Maelström” and other stories; and H. G. Wells in *The Invisible Man*, “The Story of the Late Mr. Elvesham,” and “The New Accelerator.” And yet, it is also the same method that allows mathematicians to determine the elements and properties of figures and bodies in various non-Euclidean planes.

The story by Mr. Ivanov is very well written. The author has his own style: reserved, simple, but developed. We believe that Mr. Ivanov has the qualities to become a good and interesting writer.

Valery Bryusov

*Vesy*, no. 6 (June 1909), 81.

## Alexander Blok. Excerpts from letters to Alexander Ivanov's brother, Evgeny, pertaining to "The Stereoscope"

August 9, 1909.

In the latest issue of *Vesy* Val. Bryusov praised "The Stereoscope" very well, in my opinion.
Inform Alexander Pavlovich of this.

September 3, 1909.

I wanted to tell you that I am appreciating "The Stereoscope" more and more (though I haven't reread it). I have understood it even more through Bryusov's review and through reading Wells. I am thinking a lot about it. I think that this, along with Bryusov's prose, belongs to the first "scientific" experiments of art in *Russian* literature, and I deeply welcome it. Amongst the old writers, only Pushkin had a hint of these methods and this language.

A. A. Blok, *Sobranie sochinenii v vos'mi tomakh*, vol. 8, *Pis'ma* (Moscow—Leningrad: Khudozhestvennaia literature, 1963), 290, 292.

## Max Voloshin, Review of "The Stereoscope"*

St. Petersburg is a fantastical and ghostly city. We have known this for a long time. But what constitutes its ghostliness and fantasticality, which is striking even to those who do not think about Peter, or Pushkin, or Dostoevsky? The root of that feeling lies in some elusive, purely impressionistic perceptions of its streets. I believe they are as follows.

The first time I saw St. Petersburg—this was in the winter; I was studying painting and came from Paris—I was struck by the deathly strictness of its overall tone. "It is just like a photograph," came to my mind. This was especially strange after Paris, the grayest of all cities, but a different kind of gray! There, it is a cool gray, transitioning everywhere into bluish, steely, caustic charcoal, and inky blue hues. There is nothing richer and fresher than the gray palette of Paris. Meanwhile, in St. Petersburg, every tone transitions to yellowish and brown ones. Even the variegation of smoke colors and the dark red color of government buildings do not diversify, but only emphasize the dullness of the main tone, which, with its withered and brownish hues, does indeed come close to the colors of an old photograph. Apart from that, the enormity of St. Petersburg's vistas (the prospects, the embankments of the Neva), always seen from flat ground and never from above, give the illusion not of a normal, but of a diminishing, photographic perspective. Without a doubt, St. Petersburg resembles a photograph.

From this purely visual impression comes a natural transition to the idea of the ghostly and the fantastical. A photograph captures a world that is ghostly and fantastical. Ghostly, because it is colorless, monochromatic, and flat-toned. Fantastical, because it utters casually the great words: "Stop, moment!"—and time obeys.

A painting, having passed through the camera-obscura of the artist's soul, transforms a moment into eternity. Meanwhile, a photograph captures any unremarkable moment and stops it for eternity. The main characteristic of a moment is its elusiveness, its fleetingness. That is the favorite motif of the sadly joyful Apollonian poetry. A photograph captures a ghostly, yet tangible trace of the past. This is not as apparent in a new photograph, but the older the image, the more its fantasticality shines through, due to the mechanistic way of capturing a moment of past life.

Old photographs reveal a world superficially similar to the human world, but at the same time deeply hostile towards its living essence. The most frightening things in it for a human being are his doubles, which are at the same time corpses, because what is depicted has already died. If by means of a stereoscope one then gives a flat photograph three-dimensionality, its horror increases, as if becoming tangible.

In reality, we always see flat, and only logically know about the three-dimensionality of the world. A stereoscope thus monstrously emphasizes what in our eyes exists as a subconscious inkling. In effect, it makes our vision tactile. Everything in a stereoscope is more convex and bulging than in the real world. And at the same time, it is a world of dead dolls, gray doubles of life, corpses of lived moments which have not undergone decay, like the bodies of great sinners whom the earth does not accept . . .

These are the fantastical premises that created the strange, vivid, accomplished, and very Petersburgian tale of Aleksandr Ivanov, "The Stereoscope." This completely new author, debuting with this small, elegantly published book, with drawings by Smirnova-Ivanova, presents himself as an accomplished stylist, and experienced master in the kind of logical fantastical literature that has been very little developed in Russia.

The protagonist and narrator of the story enters the inner worlds of his stereoscope: those realms "which humans are forbidden to enter, into which they can only glance." Photographs have a strange charm to them. A peculiar, secluded world looks out from them. It has no living colors. Only a dull brown and its shades rule over it, as if everything has faded . . . The ghostly doubles of things forever in the past look at you from old photographs, a mysterious sadness and a quiet terror emanating from them. And the older the photograph, the deeper its charms. A living person should not upset that dead frozen world by his invasion into its depths. When he does so, the mysterious balances of those depths are disturbed . . .

The magical stereoscope, which he purchased by chance at an antique store, has a photograph of the Hall of Zeus the Olympian in the Hermitage inserted, and the stereoscope is sealed shut. He comes home, starts to look at the image, and suddenly feels that the hall is starting to take him in, that it is surrounding him with its walls from behind, from the right and from the left. He ends up transported into the three-dimensional space hidden in the depths of the stereoscope.

The real world is replaced with a stereoscopic world with great artistry. He recognizes the smell of the Hermitage's lower halls. But in this world, there is a deep silence. He hears only the beating of his heart, and the peculiar sounds of his footsteps on the stone tiles that make up the floor of the lower halls of the Hermitage. A dead light pours in from the windows, and a photographic sky is visible. In the center of the hall, he sees the figure of the photographer who photographed it. He is motionless, because he is frozen in the moment that has become imperishable in his photograph. Eerily, with a masterful accumulation of details, A. Ivanov describes the halls of this Hermitage of the past, with its frozen human figures. "They each kept their unchanging poses, glassy eyes fixed in one eternal spot. Sometimes I would catch their gazes on me, or look directly at them. Then I would shudder . . ."

With these eyes begins the terror that gradually spreads through the whole story. He touches one of those dead doubles of life. "The skin was not cold like that of a corpse. It retained some sort of warmth, like it was the faded warmth of a living body." "The dim rays from the sky of the stereoscopic world poured only a hazy, mysterious dusky light over the brownish halls." This substitution is so natural, so probable, so reminiscent of what naturally comes to mind in the halls of the Hermitage! This substitution of colors, sounds, and light contains more fantastical horror than the events themselves.

The hero accidentally breaks the glass of a display case in the Egyptian Hall and takes one of the stone scarab beetles. Here, the horror grows, because all of the phantoms, thanks to their stereoscopicity, are corporeal. He feels on himself the gaze of an old woman, who is looking at the display case. Those eyes were especially, unbearably frightening. But, overcoming his fear, he approaches her. But something terribly frightening happens. The phantom falls to the floor. He wants to flee that world. But how?

"I was a lonely living being, lost in these dead realms." He returns to the hall where the photographer is seated, moves to the apparatus, so the back of his head is touching the lenses, and slightly turns his head left and right. He finally finds the spot from which the lens of the stereoscope looks into the hall, and imperceptibly enters back into the ordinary world. This is a striking feature, because it contains that familiar gesture, when, in order to experience the depth of a doubled stereoscopic photograph, we cross our eyes and move the card before our eyes several times, at a certain distance, until both images merge into one. This very gesture is repeated in reverse, and the three-dimensional world separates into two flat images.

The hero of "The Stereoscope," waking up in the living world which is flowing in time, finds a scarab in his pocket, completely identical to one he has seen in the Hermitage in a case, but that one is green, and this one is dark brown—it is photographic. He goes out onto the street and walks through the photographic St. Petersburg of the past. The bygone wind howls through the air. He finds the house and apartment where he lived as a child. There, he sees his motionlessly seated father, and himself as a little boy, with a book, in the nursery. These are the best pages of the story in terms of mood and sustained tone. But something is beginning to happen in the stereoscopic world: it is beginning to darken, and a reddish-brown dusk falls. He runs to the Hermitage, so as not to lose his way out. "Around me, streets crossed each other and stretched out for miles, squares spread out, and on them stood the silently frozen doubles of once living people." He runs onto the porch of the Hermitage, with its formidable gigantic atlantes, and enters the vestibule. But something had happened within that motionless world after he knocked over the old woman in the Egyptian Hall. The balance was disturbed, and some figures came into motion. The ghost of the old woman chases him through the fully darkened brown halls of the Hermitage. He flees from her in terror. He sees two other mannequins who have left their spots. He manages to reach the hall with the photographer, and, finding the point of view, slips away from this disturbed world. But, already looking from the outside into the lenses of the stereoscope, he sees that the old woman is sitting on the floor of the hall and directly looking at him. Terrified, afraid that the old woman could enter the living world through the same path as him, he grabs a hammer and smashes the magical lenses of the stereoscope.

Here is the simple plot of this fantastical story, which undoubtedly creates a strong sense of horror. Yet strangely, this horror is hidden less in the events of the story than in the masterful descriptions, creating the full illusion of a photographic world. This story is certainly a new and excellent page in the realm of Petersburgian fantastical literature, beginning with "The Queen of Spades" and *The Bronze Horseman*. The theme of a stereoscopic world also seems to me completely unused by anyone until now, if one does not count the few hints in Turgenev's "Klara Milich." It also occurred to me while reading that I don't recall any Russian writers describing the Hermitage and showing the eerie and formidable grandeur of the encumbered gigantic atlantes at its entrance.

## Notes

* This review was written for the opening issue of *Apollon* in October 1909, but was not used by the magazine's editor. A draft copy from Voloshin's archive was published by Vladimir Kupchenko in *Novyi zhurnal* (NY), no. 168–169 (September—October 1987), 233–37; it was reprinted in V. P. Kupchenko, "Eshche odin Aleksandr Ivanov," in *Litsa. Bibliograficheskii al'manakh* (Moscow-St. Petersburg: Feniks, 1993), 5–9.

Dan Ungurianu

# Alexander Ivanov's "Stereoscope" in the Context of Mystical and Fantastic Literature of the Silver Age

## Guidebooks to the Twilight Zone

All the literary works in this collection are united by three common characteristics. They were written in the early twentieth century, during the so-called Silver Age, a period of artistic renaissance in Russia and an important part of the larger European *Belle Époque*.[1] Their action takes place in St. Petersburg, one of the most beautiful cities in the world and a splendid imperial capital, which, in addition to being the cradle of modern Russian culture, became its major subject and theme. And finally, all of them belong to the mystical or fantastic genres.

The latter assertion intentionally conflates two extremely broad categories that do not necessarily intersect. Fantastic literature, with all the multitude of its varieties from gothic to fairytale and fantasy, while involving supernatural occurrences, does not have to make claims beyond the realm of fiction. Mystical literature, on the other hand, even if we leave aside overtly doctrinal texts, has potentially serious existential implications. The Silver Age saw the proliferation of mystical teachings among artists and intellectuals, who embraced spiritualism,

1 One can argue that the term "Silver Age," when applied to the turn of the twentieth century in Russia, is in many ways a misnomer; see Omry Ronen, *The Fallacy of the Silver Age* (Amsterdam: Routledge, 1997). However, this is a lost battle: the term has gained wide currency in literary and cultural studies both in Russia and abroad and has become a standard way to designate the period. Moreover, the "aura" of the term perfectly agrees with the aestheticism and decadence of the era.

theosophy, anthroposophy, and aspects of Eastern religions; they also experimented with Christianity, something that was most conspicuously manifested through Sophiology and God-seeking in the decadent and symbolist circles. All sorts of combinations of these ingredients were possible, with individual involvement ranging from mere curiosity to full-fledged participation in occult practices. Hence, a strong supernatural coloring—or a "mystical lining"—that became an integral part of the period's worldview.[2] This atmosphere is captured vividly by Vladislav Khodasevich, who reminisces of the years of his symbolist youth:

> [We] were living in a complex and difficult world, one that is no longer easy for me to describe in the way we understood it then. It was hard to breathe in the hot, pre-storm air of those years. Everything appeared ambiguous and equivocal; the outlines of objects seemed unsteady. Reality, bleeding over into consciousness, became permeable. We were living in the real world—and, at the same time, in some special, hazy, and complex reflection of it, where everything was "the same, but different." It was as if every object, every step, and every gesture were being tentatively reflected, projected onto an alternative surface, onto a screen that was close, but untouchable. Everyday happenings were transformed into visions. In addition to its obvious, primary meaning, each event took on a secondary meaning that had to be deciphered. This meaning wouldn't yield itself to us without a fight, but we knew that it was the true one. And so we lived in two worlds at once. But, as we didn't know how to uncover the laws governing the events taking place within that second world (which seemed much more real to us than the real one was), we could only wallow in our dark and troubled premonitions. We perceived everything that happened then as an omen. But of what?[3]

---

2 See Maria Carlson, *No Religion Higher Than Truth: A History of the Theosophical Movement in Russia, 1875–1922* (Princeton, NJ: Princeton University Press, 1993); Bernice Rosenthal, ed., *The Occult in Russian and Soviet Culture* (Ithaca, NY: Cornell University Press, 1997); N. A. Bogomolov, *Russkaia literature nachala XX veka i okkul'tizm* (Moscow: Novoe literaturnoe obozrenie, 1999); Julia Mannherz, *Modern Occultism in Late Imperial Russia* (DeKalb, IL: Northern Illinois University Press, 2012).

3 Vladislav Khodasevich, *Necropolis*, trans. Sarah Vitali (New York: Columbia University Press, 2019), 83.

Much of the essentially occult art from the turn of the twentieth century is not necessarily fantastic; this is true about the major mystical novels of the era: Fyodor Sologub's *Petty Demon* (1905), Andrei Bely's *Petersburg* (1913), and even Valery Bryusov's *Fiery Angel* (1908), which is steeped in the atmosphere of black magic and sorcery. Supernatural occurrences there can be explained as hallucinations of the characters, or in terms of their mental illness. Similarly, Dmitry Merezhkovsky's grand historiosophic saga, the trilogy *Christ and Antichrist* (1895–1904), which was extremely popular in Russia and also gained considerable international acclaim, is quite realistic in terms of its action. This, however, does not cancel out its mystical dimension. Let us demonstrate this point by lingering for a moment on Merezhkovsky's work, taking particular notice of its crucial scene, in which the statue of Venus arrives at the Summer Garden in St. Petersburg.

The trilogy rests on Merezhkovsky's idea of the eternal conflict between two diametrically opposed elements—the "truth of Dionysus" (or the "lower abyss") and "the truth of Christ" (or the "upper abyss")—and the yearning for their synthesis. In *Death of the Gods (Julian the Apostate)*, Merezhkovsky portrays the victory of Christianity over Julian's abortive attempt to restore the old religion. However, paganism returns with a vengeance during the Renaissance, which is described in *The Gods Resurrected (Leonardo da Vinci)*. The final book of the trilogy, *The Antichrist (Peter and Alexis)*, shows another triumph of paganism, which—with Petrine reforms—invades Holy Russia. And yet, the "Antichrist Tsar" fails to overcome a Christianity that finds refuge in the passionate faith of the Old Believers, who are full of eschatological expectations.

The central pagan symbol of the trilogy is the statue of Venus (now exhibited at the Hermitage and known as Venus Tauride), which absorbs various feminine cults of antiquity. In the opening novel of the trilogy, this statue inspires Emperor Julian to rebel against Christianity. Although he suffers a defeat and the pagan gods perish, Venus is reborn a millennium later, emerging from her grave in sixteenth-century Italy. Purchased by Peter the Great two centuries later, the statue travels to St. Petersburg:

> It was a sculpture by Praxiteles: Aphrodite-Anadyomene—she who was born of the froth of the sea, and Urania the heavenly, the ancient Phoenician Astarte, the Babylonian Mylitta, proto-mother of the earth, the great Benefactress, she who filled the sky with stars like seeds, and poured the Milky Way as milk from her breasts [...] She was as innocent and as voluptuous as

> ever, naked and not ashamed of her nakedness [. . .] She traveled further and further, from epoch to epoch, from nation to nation [. . .] until in her triumphant march she reached the last limits of Earth, Hyperborean Scythia, beyond which there was nothing but night and chaos. Rising on the pedestal, she for the first time glanced as if with surprised and curious eyes at this new alien land [. . .] at this strange city, which was akin to the settlements of nomadic barbarians, at this sky for which there was neither day nor night, at these black, somnolent, dreadful waves which were similar to the waves of the underground Styx. This country was so unlike her luminous Olympian homeland. And still the goddess smiled with an eternal smile, just like the sun would smile penetrating into dark Hades.[4]

The passage is thoroughly mystical, and yet there is nothing fantastic actually happening here. The mystical aura emerges from the evocation of mythology, and from the figurative, not literal, animation of the statue.

The episode is also full of vampirical motifs that became extremely widespread during the Silver Age. They are introduced in the description of the statue's delivery to Russia:

> Across oceans and rivers, mountains and plains, cities and, finally, through the impoverished Russian villages, dark forests and swamps, protected jealously by will of the tsar, rocking back and forth on the waves, or to the rhythmic jaunt of soft springs in her dark box, as in a cradle or a coffin, the goddess made her long journey from the Eternal City to the newly-founded town of Petersburg.[5]

"Impoverished Russian villages" is a quotation from the poem "These impoverished villages, this meager nature" (1855) by Fyodor Tyutchev. This reference is important, as it asserts that Russia is the land of Christ. Otherwise, Merezhkovsky is very likely alluding to the story of Dracula's travel from Transylvania to England. Later, vampirical motifs become even more pronounced:

---

4 D. S. Merezhkovskii, *Polnoe sobranie sochinenii*, in 24 volumes, vol. 4 (Moscow: Tip. I. D. Sytina, 1914), 30.

5 Ibid., 27.

> The crowd made way for the strange procession. The tsar's tall men-in-waiting and grenadiers bore the long black box that resembled a coffin on their shoulders with difficulty, bending under the weight. Judging by the size of the coffin, the corpse was of superhuman height. They placed the box on the ground. The sovereign—alone and without any assistance—undertook to open it. [. . .] He was in a hurry and pulled out the nails with such impatience that he scratched his hand so that blood flowed. [. . .] The last nails bent their way out, the wood made a cracking noise, the lid lifted and the box was open. At first, they saw something gray and yellow, resembling the dust of crumbled bones in a grave. These were pine shavings, sawdust, felt and bits of combed wool placed in the box as cushioning.[6]

But again, the mystical dimension here is created by allusions and innuendo, with no supernatural occurrences taking place.

While such works as Merezhkovsky's trilogy are crucial for establishing the system of metaphysical coordinates for the artistic imagination of the period, this collection includes shorter prose pieces that fall under the rubric of fantastic literature. They describe events that are outside the "normal" parameters of the real world, and some that are openly supernatural—albeit with varying degrees of certainty. The mystical component is also present, but it can be genuine and deep or more superficial, as a mere tribute to the prevailing fashion and a literary device.

***

By far the most important piece in this collection is "The Stereoscope. A Twilight Tale" (written in 1905, published in 1909). It describes the adventures of a man who accidentally enters the world of an old photograph through the device of a strange stereoscope. This gem of the fantastic literature of the Silver Age was written by Alexander Pavlovich Ivanov (1876–1933), who was not a professional writer, but rather had a degree in mathematics and for a long time earned a living as a statistician in the Ministry of Finance. At the same time, he sporadically wrote articles on artistic topics. In 1911 he published the first biography of the painter Mikhail Vrubel, a seminal pioneering figure in Russian

6 Ibid., 29–30. For more on allusions to *Dracula* in Merezhkovsky see Dan Ungurianu, *Plotting History: The Russian Historical Novel in the Imperial Age* (Madison: The University of Wisconsin Press, 2007), 160–70.

symbolist and modernist art. He also wrote the first monograph on the work of Nicholas Roerich (a prominent artist and subsequently an even more prominent mystagogue of international stature), but this remained unpublished because of the revolutionary turmoil. After the revolution, Ivanov joined the staff of the Russian Museum and, additionally, conducted courses on Russian art for university students. Ivanov had connections to the members of the *Mir Iskusstva* (World of Art) movement and was well acquainted with Alexander Blok, an iconic figure of the Silver Age and one of the greatest Russian poets. Alexander's younger brother, Evgeny, was Blok's closest friend, and Blok was very fond of the Ivanovs (three brothers, two sisters, and their mother). "Because people like them exist, it is easier to live; they are a mainstay," wrote Blok. He called Alexander "charming" and "kind" and also "a truly exceptional person, like the entire Ivanov family."[7]

As a writer of fiction, Alexander Ivanov literally is *homo unius libri*, since "The Stereoscope" was the only work he published during his lifetime. It was met with accolades from the leading symbolists. Valery Bryusov printed a short but extremely positive review in *Vesy* (The Scales), the main symbolist magazine. Maximilian Voloshin wrote a long and glowing review of "The Stereoscope" for the opening issue of *Apollon* (Apollo), another major modernist magazine, although this article remained unpublished until recently. Last but not least, Alexander Blok spoke highly of the tale in his correspondence. (These reviews are included in the Appendix.)

Perhaps it was beginner's luck, but Ivanov's first and only tale turned out to be quite a spectacular work. It grips the reader's attention and remains highly suspenseful from the beginning to the finale, creating a haunting picture of the twilight realm. From the perspective of literary history, "The Stereoscope" is likewise quite noteworthy. It presents a full-blown symbolist paradigm and can serve as a compendium of symbolist motifs. It is also firmly rooted in the tradition of Russian classical literature. At the same time, it contains fascinating innovations of plot and theme.

"The Stereoscope" clearly belongs to the so-called Petersburg text of Russian literature. This notion, developed in the 1970s by the prominent Soviet philologist Vladimir Toporov, gained wide popularity in the late 1980s and 1990s. It has perhaps become overused, but this does not cancel its validity, especially for

---

7 See L. A. Il'iunina, "Ivanov, Aleksandr Pavlovich," in *Russkie pisateli 1800–1917. Biograficheskii slovar'*, vol. 2 (Moscow: Bol'shaia rossiiskaia entsiklopediia, 1992), 368–369; V. P. Kupchenko, "Eshche odin Aleksandr Ivanov," in *Litsa. Bibliograficheskii al'manakh* (Moscow-St. Petersburg: Feniks, 1993), 5–15.

the Silver Age, when the myth of St. Petersburg was solidified and canonized in symbolist circles.[8] Drawing on the late romantic legacy and on Dostoevsky, the symbolists repudiated the often disparaging attitude towards St. Petersburg that had, in the second half of the nineteenth century, replaced Alexander Pushkin's earlier declaration of love for the city. The negativity was caused by the emergence of "critical realism," which stressed social exposés and concentrated on the darker aspects of life. Ideological filters played a further role, since St. Petersburg could be seen as the realm of soulless officialdom, the embodiment of hierarchy and oppression, a "European" city decidedly foreign to the rest of Russia, etc. The symbolists reclaimed St. Petersburg as a worthy subject of art and a uniquely beautiful place. This is described, for example, in Alexandre Benois' manifesto "The Picturesque Petersburg," published in 1902 in the opening issue of the *Mir Iskusstva* (World of Art) magazine. Moreover, the mythic potential of the city resonated in a powerful way with the neo-mythological sensibilities of the symbolist era, resulting in numerous texts and artworks blending the aesthetics and metaphysics of St. Petersburg.

"The Stereoscope" neatly fits into this mold, portraying the city as both beautiful and eerie, made of solid stone yet ghostly, setting the scene for a drama that involves a threat of perdition and a promise of salvation. Especially prominent in "The Stereoscope" are eschatological and apocalyptic motifs that have accompanied the Petersburg myth since its inception; these were especially strong during the Silver Age, but Ivanov takes some of them to new heights. Nowhere else has St. Petersburg has been so consistently and overwhelmingly presented as the kingdom of the dead as in "The Stereoscope," where the protagonist finds himself in a ghost of the city, with countless phantoms of its inhabitants, with dead buildings, motionless ripples on the water, and a frozen wind. The verbal motif of death in the tale is unceasing: words with related roots are used dozens of times (*mertvyi* [dead] appears 46 times, *umeret'* [to die] 15 times, *prizrak* or *prizrachnyi* [phantom, ghostly] 69 times). A decade later, in the wake of the post-revolutionary devastation and with a burial site appearing at the city's center in the Field of Mars, Petropolis, as the dictum went, was indeed turning into Necropolis.[9] The most horrible fulfilment of such prophecies would come true with the siege of Leningrad during World War II.

8 For the most extensive collection of Toporov's writing on the topic see V. N. Toporov, *Peterburgskii tekst russkoi literatury. Izbrannye Trudy* (St. Petersburg: Iskusstvo, 2003).

9 See Bethea, David. *Khodasevich: His Life and Art.* (Princeton: Princeton University Press, 1983), 189–90.

The very first description of the city in the tale, still in the realm of reality and full of life and color, evokes an apocalyptic cityscape from Dostoevsky that is repeated in his works three times. The most oft-quoted instance is found in *A Raw Youth* (1875): "A hundred times over, in such a fog, I have been haunted by a strange but persistent fancy: What if this fog should part and float away, would not all this rotten and slimy town go with it, rise up with the fog, and vanish like smoke, and the old Finnish marsh be left as before, and in the midst of it, perhaps, to complete the picture, a bronze horseman on a panting, overdriven steed."[10] Even more relevant for "The Stereoscope" in seasonal terms is the passage from Dostoevsky's early tale "A Weak Heart" (1848), later repeated almost verbatim in his feuilleton "Petersburg Dreams in Verse and Prose" (1862):

> One wintry January evening I was hurrying home [. . .] When I reached the Neva, I paused for a moment and cast a piercing glance along the river into the smoky, frosty, murky distance that had suddenly turned crimson with the last purple of the sunset burning out on the misty horizon. [. . .] It was bitterly cold . . . frozen steam poured from tired horses and scurrying people. [. . .] Columns of smoke rose like giants from all the roofs on both embankments and rushed upward through the cold sky, twining and untwining along the way, making it seem as if new buildings were rising above old ones and a new city was forming in the air. [. . .] It seemed, finally, that this whole world with all its inhabitants, strong and weak, with all their dwellings, shelters of the poor or gilded mansions [of the rich], at that twilight hour resembled a fantastic, magical vision, a dream which in turn would vanish instantly and rise up like steam into the dark-blue sky.[11]

The action of "The Stereoscope" likewise begins in the winter with the emphasis on the smoke above St. Petersburg: "I was walking down G-ya Street on a frosty morning, the dawn all dressed in white. The sky was gray and the air, a pale blue. Numberless white clouds of winter smoke rose from the chimneys, and tried to stay upright, but the sharp eastern wind knocked them sideways and ripped

---

10 Dostoevsky, Fyodor. *A Raw Youth*, trans. Constance Garnett (London: William Heinemann, 1956), 132.

11 Dostoevsky, Fyodor. "Petersburg Visions in Prose and Verse," translated by Michael R. Katz. *New England Review* 24, no. 4 (Fall 2003), 101.

them to shreds, making the whole city fume ominously." Here we do not have explicit musings about the possibility of St. Petersburg's disappearance, but the narrator is about to acquire the magical device that will transport him to the ghost city.

The link to the tradition of the Petersburg text is also obvious in the episode immediately following this cityscape, when the narrator stumbles upon the stereoscope. The description of the auction warehouse recalls the cheap and chaotic art shop in Nikolai Gogol's "Portrait" (1834/42). In both tales, the magical object emerges from a heap of worthless and useless items. And while the discoveries might seem accidental, both protagonists are predisposed to meet what is coming their way. Chartkov had secretly dreamed of becoming a fashionable artist, and Ivanov's narrator, we learn, had long wanted to buy a stereoscope, a device he'd admired since he was a boy, thus plotting a mental return to his childhood. Even the locations where the two stories begin are situated quite close to each other, in the commercial belly of the city between the Apraksin Dvor and the Sennoy Market.

Despite such situational and topographical proximity, there are also essential differences. In Gogol, junk unequivocally belongs to the lowly manifestations of being; it is a conduit of demonic presence and the opposite of divine harmony. The warehouse in "The Stereoscope" is of a different nature. It has a pronounced hue of antiquarian nostalgia, as the narrator discerns "quiet rustles and whispers of the past" emanating from the outmoded and worn-out items exhibited. At the same time, there is also a motif of the existential dump, which becomes extremely prominent during the modernist period and whose ontological implications are most disturbing with the introduction of Gnostic overtones. If in the world that is fallen, or even forsaken by the benevolent God, there is always a hope for redemption, here the intentions and the very nature of the Creator can be legitimately called into question. To quote Ivanov's protagonist: "The whim of the unknown optician [...] seemed strange and absurd."

The Gogolian link is also evident later in the tale with the motif of the horrible gaze, which resonates with the horrible eyes from "The Portrait" and also brings to mind Gogol's Viy, whose gaze destroys the protection of the magic circle. The old woman staring at the narrator through the lenses of the stereoscope in the finale inspires such fear (specifically, fear that she can penetrate the border between the worlds) that the narrator hurries to smash the stereoscope. This old woman combines features of three famous witches of classical Russian literature: the witch from "Viy," the old countess from "The Queen of Spades," and the pawnbroker from *Crime and Punishment*. In "The Stereoscope," as in all of the above stories, the male protagonist assaults the "witch"—but these assaults are not all exactly the same. Whereas in Gogol the witch is the clear perpetrator, in Pushkin and Dostoevsky the aggressors are the young men. In Ivanov we have both scenarios. At first, the instigator is the protagonist, who disturbs the peace of the realms of the stereoscope, breaks a display case in the Egyptian Hall, steals the scarab, and also, albeit inadvertently, topples the old woman. But later, during the chase, he acts in self-defense, pushing her away. Additionally, in Ivanov there emerges a considerable ambiguity concerning the motivation of the "witch." The old woman acts as the guardian of her world, like the old countess who guards the secret of the three cards and the pawnbroker who guards her treasure chest. At the same time, as the narrator suggests quite unexpectedly, she might be motivated by *love*: not the vampirical love of Gogol's witch, but rather by the liking she took to the unknown child she saw in the museum (the narrator himself, as a boy) whom she wants to protect against an intrusion. Even with this interpretation, however, the overall scenario is ominous, as the boy remains forever caught in the old woman's somber world.

Another theme with a rich literary lineage is that of doppelgangers. It came to prominence during the romantic period, remained quite productive in post-romantic literature, and flourished at the turn of the twentieth century in Russia and Europe alike (famous European examples include Meyrink's novel *The Golem*, 1915, and the horror film *The Student of Prague*, 1913, with several subsequent remakes). In Ivanov, it occupies a central place, as the frozen photographic figures are said to be phantoms or doubles of people who once existed in reality. *Dvoinik* [double] is one of the most frequently used words in the tale, appearing 46 times. All of the people in the city, it seems, shed a double of themselves in April 1877, when the mysterious photographer took the picture that was later sealed into the stereoscope. Thus, in terms of the sheer size of the doppelganger population, "The Stereoscope" would easily qualify for the Guinness Book of Records: in 1877, about 800,000 people resided in St. Petersburg, and that does not account for visitors, horses and other animals, or the buildings and other structures and objects that likewise produced their own doubles.

Closely related to the doppelgangers are motifs of the puppet / dummy / mannequin / automaton. These already formed one semantic continuum during the romantic era. All were seen to invite the possibility of a diabolic presence through their sinister travesty of life, belonging, simultaneously, to the category of the undead. Puppets and automatons could be actual, as in Hoffmann, or more figurative, as in Gogol's "Portrait," which served as an obvious source for "The Stereoscope." Looking at commercial pseudo-art, the young artist Chartkov muses that it appears to be produced not by a human being, but a crudely made automaton. Almost immediately afterwards, falling under the spell of the portrait, he loses his will, buying the painting he did not want to buy and walking home with his purchase as if "mechanically" (*mashinal'no*). Eventually, he is transformed into an automaton, becoming a fashionable artist who, with a habituated hand, churns out prettified yet lifeless portraits of wealthy patrons. In Gogol, these motifs are numerous and consistent, from the early Dikanka tales to "The Overcoat," where representations of the protagonist, Akaky Akakievich, span from a copying automaton, a human Xerox machine of sorts, to an avenging cadaver roaming the streets of St. Petersburg.

In Ivanov, we encounter multiple designations for the old woman who comes to life and begins to chase the protagonist. She is called *fantosha*, an obsolete word derived from the French *fantoche* [puppet], or *avtomat* [automaton]; other times *kukloobraznyi dvoinik* [a doll-like double] or *strashnyi dvoinik* [a horrible double] of the person who is no longer alive. She is a walking cadaver of sorts, filled with *mertvennaia zloba* [deadly malice].

All this dovetails neatly with the symbolist imagination and finds fascinating parallels in the thoughts of Ivanov's brother Evgeny, a person of keen religious and mystical sensibility who, in addition to his friendship with Alexander Blok, was close to such prominent cultural figures of the day as Dmitry Merezhkovsky and Zinaida Gippius, Vasily Rozanov, and Andrei Bely. Evgeny Ivanov experienced acute existential fear of universal "automatization" in modern society that sucked away life from people leaving in their place empty shells. He described his conversation about this with Blok, who would touch upon similar motifs in his drama "The Puppet Show" (1906): "An invisible void (from Wells) is walking around the city in 'human dress' [. . .] A mannequin, a mask, an automaton. A dead man, a doll that pretends to be alive [. . .] I was talking about the void at the Bloks. Sasha (Al. Blok) is well aware of this. He even showed on a chair, bending to the side, how a void, sitting by the table, would suddenly lean sideways, dropping its hands."[12]

In his unfinished essay "The Mirror and the Automaton" (1906–1908), Evgeny Ivanov envisions a catastrophic onslaught of automatons, a zombie apocalypse of sorts (to use a term from later developments in the horror genre): "Automatons will crawl out of their dark corners and will crush and smash everyone [. . .] and the people will croak from the fear of [. . .] the coming automatons." He even prophesies that the Antichrist is the "ultimate great Automaton,"

---

12 E. P. Ivanov, "Vospominania i zapisi Evgeniia Ivanova ob Aleksandre Bloke," introduction by D. E. Maksimov, publication and commentary by E. P. Gomberg, D. E. Maksimov, A. M. Bikhter, in *Blokovskii sbornik*, ed. Iu. M. Lotman (Tartu State University, 1964), 392.

"the great Cadaver."[13] In Alexander Ivanov, there is no talk of the Antichrist, but a zombie assault is underway, as not only the old woman, but also some other doubles begin to stir after the protagonist disturbs their tranquility.

With all the importance of the mannequins coming to life in "The Stereoscope," it is a secondary horror plot, in the direct sense of the word, since this is something that occurs only on the second day of action, during the protagonist's second trip. It is also quite traditional, involving the archetypal situation when a human is attacked by monsters. The primary horror plot in Ivanov is much more unusual and is based not on action, but the lack thereof, as the prevailing feeling of existential angst is created by the eerie immobility of the world that froze at the moment the photograph was taken. This can be linked to such cherished symbolist notion as "moments" (*migi*), existential units marked by unusual lucidity and even epiphany. In the immobile universe of the stereoscope, lit by dim, brownish light, the valence of the "moment" is inverted. Instead of fulness of life, there is only sadness and deadness, a travesty of immortality—or its somber version: if not hell, then perpetual limbo.

Similar motifs are found in Blok, for example, in his poem "Cleopatra" (1907), where an effigy of the Egyptian queen, who is "neither dead nor living," is put on display at a waxworks cabinet in St. Petersburg. The Egyptian connection is in itself noteworthy, as important episodes in "The Stereoscope" take place in the Egyptian Hall of the Hermitage. The quintessential land of mystery with its cult of the dead, Egypt offered rich opportunities for the symbolist imagination.[14] Importantly, wax effigies belong to the same category as doubles, puppets, and automatons. In fact, Ivanov on several occasions compares the inhabitants of the stereoscopic realms to life-size wax figures. Since some of the exhibits in waxworks cabinets were equipped with mechanisms, as was the case with the wax Cleopatra described in Blok's poem, they could be set into motion. The stillness of wax effigies, combined with repeated mechanical movement, contribute to the sensations of limbo and of a vicious circle.

Circular motion, the Nietzschean "eternal return," is a crucial category for the symbolists and for modernism in general. It can be loaded with both positive and negative metaphysics, the latter coming to the forefront in Blok's "Cleopatra" and also in Ivanov. The trajectory of the movement in the tale is predominantly circular: in the Hermitage, the protagonist walks and runs

---

13 O. L. Fetisenko, "'Skrizhali kul'tury' Evgeniia Ivanova," *Khristianskoe chtenie*, no. 3 (2015), 240, 234.

14 For additional Egyptian references in the tale see S. Shargorodskii, Commentary to A. P. Ivanov, *Stereoskop. Sumerechnyi rasskaz* (Salamandra, P.V.V., 2013), 54–63.

in circles, both on the first floor, around his entry point in the Hall of Zeus, and on the second floor, around the stairwell. His sortie into the ghostly St. Petersburg also follows a circular path. Additionally, the tale is full of repetitions in terms of motifs, themes, situations that further enhance the circular trajectory. As was mentioned, the entire plot is rooted in the protagonist's desire to relive the magic of stereoscopes he experienced in childhood. The Abu-Simbel colossi, the subject on view in his first stereoscopic photo, will be reincarnated in the gigantic atlantes at the portico of the New Hermitage. The human figure on the enormous hand of a colossus (a sitting Arab) will echo the figure of Nike standing on the orb held by Zeus the Olympian. The gigantic head on a pedestal in the museum will find parallels in the engraving of a gigantic severed head in the book read by the protagonist as a boy. The very clutter of old artifacts in the auction warehouse presages the assembly of heterogeneous exhibits in the Hermitage. The old woman, the guardian of the twilight world, has a counterpart in the real world, the old Marya, the servant who watches over the apartment and checks on the protagonist. These correspondences are only partial, but this is very much in tune with the symbolist variations on the veil of Maya or, to use the famous line from Blok, "the icy ripples on the canal."

There is another important peculiarity to Ivanov's tale that can be explained through the symbolist worldview. In "The Stereoscope," we find a situation opposite of the proverbial "butterfly effect." In Ray Bradbury's "Sound of Thunder" (1952), a minuscule interference into the past during time travel (the accidental killing of a butterfly) produces an avalanche of consequences that drastically affects the course of history. In "The Stereoscope," the time traveler deliberately breaks a museum case and steals an exhibit, but there are no ramifications for the present. Moreover, the protagonist keeps his booty and brings the stolen scarab back to the real Hermitage in order to compare it with its double, which is safe and sound in its intact case. This is conclusive evidence, which completely excludes all Todorovian hesitation and proves that the narrator's journey was not a dream. The curious lack of consequences for the present is rooted in the symbolist concept of multiple realities that exist independently, although they may intersect and have substantial correspondences.[15] This version of a multiverse, with its potential infinity of dimensions, is quite different from the

15 On the symbolist concept of multiple realities, *mnogomirie,* and its comparison to the romantic binary picture of the world, see Z. G. Mints, "O nekotorykh 'neomifologicheskikh' tekstakh v tvorchestve russkikh simvolistov," in *Tvorchestvo A. A. Bloka i russkaia kul'tura XX veka. Blokovskii sbornik III. Uchenye zapiski Tartuskogo gosudarstvennoko universiteta* 459 (1979), 90–91.

hierarchical binary world of the romantics or the positivists' linear temporal plane with intertwining chains of cause and effect.

Related to this is also the prominence of Ivanov's literary models and the obvious intertextuality of his tale. Some of Ivanov's likely sources were named by his first reviewers and include Nikolai Gogol, E. T. A. Hoffmann, Ludwig Tieck, Ivan Turgenev's mystical tale "Klara Milich. After Death," Edgar Allan Poe, and H. G. Wells. Recent scholars further expanded this list by adding Dante's *Hell*, variations of the Sleeping Beauty fairytale (including Vasily Zhukovsky's poetic version and, potentially, the eponymous ballet by Tchaikovsky), and Guy de Maupassant's novella "The Night (A Nightmare)."[16] Reflecting on this matter, Innokenty Oksenov, in his otherwise somewhat naïve review of the 1918 edition, makes a well-founded conclusion: "The author of 'The Stereoscope' is undoubtedly very cultured" (in the sense that he was influenced by numerous works of literature).[17] Needless to say, intertextuality is an immensely broad phenomenon with multiple manifestations, from Bible cross-references to post-modernist hypertexts, but here we again encounter a peculiar symbolist phenomenon. The intertextual element in realistic literature tends to be quite weak, often non-existent, and understandably so, since the main point of reference is real life. At the turn of the twentieth century there is an explosion of intertextuality, the nature of which is aptly summarized by Zara Mints in her work on the neo-mythological aspects of symbolism: "The symbolist 'text-myth' is in particular 'literature about literature', a poetically conscious play with diverse traditions, a whimsical variation of their images and situations that eventually creates the image of the tradition itself. The constant delineation of the 'theme of culture' as one of the main themes can be seen as yet another manifestation of the symbolist panaestheticism."[18] Thus intertextual and (broadly speaking) cultural references make up an important layer of reality in the symbolist multiverse. In this respect, the fact that the narrator repeats on several occasions that he propped up the stereoscope by placing it on a heap of books can be seen as a self-referential note.

---

16 M. V. Biriukova, "Modernistskaia metafora 'gorod-grob' v kontekste simvoliki goroda-muzeia," *Voprosy muzeologii* 6, no. 2 (2012), 20; T. V. Tsiv'ian, "Kamen' v 'Stereoskope' Aleksandra Ivanova: Personazh ili anturazh?" in *Dialog s kamnem: ot prirody k kul'ture*, ed. M. V. Zav'ialova and T. V. Tsiv'ian (Moscow: MGU, 2016), 124; Olga Zolotareva, "The Image Responds: Photographic Aura in Aleksandr Ivanov's 'Stereoscope,'" *Journal of Modern Literature* 45, no. 3 (2022), 64–65.

17 Innokentii Oksenov, Review of A. Ivanov, "Stereoskop," *Kniga i revoliutsiia*, no. 7 (1921), 57.

18 Mints, "O nekotyryx neomifologichekikh tekstakh," 94.

There is one more conspicuous feature of "The Stereoscope" that was emphasized by its first reviewers. Bryusov, Blok, and Voloshin—all three quintessential symbolists—as if echoing one other, praise the irresistible logic and perfect realism of the tale. Does not this run against the general perception of symbolist art, which is both misty and mystical? A conspicuous example of the latter paradigm is found in another piece by Ivanov that was written in 1906, but published only in the 1990s,"The Hillfort" ("Gorodishche"). This story was inspired by the essay "On the Burial Mound" ("Na kurgane," 1898) by Nicholas Roerich, and by his Slavic-themed paintings that later would culminate in the famous set designs for Stravinsky's *Le Sacre du printemps*. The plot is similar to that of "The Stereoscope." The protagonist, a modern person on a hunting trip, stumbles upon an ancient hillfort lost in a forest that is uncannily familiar to him, as if seen in a recurrent dream from childhood. Visions from bygone years expand and envelop him:

> Forefathers appear on the nocturnal hill, separated from him by the incomprehensible distance of the Past, alien, superhuman, vague giants. He is scared by their murky presence. They look at him from the neighboring hills through the obscure distance of the Bygone, standing, sitting, bending, their speech coming from there as a mingling rustle of echoes in the naked walls of a deserted abode. Did he see them in his dreams as horrifyingly gigantic as they now emerged from his Memory? Or were they thus transformed by the great distance of the Past? Perhaps it made them frightening and monstrous, since a human being is not allowed to cross with impunity certain borders? He was scared, but joy overcame fear when he was thinking about the great miracle that transported him beyond these mysterious borders.[19]

As he relives the past and navigates the terrain known to him from his dreams, the hero discovers an ancient grave. Digging into it, he finds a skull that belonged to his ancestor Slovut, killed in an ancient battle, who might be his own former incarnation, or his double, or actually himself. What follows is a variation on *Hamlet*'s scene with Yorick's skull, but one in which Hamlet is peering at the skull of Hamlet:

---

19 Ivanov, A. P. "Gorodishche," introduction and publication by L. A. Il'iunina and E. R. Obatnina. In *Litsa. Bibliograficheskii al'manakh* (Moscow-St. Petersburg: Feniks, 1993), 24.

> With one hand he was touching the bulges and ridges of the skull, with the other he palpated under the hair and skin the bones of his own head and, to his amazement, he realized that these two skulls were like twins, identical in all their cavities, two doubles, a dead one and a living one! He then lifted the skull and held it against his face, looking, as if enchanted, into its empty eye sockets, as he sometimes would look at his face in the mirror and a strange horror would arise, but he couldn't tear himself away! These were the bones of the ancient Slovut, these were the remains of a forefather who died here. My God! It was the skull of his own Past self, his ancient skull of yore![20]

Similarly, in "The Stereoscope," the protagonist miraculously crosses the border between temporal planes and encounters his own double. The vocabulary in the two stories is almost identical, and yet their modalities are markedly different. "The Hillfort" is impressionistic, oneiric, and highly emotional. "The Stereoscope" is also replete with strong emotions: fear (*strakh* is used 18 times, *strashnyi* 33 times, *uzhas* 16, and *zhutkii* or *zhutkost'* 17), sadness (*grust'*, *grustnyi*, or *grustit'* appear 19 times), and joy (*radost'* or *radostno* appear 12 times). However, the overall feeling is much more "lapidary," in the literal sense of the word, because of the prominence of stone in the settings and the sense of universal petrification, and also "dimmer," like the sepia light in the stereoscopic world. Perhaps because of this Blok spoke of a scientific kind of art in "The Stereoscope," and Bryusov saw in it "the same method that allows mathematicians to determine the elements and properties of figures and bodies in various non-Euclidean planes."

With all that, "The Stereoscope" is a quintessential symbolist text, no less so than "The Hillfort." One should bear in mind that "realism" was the term readily appropriated in symbolist circles to describe their art and also their religious philosophy.[21] This includes the assertion that the reality discovered by them is of a higher nature, and is also a corollary of objective idealism, which posits the independent existence of spiritual phenomena. Despite its anti-positivist thrust, symbolism inherited the respect for the scientific paradigm characteristic of the age. This can be seen even in the occult practices: the most widespread of these was spiritism, which is arguably in tune with quasi-scientific approaches in that

---

20 Ibid., 38.

21 Gennadii Obatnin, *Ivanov-mistik. Okkul'tnye motivy v poezii i proze Viacheslava Ivanova (1907–1919)* (Moscow: Novoe literaturnoe obozrenie, 2000), 45–74.

the séance is an experiment of sorts that can be documented and repeated. A tension between the mystical and the scientific was felt by some symbolists, including Bryusov, who was perhaps a skeptic at heart but nonetheless diligently indulged in black magic. Here is what he writes in the preface to *The Fiery Angel*, posing as a mere publisher of an old manuscript:

> Concerning the author's belief in everything supernatural, he was in this respect just keeping up with his time. However strange it may seem, the accelerated development of magical teachings began exactly during the epoch of the Renaissance and lasted through the entire 16th and 17th centuries. The vague sorcery and fortunetelling of the Middle Ages in the 16th century were reworked into neat scientific disciplines, of which the scholars counted twenty [. . .] The spirit of the time that sought to rationalize everything could turn even magic into a defined rational doctrine, endowing fortunetelling with sense and logic, finding a scientific explanation for flights to black sabbath, etc. Believing in the reality of magical phenomena, the author of the Tale only followed the best minds of his age.[22]

"Believing in reality of the magical phenomena" is a formulation that could be easily applied not only to the sixteenth and seventeenth centuries, but also to Bryusov's own epoch. Despite the obvious irony, this was yet another manifestation of the cyclical model of time that was among the persistent fixations of symbolism.

Thus "The Stereoscope" clearly utilizes the existing mold of symbolist literature and also, as part of this paradigm, plays with the previous literary tradition. With all that, some of its aspects are quite innovative. In terms of theme, it is one of the earliest examples of museum fiction, a sub-genre that became productive during the high modernist period and also migrated into film, including the museum episode of the cult Soviet cartoon *Well, Just You Wait* (Episode 12, 1978), the *Night at the Museum* franchise (2006–present), and the arthouse treatment of the topic in a historiosophic and mystical vein given by Alexander Sokurov's *The Russian Ark* (2002).[23] "The Stereoscope" is the first work of fic-

---

22 Briusov, V. Ia. *Ognennyi angel* (Moscow: Skorpion, 1909), vii.

23 See Dan Ungurianu, "Khranilishche. Zametki o topose muzeia v russkoi literature 1920–30-kh gg," in *Russian Literature and the West: A Tribute for David M. Bethea*, ed. Alexander Dolinin, Lazar Fleishman, and Leonid Livak, vol. 2 (Stanford Slavic Studies, vols. 35–36; Stanford: Dept. of Slavic Languages and Literatures, Stanford University, 2008), 186–211.

tion set in the Hermitage and the first work that brings into focus the splendid gigantic atlantes at the portico of the museum, which have become a recognizable symbol of St. Petersburg. Additionally, "The Stereoscope" appears to be one of the first works of literature centered around a photograph and, arguably, anticipates important developments in modern theory of photography.[24]

Some elements of the plot in Ivanov's tale are also unusual. The overall situation has many antecedents and can be described as travel to a different realm or some kind of enchanted space. This is an archetypal plot found in numerous cultures, from katabasis in Greek mythology to various Russian legends.[25] Especially pertinent is that of the city of Kitezh, since it was popularized during the Silver Age and figures prominently in the final novel of Dmitry Merezhkovsky's trilogy (*Peter and Alexis. The Antichrist,* 1905) and in Nikolai Rimsky-Korsakov's last opera (*The Legend of the Invisible City of Kitezh,* 1907). Also relevant are literary works about time travel, including H. G. Wells's *Time Machine* (1895) and Mark Twain's *Connecticut Yankee in King Arthur's Court* (1889). The latter is particularly noteworthy, since it involves accidental travel to the past, just like in "The Stereoscope," something that has nowadays become an extremely productive genre in science fiction and fantasy. One can also recall Prince Vladimir Odoevsky's story "Town in a Snuffbox" (1834), in which a boy falls asleep and, in his dream, enters a music box, a magical device in a compact container (much like the stereoscope), and meets its miniature inhabitants, which make the mechanism work.

However, in all of the above examples, even (to a degree) dark Hades, the visitors find themselves in a world full of life and movement—but the protagonist of "The Stereoscope" travels to a totally frozen, immobile realm. In this respect, the closest analogy is found in some fairy tales. One of them is mentioned by the narrator, who says that the enormous dead Peterburg reminded him of the Arabic tale of the City of Brass (which creates yet another "correspondence": a link to the Arab in the first stereoscopic photograph seen by the narrator in childhood). In this story from *One Thousand and One Nights,* travelers enter a city full of wares and treasures . . . yet completely lifeless, since all of its inhabitants starved to death. The tale also features the motif of punishment for stealing

---

24 See Zolotareva, "The Image Responds"; O. M. Annanurova, "'Neiz'iasnimoe chuvstvo': Opyt vospriitia stereoskopicheskoi fotografii v rasskaze A. Ivanova 'Stereoskop,'" *Novoe literaturnoe obozrenie* 149, no. 1 (2018), 414–427; Katherine M. H. Reischl, *Photographic Literacy: Cameras in the Hands of Russian Authors* (Cornell University Press, 2018), 55.

25 N. A. Krinichnaia, *Russkaia mifologiia. Chelovek na pereput'e mirov. Bylichki, byval'shchiny, legendy, pover'ia o poiskakh i posescheniiakh zapovednykh mest i mirov* (Moscow: Akademicheskii proekt, 2023), 8–12, 106–107.

from the dead, and of some cadavers seeming to come to life. *The Sleeping Beauty* may provide an even closer analog. The tale was known in Russia in both the Charles Perrault and Grimm Brothers versions, and was also rendered in verse by Vasily Zhukovsky as "The Sleeping Princess" (1831). Although illustrations of the fairytale tend to emphasize slumbering, the texts of all of the three versions contain descriptions of the world that came abruptly to a standstill, with people frozen in mid-action as in "The Stereoscope."[26] Even the fire and smoke in the palace kitchen are in suspended animation, just like water and wind in the stereoscopic St. Petersburg:

> The cook is asleep in front of the fire,
> And the fire, engulfed in sleep,
> Doesn't blaze nor burn,
> But stands still with a sleepy flame.
> And above it doesn't move
> The sleepy smoke, curled up in a puff.
> And all the vicinity and the palace
> Are engulfed in dead sleep
> [...]
> In the courtyard he encounters
> A multitude of people, and everyone sleeps.
> One stands as if riveted,
> Another walks without moving,
> Another stands with his mouth open,
> And on his lips keeps silence
> An unfinished conversation.
> Another, feeling sleepy, was going to lie down,
> But he didn't succeed,
> As the magic sleep got hold of him
> Prior to the ordinary sleep,
> And, immobile for three centuries,
> He is neither standing nor lying,
> But, ready to fall down, sleeps.[27]

---

26 This is the case, for example, with Gustave Doré. Although some of his characters are stopped in mid-action, the vast majority of them are lying, squatting, crouching or leaning on something in their sleep. A later illustration by Valery Kurdiumov in the 1915 Sytin edition of Zhukovsky focuses on figures who froze while moving.

27 V. A. Zhukovskii, *Spiashchaia tsarevna* (Lenigrad: Detizdat, 1939), 12–13.

Later cinematic takes on this motif can be found in *Paris qui dort* (dir. by René Claire, 1924), this one with a sci-fi premise, and in the properly fairytale mode, in *The Tale of Tsar Saltan* (dir. by Alexander Ptushko, 1966), which includes an episode, absent from Pushkin's original, with a city frozen in mid-motion.

Other antecedents for "freezing" can be found in *tableaux vivants,* static compositions made up of live human beings. This synthetic form of art, involving aspects of painting, sculpture, and theater, flourished throughout the nineteenth and early twentieth centuries in various settings, from royal courts to fairground booths. Its relationship to painting proper could be twofold.[28] In some instances, *tableaux vivants* were inspired by paintings, as for example was the case with Karl Bryullov's monumental apocalyptic painting "The Last Day of Pompeii" (1833), which produced a deep impact on contemporaries. *Tableaux* based on Bryullov's masterpiece appeared as part of carnival entertainment in Russian cities from the mid-1830s into the 1860s. But a *tableau* could also precede a painting, as was sometimes the case with the famous historical painter Konstantin Makovsky. An aficionado of Russian traditions, he arranged in his studio a number of *tableaux* from the life of the upper classes from the Muscovite period, using as props genuine antiques and involving modern-day aristocrats, descendants of the boyars of yore. One of these *tableaux* was photographed and became the basis for his famous painting "A Boyar Wedding Feast" (1883). Lately, this art form has experienced a curious renaissance. It can be observed in the performances of street artists (also being a variety of sculpture coming to life), it is a frequently used device in modern ballet and opera performances, and it is practiced by visitors to museums who take photos of themselves impersonating the very artworks that supply backdrops for their tableaux.

By the 1820s and 1830s, the influence of *tableaux vivants* could be felt on literature. For instance, historical novels were often compared to a series of living pictures from a certain epoch. The above-mentioned "The Last Day of Pompeii" by Bryullov was also reflected in literature. Ivan Lazhechnikov, in his *Ice Palace* (*Ledianoi dom,* 1835), one of the most popular Russian historical novels, evokes the painting twice, including the following episode where numerous people in the noisy marketplace are struck by fear:

---

28 N. N. Mut'ia, "Teatral'nost' russkoi salono-akademicheskoi zhivopisi vtoroi poloviny XIX veka," in *Nauchnye Trudy. Rossiiskaia akademiia khudozhestv. Institut im. I. E. Repina* 28 (January—March 2014), 58–67.

> All of a sudden the call of a sentry rings out. It sounds like the voice of a herald bringing tidings of the end of the world. Thereafter all falls silent, all movement ceases, and the pulse stops beating as if life has been extinguished in one fell stamp of an angry god's heel. Scales, measuring sticks, legs, arms, mouths all freeze in the same position in which they have been caught by that call.[29]

The most famous instance of a *tableau vivant* in Russian literature is found in Gogol, himself a student of painting and an author with an exceptionally strong visual component in his artistic imagination.[30] An admirer of "The Last Day of Pompeii," he fashioned the finale of his play *Inspector General* (1835) after Bryullov's masterpiece—this is the famous "mute scene" in which numerous characters freeze in poses meticulously described by the author. The concluding stage direction reads: "The petrified group maintains such a position for almost a minute and a half. The curtain falls." Another spectacular *tableau vivant* is found in Tchaikovsky's ballet *The Sleeping Beauty* (libretto by Ivan Vsevolozhsky and Marius Petipa) that premiered at St. Peterburg's Mariinsky Theatre in 1890 and became one of the most successful classical ballets. As the Lilac Fairy casts a spell on Princess Aurora and her parents' kingdom, numerous characters on stage freeze and later come back to life when the spell is reversed.

However relevant these examples may be, in one important respect Ivanov's plot is different, namely, the realm entered by his protagonist is a photograph, that is, a kind of picture. There are numerous examples of pictures or statues that come to life, starting with the myth of Pygmalion. In the Russian tradition, textbook cases involve Pushkin's "Stone Guest" and "Bronze Horseman," Gogol's "Portrait," and Lermontov's "Shtoss."[31] But this situation applies only to the secondary plot of "The Stereoscope," when some doubles come to life and start moving. The primary plot has a different trajectory, as it involves a living person drawn into a picture. There are partial antecedents in romantic tales based on the notion of the model and the portrait as connected vessels of sorts, with a danger of artistic transference, the draining of the living person

---

29 I. I. Lazhechnikov, "Ledianoi dom," in his *Sochineniia v dvukh tomakh*, vol. 2 (Moscow: Khudozhestvennaia literature, 1986), 84.

30 See Nikolai Firtich, "The Inclusive Vision: Gogol, the Avant-Garde, and the Russian Cubo-Futurist Strategies of Depiction," *Short Story Criticism* 287 (2020), 242–44.

31 See Roman Jakobson's pioneering work "The Statue in Pushkin's Poetic Mythology," in his *On Verse, its Masters and Explorers* (Selected Writings, vol. 5; Mouton: The Hague, 1979), 237–280.

into his own image. This motif is present already in Gogol (the story of how the portrait was painted), in Konstantin Aksakov's "Walter Eisenberg" (1836), and Edgar Allan Poe's "Oval Portrait" (1842). Oscar Wilde's *Picture of Dorian Gray* (1890) ultimately rests on the same premise. However, this is different from entering the picture. A closer parallel is found in Lewis Carroll's *Through the Looking-Glass* (1871), but while the general situation of a magical conduit into another dimension is similar, a mirror is not a picture.

The motif of entering a picture will gain currency later in the twentieth century. It is prominent in the work of Vladimir Nabokov, who employs it on three occasions: in his early short story "La Veneziana" (1924, published in 1995), in the novel *Glory* (1932), and also in his autobiography. It is central to "The Man Who Was Milligan" (1914), one of Algernon Blackwood's tales of the uncanny. C. S. Lewis makes a painting a gateway to Narnia in *The Voyage of the Dawn Treader* (1952). Variations of this motif may also involve cinema. In the Soviet animated film "Petya and the Little Red Riding Hood" (1958, script by Vladimir Suteev), a boy sneaking into the movie theater accidentally enters the screen and joins the action of the projected feature. The motif also appears in films about artists: the Soviet Georgian *Pirosmani* (1968, dir. by Giorgi Shengelaia) and the Swedish *Adventures of Picasso* (1978, dir. by Tage Danielsson).

There are some important antecedents to this motif. In European literature, it is found in Hans Christian Andersen's "Ole Lukøje" (1841), where the title character first makes a painting come to life and then puts a boy inside it. In all likelihood, a translation of Andersen's fairy tale into English was the source of the motif in both *Glory* and *Speak, Memory!*[32] Much older antecedents exist in China, and while they were not known in Europe for hundreds of years, the story of the great Wu Daozi, the eighth-century painter who entered a mural of his own creation, was mentioned by Herbert Allen Giles in his *Introduction to the History of Chinese Pictorial Art* (1905). Interestingly, this legend drew the attention of two prominent Western theoreticians: Walter Benjamin in his "Work of Art in the Age of Its Technological Reproducibility" (1935) and Siegfried Kracauer in his *Theory of Film* (1960). Additional instances are found in Pu Songling's *Strange Tales*, a collection from the turn of the eighteenth century. In one novella, a traveler enters a mural in a monastery and marries a fairy depicted there. In another vignette, a Daoist monk can hide in his own picture (here an artist becomes a magician, as in Russian lore about Stenka Razin, who escaped prison on a boat he drew on the wall of his cell). English translations of the

---

32 Aleksandr Dolinin and Grigorii Utgoff, Commentary to *Podvig*, in Vladimir Nabokov, *Sobranie sochinenii russkogo perioda v 5-ti tomakh* (St. Petersburg: Simpozium, 2004), 718.

collection appeared in 1880 and 1915 (Russian in 1922–23). Hence, perhaps, the Chinese print and the collection of Chinese stories by Lafcadio Hearn that figure prominently in Algernon Blackwood's "Milligan."

One can also cite various developments in visual arts or crossbreeds between visual arts and fairground booth attractions involving *tromp l'oeils* that blur the border between the picture and the spectator. In Charles-André van Loo's "Cupid Shooting the Bow" (1761), displayed in the Pavlovsk Palace, the god of desire seems to be aiming his arrow at the onlookers regardless of their viewpoint. Something similar happens in two large paintings in the Russian Museum. Vasily Polenov's "Christ and the Woman Taken in Adultery" (1888) portrays a donkey who "follows" the spectators, much to the amusement of younger visitors who do not care about the adult subject matter. When one moves along Vasily Surikov's "Stepan Razin" (1906), it seems that the boat carrying the Cossack chieftain turns, heading for the expanse of the Volga. Dioramas and panoramas that combined two-dimensional and three-dimensional representations flourished into the mid-twentieth century. And some contemporary multimedia exhibitions, often with augmented reality components, seek to transport the viewer inside of masterpieces of painting, which is in a way an extension of the older stereoscopic photography and the subsequent 3D film.

Whatever the trajectory of the motif of entering a picture, Ivanov can be credited for employing it both fully and early, perhaps even first, in Russian and European literature of the twentieth century, which is no small achievement. Most important for this collection, Ivanov created an atmospheric mystical masterpiece, which, to quote Voloshin's review, "is certainly a new and excellent page in the realm of Petersburgian fantastical literature, beginning with 'The Queen of Spades' and *The Bronze Horseman.*"

***

Unlike Alexander Ivanov, Alexander Alexeyevich Izmailov (1873–1921), was a professional man of letters. He wrote prose, poetry (including some very apt parodies), and drama, but above all is remembered as one of the most prolific and influential literary critics of the day. Izmailov was not a symbolist, his own work being closer to the late offshoots of the realistic tradition. But his tale "The Antiquarian" (1903) fits well into the Silver Age mold, not least for its mystical overtones. He published several tales of the uncanny and a collection entitled *Mystical Tales* (1912), some of them with a humorous touch (for example, exposés of spiritism), yet others quite serious in tone. "The Antiquarian" belongs to the latter category and tells the story of mysterious letters from a supposedly omniscient anonymous mentor who seeks to provide moral guidance for modern-day intellectuals.

The tale is full of literary allusions. As in "The Stereoscope," the references to Gogol's "Portrait" are quite obvious, and they serve as a starting point for the main action. From the medley of one of St. Petersburg's markets emerges something extraordinary: rare mystical books and the enigmatic antiquarian. After the book seller disappears, his store space is occupied by a dealer in frames and cheap pictures (cf. the shabby art shop at the beginning of "The Portrait"). The suspiciously agile lame boy who spies on the narrator is a literary relative of the nimble blind boy from Mikhail Lermontov's "Taman." The antiquarian claims that in guiding the narrator he is only fulfilling someone else's will. This resonates with the words of the countess's ghost in "The Queen of Spades," who says that she came to Hermann not of her own will. The confusion with signs in the finale is somewhat reminiscent of Lermontov's ghost story "Shtoss," while the general motif of signboards is quite prominent in Gogol.

Overall, the antiquarian in Izmailov's tale does not at all resemble his historical namesake Alexander Labzin, a grandee and a major public intellectual. Ascetic, dry, and moralistic, he rather reminds one of the most famous freemason of classical Russian literature, Osip Bazdeev, Pierre Bezukhov's teacher in Leo Tolstoy's *War and Peace*. There are countless references to old mystical books, which is appropriate given the antiquarian aspect of the story and creates an aura of historical stylization. Quite in tune with the sensibility of the age is also the repetition of a cycle, a metempsychosis of sorts, as the literati of early twentieth-century St. Petersburg are haunted by inexplicable echoes from the golden age of freemasonry in Russia, a hundred years gone.

***

Sergei Abramovich Auslender (1886–1937) was introduced into St. Petersburg's artistic and intellectual elite as a young man by his uncle and mentor Mikhail Kuzmin, a prominent figure of the Russian Silver Age. He collaborated in major modernist magazines and was an active participant in literary and theatrical life. Auslender did not accept the Bolshevik revolution and supported the Whites, becoming a press secretary for the "Supreme Ruler of Russia" Admiral Kolchak. After the civil war, Auslender settled in Moscow, renewing his involvement with theater and writing books for children about the revolutionary and liberation movements. During the Great Terror, he was arrested and executed.

"The Night Prince" appeared in 1909 in the opening issue of *Apollon,* a leading modernist literary and artistic magazine, with illustrations by Mstislav Dobuzhinsky, an important member of the World of Art circle. In 1912, the tale was included in his second collection of stories, in the section entitled

"Petersburgian Apocrypha." St. Petersburg figures prominently in the work of Auslender, who repeatedly confesses love for Russia's Northern Capital: "This city inebriates me. [. . .] It teaches one to be light, trim, elusive, always prepared for the most fantastic adventure or heroic deed, and at the same time independent, reserved, not revealing one's mysteries to anyone. That is what this magical, cold, and free Petersburg teaches."[33] Nikolai Gumilev, a prominent poet and the founder of Acmeism, praises his friend Auslender as the quintessential Petersburgian writer both in theme and style:

> Sergei Auslender is a writer-architect; in combining words he values not coloristic effects, nor the musical rhythm or lyrical excitement, but rather the purity of lines and harmonic equilibrium of parts subordinated to one idea. His teachers were Rastrelli, Quarenghi, and other creators of the wondrous palaces and temples of his much beloved Petersburg. More than any other Russian writer, Sergei Auslender is a Petersburgian. He feels the city as it was when it was only piles and beams, just-born of Peter's will; when it was movingly naïve in the 1820s; now, when it is taut and splendid. His heroes are also Petersburgians [. . .] and, needless to say, only in Petersburg can they go through such unexpected and enigmatic adventures.[34]

"The Night Prince," which is among Auslender's best pieces, relates one such adventure. Its young protagonist Misha Trubnikov is crowned as a prince for the night by some kind of secret society, and then undergoes sexual initiation.

It is assumed by most commentators that the action of the tale takes place in the 1820s or 1830s, during Pushkin's era. The text does not mention specific dates, but there are a number of clues. An important location in the tale is the bridge with sculptures on the Catherine Canal, close to Nevsky Prospect. This has to be the Bank Bridge with its figures of winged lions (also known as gryphons), which was constructed in 1826. The protagonist and his friend attend a ballet featuring Avdotya Istomina, the legendary dancer described by Pushkin in the celebrated passage from the first chapter of *Eugene Onegin*, who retired in 1836. The Pushkinian connection is further enhanced by the fact that Misha,

---

33 Sergei Auslender, *Peterburgskie apokrify. Roman povesti i rasskazy* (St. Petersburg: Mir, 2005), 91.

34 N. S. Gumilev, *Polnoe sobranie sochinenii v desiati tomakh*, vol. 7. *Stat'i o literature i iskusstve, obzory, retsenzii* (Moscow: Voskresen'e, 2006), 144.

coming to the city for the Christmas holidays, is a "lyceum" student: the only institution under this name was the Imperial Lyceum in Tsarskoe Selo, Pushkin's alma mater, from which he graduated in 1817 as a member of the inaugural class.

There are, however, some details that point to an earlier historical period. In addition to Istomina, there seem to be only two more "documented" historical characters in the tale: the popular Gypsy singer Stepanida performing the latest romance, "Sure Signs," and the masterful Gypsy dancer, who remains anonymous. The description of these characters and the romance are taken virtually verbatim from the diaries of Sergei Zhikharev (they are also quoted in the readily available *Old Petersburg* by Mikhail Pyliaev). Both of these episodes belong to the year 1805, which is part of a very different epoch. A conspicuous and intentional mixture of epochs is found in Nadenka's outfit in the end, which combines fashions from the *ancien régime,* the 1790s, and the Empire style.

A similar extension of chronology is also found in the overall artistic framework of the tale. Like many of Auslender's early works, "The Night Prince" pays tribute to the trend of literary stylization, found in Merezhkovsky, Bryusov, Kuzmin, and Boris Sadovskoy. While the general atmosphere of the tale is that of the 1820s and 1830s, there are incursions of the eighteenth century: through the archaic ring of the epigraph and the style of the letter in the beginning and, most prominently, through the presence of narrative chapter subtitles that are modeled after eighteenth-century adventure novels.[35] Additionally, the eighteenth century "intrudes" in the episode involving the plate depicting Madame de Pompadour. A dual set of chronological indices is very much in tune with the retrospectivist current in the World of Art circle; its two favorite epochs were the eighteenth century and the first decades of the nineteenth. This also finds parallels in two of Pushkin's major prose works. In "The Queen of Spades," the action takes place in the present (that is, the 1830s), but there are constant intersections with the eighteenth century: flashbacks to the time when the countess shone as the Venus of Moscow at the royal court in France, her mansion built in the architectural style of a bygone era, her adherence to the fashion of the 1770s, Hermann's thoughts about her lucky lovers of yore. In *The Captain's Daughter* there is actually a triple chronology: the main action takes place in the 1770s, but Grinev writes his memoirs much later, during the reign of Alexander I, and the "editor" publishes them even later, in 1836.

---

35 For this and also for quotations from Pushkin in Auslender's tale see N. D. Tamarchenko, "Skrytaia tsitata kak otsylka k zhanrovoi traditsii," *Reosiayeongu* [Russian Studies, South Korea] 19, no. 2 (2009): 46–55. Tamarchenko suggests that, although the chapter subtitles are an eighteenth-century element, the "The Night Prince" with its six main chapters and an epilogue is structurally modeled after "The Queen of Spades."

As one might expect, allusions to Pushkin in "The Night Prince" are prominent and numerous. The flight of Istomina at the ballet performance and the coachman's shout "Make way! Make way!" are almost direct quotations from the first chapter of *Onegin*. There, they are likewise related to the adventures of a young aristocrat in St. Petersburg, with all the difference between the main characters: the confident dandy Eugene and the awkward teenager Misha in his school uniform. No less prominent are the ties to "The Queen of Spades." Like Hermann, Misha confronts a pictorial representation of a young beauty (actually two of them), and he likewise verbally threatens the "witch." Like Hermann, who steps back in fear and falls when the dead countess winks at him at the funeral, Misha makes a clumsy step and falls down on the staircase of the theater under the smile of the mysterious lady. Roaming the streets of the wintry city, each protagonist has a mystical encounter that decides his fate. For Misha, it occurs in the middle of a snowstorm, just as it does for Petrusha Grinev from *The Captain's Daughter*.

There is also a layer of German allusions, most prominently to Goethe (the carousing and singing students at The Pink Swan are reminiscent of the students at Auerbachs Keller in *Faust*) and E. T. A. Hoffmann, the quintessential German writer of the fantastic (in the late nineteenth and early twentieth centuries in Russia the fantastic genre was often called *hoffmanniana*).[36] Auslender employs a number of common romantic motifs that were revitalized during the symbolist era. In addition to the nocturnal chronotope, this includes doubles and mirrors, sliding through the unstable borders between realities, pictures coming to life (Marquise de Pompadour, the bather) and living people turning into a picture (a *tableau vivant* at the end of the ballet and two shadows merged in a kiss in the window of a carriage, a graphic vignette in the spirit of *Mir Iskusstva*).

The overarching motif of the tale is markedly symbolist, most famously associated with Alexander Blok, and involves pursuit of the Beautiful Lady, the mysterious Stranger, an epitome of eternal femininity and a reflection of Divine Wisdom. There is a series of her incarnations in the tale, real and imagined, fleeting or significant, lofty and vulgar, but all of them attractive and tempting in their own way. They include: a) the depiction of Marquise de Pompadour on a plate; b) Misha's cousin and his first love Nadenka; c) the painting of a bathing girl in the study of Misha's uncle (in addition to the motif of a revived picture, we also have here the symbolist motif of multiple and deceptive veils); d) the

36 A. M. Gracheva, Introduction and commentary to Sergei Auslender, *Peterburgskie apokrify. Roman povesti i rasskazy* (St. Petersburg: Mir, 2005), 22.

legendary prima Istomina (and her seductive character in the ballet); e) the young lady in the theater who dropped her playbill; f) the chubby cupid played by a student ballerina and the love interest of Misha's friend; g) the mysterious lady in the theater who becomes the prize of the Night Prince; h) Shakespeare's Jessica from *The Merchant of Venice* mentioned by Zillerich; i) the Gypsy singer Stepanida; j) the hostess of the night ball; k) the Moorish girl in an immodest red dress, the servant of the mysterious lady; l) Misha's numerous mistresses in the epilogue.

Far from the high mystical meaning of the quest for the Beautiful Lady in the early works by Blok, the outcome of Misha's adventure is rather trite, as he becomes a rake seducing high-society ladies. But one should keep in mind that the symbolist paradigm includes the possibility of the fall, both for the Lady and her Knight. Besides, Misha does not in the end stoop so very low, not even as low as his friend Pakhotin, whose name is likely to be derived from *pokhot'* [lust] and who bewilders the inexperienced boy with lewd stories. Rather, Misha "graduates" to being somebody like Onegin of the first chapter, who is not yet bored with the "science of the tender passion."

Last but not least, one should note the fascinating similarities between "The Night Prince" and Mikhail Bulgakov's masterpiece *The Master and Margarita* (1928–1940). They begin with Misha's conversation with a mysterious stranger on the bridge; recall Bulgakov's opening chapter, "Never Talk to Strangers." Like Bulgakov's Woland, Zillerich inexplicably knows everything about his interlocutor, including his thoughts. In "The Night Prince" there is no single lord of darkness, as the secret society is represented by two competing leaders, Zillerich and the baron. In a way, they combine the roles that in Bulgakov are distributed between Woland and the mischievous members of his retinue. Both works culminate with a grand ball for which the main characters are crowned. In the aftermath of these balls, the characters are re/united with their loves. Incidentally, in both works the color associated with love is yellow: in Auslender, this includes the yellow dress of Marquise de Pompadour, Istomina's yellow veil, and the yellow rose that leads Misha to the mysterious lady; in Bulgakov, the bouquet of yellow flowers Margarita holds during her first encounter with the Master. The commentary accompanying the recent edition of Auslender's prose cautiously terms such parallels "typological."[37] But given Auslender's status (not a writer of first importance, he was nonetheless a notable figure of the Silver Age), the venue of his tale's first publication, and

---

37 Ibid., 23.

the fact that in the 1920s he and Bulgakov knew each other personally and belonged to the same literary circle in Moscow, it is reasonable to suggest that "The Night Prince" could have been among the sources for *The Master and Margarita.*

***

Count Alexey Nikolayevich Tolstoy (1882–1945) is by far the most famous and successful writer of all our authors. He began his literary career in the 1900s and by 1917 was a notable man of letters. Opposed to the Bolshevik revolution, he emigrated to Europe but returned to Russia in the 1920s to a warm welcome. After Maxim Gorky's death in 1936, Tolstoy, jokingly nicknamed "the Red Count," became one of the patriarchs of Soviet literature and was showered with all sorts of official honors. His output is prolific and includes a compelling epic of the revolution and the civil War (*The Road to Calvary*, 1922–1941); one of the best Russian historical novels (*Peter I*, 1934–1945); first rate science fiction novels (*Aelita*, 1923, *The Hyperboloid of Engineer Garin*, 1927); a deep remake of *Pinocchio* (*The Golden Key, or The Adventures of Buratino*, 1936), which acquired a cult status and became part of Russian popular culture; many plays; and numerous tales and short stories in a variety of genres.

"The Satyr" (1912), with its pervasive eroticism and amorous adventures, is an excellent counterpart to "The Night Prince." The protagonist, a promiscuous young woman called Lyubochka (from Lyubov/Love), can be seen as a lowered incarnation of the Beautiful Lady. When the story begins, the city is enveloped by fog—an oft-recurring meteorological condition in the Petersburg text of Russian literature. There is indeed a definite connection to the classical tradition, mainly to Gogol. The fog and the romantic pursuit through the streets of St. Petersburg find parallels in "Nevsky Prospect" (1835). There are also echoes from "The Nose" (1836), as an unusual creature becomes the talk of the town, and "The Overcoat" (1842), in the mention of a man bumping into a horse's muzzle in the middle of the street. The ending of Tolstoy's story, in which the satyr flees, scared by the insatiable ambitions of his bride, can be seen as a take on the finale of Gogol's play *The Marriage* (1842), in which the bridegroom escapes through the window. As he leaves, the satyr repeats almost verbatim the words of another Gogol fugitive, Khlestakov from *The Inspector General:* "I'll be back right away, right away."

In 1913, Tolstoy published a reworked version of the story. Entitled "The Faun," this version implied that the amorous adventure was just the heroine's dream. Tolstoy also retouches his literary allusions, arguably taking as a main point of reference Dostoevsky's "White Nights" (1848), which likewise includes a romantic pursuit. Tolstoy introduces into the first paragraph the word "dreamers" (*mechtateli*), which is central for "White Nights," both as a verbal motif and the key to the overall reading of the tale. In the description of the fog, Tolstoy removes the mention of the horse's muzzle, which is a recognizable detail from "The Overcoat," and adds instead the color yellow, the signature hue of Dostoevsky's Petersburg.

The classical tradition in the story is mixed with modernity, and this is perhaps most visible in the character of Lyubochka, who is layered with all sorts of fashionable symbolist and decadent clichés and stereotypes. But they are presented ironically, as symbolism as a literary movement was by that time in decline. Lyubochka also reflects signs of modernity outside literature: she dwells in a tall building on the seventh floor in an apartment equipped with a telephone, which she uses for improvised phone sex (this is, perhaps, one of the earliest scenes of this kind in literature). She buys a posh postcard with a depiction of a zeppelin carrying flowers in its basket, an item belonging to the ubiquitous mass culture with a nod to modern technology. Her dreams of fame include celebrity status, gossip columns in the press, nude photographs, automobiles, tours of Europe and the US, and huge honorariums.

This kind of civilization is seemingly incompatible with the ancient deities and mythological creatures, but the placement of a satyr into contemporary St. Petersburg is itself a tribute to modern fashion. For several years on the eve of World War I, there was a wave of classical revival in architecture, visual arts, book illustration, decorative arts, and literature; an important herald of this current was the launch of the magazine *Apollon* in 1909. As was mentioned, Auslender's "The Night Prince" appeared in its first issue, and for good reason. Interest in the 1820s and 1830s, the epoch of Empire style (which was a late offshoot of the Neoclassic style), was very much in fashion. A characteristic motif of the time was the juxtaposition—contradictory, striking, and piquant—of classical antiquity and the modern urban environment. This is exemplified by Nikolai Remizov's often-reproduced 1911 poster for *Apollon,* in which the radiant Olympian god rises against the dark mass of the cityscape with its towering buildings, chimneys, and electrical wires. In this logic, Lyubochka, however vain and dissolute, is yet another iteration of Venus appearing from the fog under the northern skies of St. Petersburg.

Since *The Master and Margarita* was mentioned in connection with "The Night Prince," one can point to several parallels between Bulgakov's novel and Tolstoy's story that are most likely "typological" but nonetheless curious: the fog that suddenly falls upon the great city (cf. darkness descending upon

Jerusalem), a discrepancy between the "beastly" build of the stranger and his modern urban attire (cf. Azazaello), the sudden jump of a supernatural creature onto a moving vehicle (cf. Behemoth the cat leaping onto the tram). Additionally, in the later version of the story (which Bulgakov could have read, as it was included in Tolstoy's collected works), one can point to the elusiveness of the stranger who is in vain hunted by the police (cf. the futile attempts to apprehend Woland and his retinue) and the invitation to the heroine to join a grand sabbath in the nude.

***

A. Bezhetsky was the pen name of Alexey Nikolayevich Maslov (1852–1922). A career officer in the engineer troops, he retired as a four-star general. He published on military matters and also wrote fiction, but he remained, so to speak, a subaltern officer in the realm of literature (although Chekhov praised his war stories). By far the oldest author in this anthology, Bezhetsky, like his younger contemporaries, paid tribute to the fashionable mystical genre and in 1914 published a collection entitled *The Unknown*, which includes "The Wax Museum." The story begins as a romantic adventure, but things go awry: the beautiful stranger sets up a date with the protagonist in a wax museum, where uncanny things start to happen. As was discussed in connection with "The Stereoscope," waxworks were a prominent topic at the turn of the century. In addition to the above-mentioned poem "Cleopatra" (1907) by Blok, one can recall Gustav Meyrink's novella "Wachsfigurenkabinett" (1907), whose title was used for an entire collection of his stories. Even when employed in a perfectly realistic setting, a wax effigy could convey a mystical aura, as in Sir Arthur Conan Doyle's "The Adventure of the Empty House" (1903), where an animated wax double of Sherlock Holmes (whose death has just been revealed to Dr. Watson as a hoax) creates a fatal illusion for a would-be assassin. His bullet lodges in the wax, leaving Holmes both dead and alive, again. The topic continued into the 1920s and 30s. In Soviet literature, it appears in Kavalerov's dreams of glory in Yury Olesha's *Envy* (1927) and, most extensively, in Yury Tynyanov's historical tale "The Wax Persona" (1931). In cinema, the famous take on the theme is *Das Wachsfigurenkabinett* (1924), a German expressionist film directed by Paul Leni, although there are also later variations, for example, the American comedy horror *Waxwork* (1988) and its sequel *Waxwork II: Lost in Time* (1992) directed by Anthony Hickox.

"The Wax Museum" very vividly illustrates the connection between the romantic origin of the theme of the doll / automaton / waxworks and its early nineteenth-century variations. The adventure that involves wax figures coming to life emerges as a projection of the ballet *Coppélia,* which is loosely based on Hoffmann's *The Sandman.* There are also Gnostic motifs characteristic of the Silver Age, for example, the remark about "the mysterious and invisible hand of the master" who sets into motion the numerous wax figures at the ball of automatons (cf., the reference to the unknown optician in "The Stereoscope"). Let us also note similarities between Bezhetsky's story and two subsequent works of Russian literature of much greater importance, although here we most likely deal with typological parallels. The final episode of the show in the museum, announced as the "most interesting act," involves the decapitation of a living woman whose severed head continues to speak. This brings to mind the tearing off of the head of George Bengalsky at the Variety Theatre in Bulgakov's *Master and Margarita.* The talkative yet incoherent guide, the missing exhibit, and the strangely expanding space (also prominent in Bulgakov) bring to mind Vladimir Nabokov's "The Visit to the Museum" (1938), a later masterpiece in the genre of mystical Petersburg tales.

***

Alexander Stepanovich Grin (1880–1932) was recognized as a classic of Soviet literature only posthumously, a quarter-century after his death. Prior to that, his literary reputation took twists and turns, very much like his biography. He was a sailor, a railroad worker, a sword swallower in a traveling circus, a gold-miner, a soldier, a deserter, an agitator for the Socialist Revolutionary party, a gambler, and a writer. Arrested multiple times under the old regime for anti-government activities and sentenced to prison or exile, he made several escapes. A perennial non-conformist, Grin did not fully blend into Soviet life and spent his last years in relative seclusion in the Crimea. Grin's literary modalities vary from realism to mysticism, his hallmark genre being neo-romantic fantasy, with action usually taking place in fictional countries, dubbed collectively as Grinlandia by a later critic. Two of his masterpieces of that kind, *She Who Runs on the Waves* (1928) and especially *Scarlet Sails* (1923), enjoy lasting popularity. The latter novel gave its name to the annual festival held in honor of graduating students during the white nights in St. Petersburg and featuring a ship under scarlet sails on the Neva, a symbol of hope and dreams that come true.

Like our opening piece, Grin's short story "The Club Sponger" involves a magic stereoscope. There are, however, no discernable echoes from Ivanov's tale. The trajectory of the situation is quite different, as the hero does not enter the stereoscope, but rather a mysterious lady emerges from it, as in Turgenev's tale "Klara Milich." The casual mention of a stereoscope with an assortment of photos placed alongside journals on a table in the reading room of a gaming club attests to the widespread popularity of the device.[38]

Grin wrote "The Club Sponger" during one of the most dramatic periods of Russian history, which brought about the end of the imperial period and, in a sense, the end of St. Petersburg. The story was published in the first issue of the 1918 *Ogonyok* magazine, its action taking place (or at least, commencing) in the very recent past, the fall of 1917. The introductory part of the story represents a curious documentary source of sorts, as it describes the murky and chaotic atmosphere in Petrograd during the time between the downfall of the monarchy and the Bolshevik Revolution. One is tempted to interpret the story on a historical (or metahistorical) level, with its musings about efforts to return to a happier time in the past which are doomed and instead result in leaps forward, into uncertainty and death. But while the historical frame is important, the plot is first and foremost existential and also reminds one of Balzac's *La Peau de Chagrin* (1831), which likewise begins with a detailed description of a gaming club. Both protagonists are driven into a corner, lose the last of their money on cards, and are on the verge of suicide. As they contemplate drowning themselves, miraculous encounters occur. In Balzac, the magical object that comes into the possession of the protagonist functions with a *quid pro quo* certainty. In Grin, it involves a gamble. The outcome, however, is similar: a shrinking of life.

The theme of gambling, which entered European romanticism with E. T. A. Hoffmann's "Spielerglück" (1820), is extremely prominent in Russian classical literature.[39] For the most part it is connected to card games, later variations being the roulette in Dostoevsky (*The Gambler*, 1871) and, mutatis mutandis, the chess in Nabokov's *The Defense* (1930). Associated with this theme are the notions of chance, fate, and the intersections of different planes of reality, something that was in tune with both romantic and modernist sensibilities. The card theme has a direct link to the Petersburgian tradition (Pushkin's "The Queen of Spades" and Lermontov's "Shtoss"), but Grin's story also contains an allusion to American literature, directly mentioning a character from Bret Harte's work.

---

38 Various aspects of stereoscopic photography in pre-revolutionary Russia were reflected in the exhibition "Why Do We Need Two Eyes?" held at St. Petersburg's Rosfoto Museum (November 2023—March 2024): https://rosphoto.org/events/zachem-nam-dva-glaza/

39 See Yury Lotman's pioneering work on the topic of cards in Russian literature: Yu. M. Lotman, "'Pikovaia dama' i tema kart i kartochnoi igry v russkoi literature nachala XIX veka," in his *Pushkin: Biografiia pisatelia. Stat'i i zametki, 1960–1990* (St. Petersburg: Iskusstvo, 1995), 786–814.

A game of cards plays an important role in another mystical story by Grin, "The Gray Automobile" (1925), which served as the basis for a horror film produced during the late Soviet years, *Mister Designer* (dir. by Oleg Teptsov, 1988). The film considerably alters many aspects of Grin's story and shifts the action from a contemporary fictional country to St. Petersburg of 1908–1914. A stylish, atmospheric piece with spectacular Art Nouveau sets, *Mister Designer* is a veritable treasury of mystical themes, which include: an artist venturing into forbidden realms, transfer of life from a living person to a wax effigy and a wax effigy coming to life, invasion of automatons into the world of the living, an ominous automobile as both an apocalyptic motif and a variation of a machine acquiring a life of its own, vampirical motifs, and a fatal gambling duel. In the film, there are also open references to major texts of St. Petersburg's tradition: Tchaikovsky's opera *The Queen of Spades* based on Pushkin's tale, Blok's *The Puppet Show* and also his "The Commander's Footsteps," in turn referring to Pushkin's "The Stone Guest." Thus, a story by Grin inspired a quintessential mystical tale of St. Petersburg of the Silver Age, albeit in a different medium and some seven decades after the end of the epoch.

***

Ivan Sozontovich Lukash (1892–1940) began his literary career in 1910 as a poet of the Ego-Futurist circle. An active supporter of the February Revolution, he opposed the subsequent Bolshevik takeover. Lukash fought against the Reds in the Volunteer Army and left Russia in the 1920 together with the remnants of the defeated White forces. In emigration, he published a number of historical novels and tales and worked in a variety of genres. Among other things, in the 1920s in Berlin he collaborated with his friend, the young Vladimir Nabokov, on projects for stage and screen.

"Hermann's Card" (1922) serves as an eloquent postscript to this collection, since it portrays the late days of the imperial capital from both temporal and spatial distance, with the author looking back at the city of his youth from exile in Europe after the apocalyptic premonitions inherent in the Petersburg text finally became realized, at least for the given historical era. The story continues the theme of cards, with a plot very similar to that of "The Club Sponger." The protagonist is a gambler whose luck runs out, but who decides to challenge fate one last time. The story also has overt Gnostic overtones frequently found in modernist texts; here they are connected to the thoughts of the protagonist about a hierarchy of players and the universe governed by the blind gamble of multiple demiurges.

Perhaps the most conspicuous feature of "Hermann's Card" is its use of the literary tradition. During the symbolist era, even the writers who are by no means full-fledged symbolists treat culture as a crucial dimension of reality. Hence the numerous allusions we have seen in all of our authors. Lukash takes this to an extreme, not merely engaging the tradition, but openly recycling it. His protagonist, roaming in despair the streets of St. Petersburg during a white night (which is a signature season in St. Petersburg as both a natural and existential phenomenon), encounters Hermann from "The Queen of Spades." Accompanied by Hermann to the gambling house, he, as the title implies, bets on the same sequence of cards, with the same devastating result. In 1932, Lukash recycled another of St. Petersburg's mystical classics (and another cards tale), Lermontov's "Shtoss," completing and expanding the unfinished piece. This is a very blunt handling of the tradition, wanting in subtlety, but remarkable for laying bare the device.

Something similar happens to the historical and topographical references in "Hermann's Card." As with many of his fellow émigrés from intellectual and artistic circles, Lukash's attitude towards Russia's past was ambivalent, exhibiting enthusiastic embrace of the February Revolution but condemnation of the more radical Bolshevik phase. Lukash and his ilk were at the same time heirs to the revolutionary tradition and its opponents. This uneasiness can be seen in Nabokov's novel *The Gift* (1938), which involves the nineteenth-century radical Nikolai Chernyshevsky, who was claimed as a founding father both by the Soviets and many émigré intellectuals. Parts of the novel were actually censored by *Sovremennye zapiski*, a leading émigré magazine that considered Nabokov's treatment of Chernyshevsky unacceptable.

The opening lines of "Hermann's Card" mention the Executive Committee, the governing body of the People's Will, the radical party, which in 1881 organized the assassination of Alexander II. At the same time, all sorts of Executive Committees were a hallmark of the 1917 revolutions and the ensuing civil war. So the very first line of the story both announces the theme of revolution and treats it with characteristic ambivalence. On the one hand, there is an implied disapproval of the revolutionary terror, on the other, an implied sympathy for the revolutionaries. Value judgments aside, the sheer number of historical events and characters mentioned in the beginning of the story is quite high and spans the eighteenth and nineteenth centuries. Even more numerous are details of the city's topography, its streets, squares, waterways, buildings, and monuments. Most of the pieces in this kaleidoscope have very little direct relevance for the plot and could be easily replaced with other events and place names. Here we again deal with the phenomenon of recycling of sorts, which is quite widespread in the émigré literature and, in particular, in the work of St. Petersburg authors who, in their prose and poetry, strive to create a comprehensive catalogue of the lost city, with its landmarks, signboards, sounds, smells, tastes, and the most minuscule material and immaterial details, whether attractive or not. This trend is exemplified by the title of Sergei Gorny's book *Only About Things* (1937) that was printed in Berlin by the publishing house appropriately named Petropolis. As Lukash puts it in his preface to an earlier book by Gorny, *Saint Petersburg. Visions* (1925):

> [The Fairy of] Recollection gave him her magic box. Stored in this box are figurines, toy soldiers, toy street organs, tiny houses, arches of bridges, tiny carriages, baby streetlamps, corners of signboards, shreds of blue tram tickets, a pair of rusty Jackson Haines skates, a rubber ball, somebody's galosh with a copper letter, drops of rain, a handful of Petersburg's snow, bits of Petersburg's granite. His box has everything that is forgotten and unforgettable.
>
> With words of love and pain, quiet incantations, Gorny opens the Fairy's gift. And everything comes to life: signboards, streetlamps, carriages, railings.
>
> Here a Petersburgian cabby, alive, his blue lap open, is lowering from the seat his foot in a brownish felt boot, skates are gliding along the Neva ice, a general is being buried to the tunes of a military march. The funeral procession must be moving along Voznesenky Prospect.
>
> Here rise in the radiant distance the ghostly ripples of Petersburg's streets, the noise of steps, voices. They keep coming closer and closer, and carry you away. Sergei Gorny remembers everything, sees everything, that which we didn't notice and that which we forgot. As if imprinted on his retina is all of St. Petersburg, with its domes, colonnades and avenues, to the slightest chips in wooden paving blocks, to the rusty speckles on an old signboard. [...]
>
> This little St. Petersburg is the fairy tale of what has already been and what will be again someday.[40]

---

40 Ivan Lukash, Introduction to Sergei Gornyi, *Sankt-Peterburg (Videniia)* (Munich: Izdatel'stvo Milavida, 1925), 5–6. For a similar phenomenon in émigré poetry see Roman Timenchik, "Peterburg v poezii russkoi emigratsii," *Zvezda* 10 (2003), 44.

Strongly colored by the acute nostalgia emerging from Russian historical circumstances, this documentary literature of sorts has parallels with more general contemporary developments. It echoes the modernist obsession with time epitomized by the very title of Marcel Proust's *À la recherche du temps perdu,* which was rendered in the first English translations as *Remembrance of Things Past.* Additionally, it can be considered a version of the "literature of fact," albeit with the retrospective focus, which is in direct opposition to the futurist elan of the Soviet 1920s. In the context of this collection, one cannot help but notice that Lukash's catalogue of St. Petersburg visions has curious similarities with Ivanov's "Stereoscope," although without the latter's somber sepia tones. There is a magic photograph of the entire city of St. Petersburg, packed into a little box and miraculously brought to life.

Ultimately, invocation of the bygone world provides only an illusion of a return and creates a vicious circle, or rather a vicious circle to the second degree, as in Lukash's story. Its protagonist finishes like Hermann, who is locked up in a psychiatric hospital and endlessly repeats the cards in the fatal sequence. As was discussed in connection with "The Stereoscope," such cyclicity is in tune with modernist imagination and echoes, for example, one of the most oft-quoted texts of St. Petersburg's Silver Age, the miniature poetic masterpiece by Blok "Night, street, lamp, drugstore" (1912): "There is no way out. You will die, and everything will be repeated as before." Hermann in Lukash introduces himself as "the eternal mask." The masquerade is yet another signature motif from the Silver Age; here it is a peculiar masquerade of ghosts emerging from dark mirrors. This, one can remark in conclusion, points to a major work from a later period, Anna Akhmatova's *Poem Without a Hero* (1940–1962), which brought into vogue the notion of the Silver Age and also put important finishing touches on the myth of St. Petersburg in Russian literature.

# Works Cited


Annanurova, O. M. "'Neiz'iasnimoe chuvstvo': Opyt vospriiatiia stereoskopicheskoi fotografii v rasskaze A. Ivanova 'Stereoskop.'" *Novoe literaturnoe obozrenie* 149, no. 1 (2018): 414–427.

Auslender, Sergei. "Nochnoi prints. Romanticheskaia povest'." *Apollon* 1 (October 1909), Literaturnyi al'manakh, 33–69.

Auslender, Sergei. "Nochnoi prints. Romanticheskaia povest'." In *Russkaia istoricheskaia povest'*, in 2 volumes. Edited by Iu. Beliaev. Vol. 2, 707–732. Moscow: Khudozhestvennaia literatura, 1988.

Auslender, Sergei. "Nochnoi prints. Romanticheskaia povest'". In *Rasskazy. Kniga II*, by S. Auslender, 11–45. St. Petersburg: Apollon, 1912.

Auslender, Sergei. *Peterburgskie apokrify. Roman povesti i rasskazy.* St. Petersburg: Mir, 2005.

Belodubrovskii, E. B., and D. K. Ravinskii, eds. *Stereoskop. Antologiia peterburgskoi fantastiki*, St. Petersburg: Fond kul'tury, 1992. 2nd edition: *Nochnoi prints. Sankt-Peterburgskaia fantastika Serebrianogo veka.* St. Petersburg: Renome, 2020.

Bethea, David. *Khodasevich: His Life and Art.* Princeton: Princeton University Press, 1983.

Bezhetskii, A. "Muzei voskovykh figur." In *Nevedomoe... Fantasticheskie rasskazy*, by A. Bezhetskii. St. Petersburg: Tip. A. S. Suvorina, 1914.

Biriukova, M. V. "Modernistskaia metafora 'gorod-grob' v kontekste simvoliki goroda-muzeia." *Voprosy muzeologii* 6, no. 2 (2012): 18–25.

Bogomolov, N. A. *Russkaia literature nachala XX veka i okkul'tizm.* Moscow: Novoe Literaturnoe Obozrenie, 1999.

Briusov, V. Ia. *Ognennyi angel.* Moscow: Skorpion, 1909.

Carlson, Maria. *No Religion Higher Than Truth: A History of the Theosophical Movement in Russia, 1875–1922.* Princeton: Princeton University Press, 1993.

Davydova, L. I. Introduction, commentary, and supplementary materials. In *Stereoskop. Publikatsia rasskaza A. Ivanova s kommentariiami i prilozheniiami*, by A. Ivanov. St. Petersburg: Izdatel'stvo Gosudarstvennogo Ermitazha, 2003.

Dolinin, Aleksandr, and Grigorii Utgoff. Commentary to *Podvig.* In *Sobranie sochinenii russkogo perioda v 5-ti tomakh*, by Vladimir Nabokov, 714–42. St. Petersburg: Simpozium, 2004.

Doré, Gustave. Illustrations to "La Belle au bois dormant." In *Les contes de Perrault.* Paris: J. Hetzel, 1862.

Doré, Gustave. Illustrations to Ariosto, Ludovico. *Roland furieux: poème héroïque.* Paris: Hachette, 1879.

Dostoevsky, Fyodor. "Petersburg Visions in Prose and Verse." Translated by Michael R. Katz. *New England Review* 24, no. 4 (Fall 2003): 99–116.

Dostoevsky, Fyodor. *A Raw Youth.* Translated by Constance Garnett. London: William Heinemann, 1956.

Dushechkina, E. *Russkaia elka. Istoriia, mifologiia, literatura.* Moscow: Novoe literaturnoe obozrenie, 2024.

Fetisenko, O. L. "'Skrizhali kul'tury' Evgeniia Ivanova." *Khristianskoe chtenie,* no. 3 (2015): 226–42.

Firtich, Nikolai. "The Inclusive Vision: Gogol, the Avant-Garde, and the Russian Cubo-Futurist Strategies of Depiction." *Short Story Criticism* 287 (2020): 242–276.

Geno, A., and Tomich, eds. *Pavel I. Sobranie anekdotov, otzyvov, kharakteristik, ukazov i proch.* St. Petersburg: Sinodal'naya tipografiia, 1901.

Gracheva, A. M. Introduction and Commentary. In *Peterburgskie apokrify. Roman povesti i rasskazy* by Sergei Auslender, 5–38, 665–709. St. Petersburg: Mir, 2005.

Grin, A. "Klubnyi arap." *Ogonek* 1 (1918): 12, 14–18.

Gumilev, N. S. *Polnoe sobranie sochinenii v desiati tomakh,* vol. 7. *Stat'i o literature i iskusstve, obzory, retsenzii.* Moscow: Voskresen'e, 2006.

Il'iunina, L. A. "Ivanov, Aleksandr Pavlovich." In *Russkie pisateli 1800–1917. Biograficheskii slovar',* vol. 2, 368–369. Moscow: Bol'shaia rossiiskaia entsiklopediia, 1992.

*Istoricheskii ocherk Imperatorskogo byvshago Tsarskosel'skogo nyne Aleksandrovskogo litseia za pervoe ego piatidesiatiletie, s 1811 po 1861 g.* Edited by I. Seleznev. St. Petersburg: tip. V. Bezobrazova i komp., 1861.

Ivanov, A. P. "Gorodishche." In *Litsa. Bibliograficheskii al'manakh,* edited by L. A. Il'iunina and E. R. Obatnina, 16–39. Moscow-St. Petersburg: Feniks, 1993.

Ivanov, A. P. *Stereoskop. Publikatsia rasskaza Sumerechnyi rasskaz.* St. Petersburg: Sirius, 1909.

Ivanov, A. P. *Stereoskop. Publikatsia rasskaza A. Ivanova s kommentariiami i prilozheniiami.* Introduction and commentary by L. I. Davydova. St. Petersburg: Izdatel'stvo Gosudarstvennogo Ermitazha, 2003.

Ivanov, A. P. *Stereoskop. Sumerechnyi rasskaz.* With commentary by S. Shargorodskii. Salamandra, P. V. V., 2013.

Ivanov, E. P. "Vospominania i zapisi Evgeniia Ivanova ob Aleksandre Bloke." In *Blokovskii sbornik,* edited by Iu. M. Lotman, 344–424. Tartu: Tartusskii gosudarstvennyi univesitet, 1964.

Izmailov A. A. (Smolenskii). "Bukinist. Rozhdestvenskii rasskaz." *Novaia illiustratsiia* 51–52 (1903): 410–416.

Izmailov, A. A. (Smolenskii). "Bukinist. Iz knigi Misticheskikh rasskazov." In *Oseni mertvoi tsvety zapozdalye,* by A. A. Izmailov, 113–142. St. Petersburg: Energiia, 1906.

Jakobson, Roman. "The Statue in Pushkin's Poetic Mythology." In *Selected Writings,* vol. 5. *On Verse, Its Masters and Explorers,* by Roman Jakobson, 237–280. Mouton: The Hague, 1979.

Khodasevich, Vladislav. *Necropolis.* Translated by Sarah Vitali. New York: Columbia University Press, 2019.

Kozakov, Mikhail. "Petrogradskie dni." *Novyi mir* 11 (November 1957): 113–185.

Krinichnaia, N. A. *Russkaia mifologiia. Chelovek na pereput'e mirov. Bylichki, byval'shchiny, legendy, pover'ia o poiskakh i poseshcheniiakh zapovednykh mest i mirov.* Moscow: Akademicheskii proekt, 2023.

Kupchenko, V. P. "Eshche odin Aleksandr Ivanov." In *Litsa. Bibliograficheskii al'manakh,* 5–15. Moscow-St. Petersburg: Feniks, 1993.

Kuz'michev, Kirill. *Tret'e izmerenie. Rossiia Aleksandra II vo frantsuzskoi stereofotografii.* St. Petersburg: Kriga, 2018.

Lazhechnikov, I. I. *Ledianoi dom.* In *Sochineniia v dvukh tomakh,* vol. 2, by I. I. Lazhechnikov, 5–294. Moscow: Khudozhestvennaia literatura, 1986.

Lotman, Yu. M. "'Pikovaia dama' i tema kart i kartochnoi igry v russkoi literature nachala XIX veka." In *Pushkin: Biografiia pisatelia. Stat'i i zametki, 1960–1990,* by Yu. M. Lotman, 786–814. St. Petersburg: Iskusstvo, 1995.

Lukash, Ivan. "Karta Germanna." In *Chert na gauptvakhte. Tri peterburgskikh istorii,* by I. Lukash, 79–98. Berlin: Izd. E. A. Gutnova, 1922.

Lukash, Ivan. Introduction. In *Sankt-Peterburg (Videniia),* by Sergei Gornyi, 5–6. Munich: Izdatel'stvo Milavida, 1925.

Makovskii, S. K. *Siluety russkikh khudozhnikov.* Moscow: Respublika, 1999.

Mannherz, Julia. *Modern Occultism in Late Imperial Russia.* DeKalb, IL: Northern Illinois University Press, 2012.

Merezhkovskii, D. S. *Polnoe sobranie sochinenii,* in 24 volumes, vol. 4. Moscow: Tip. I. D. Sytina, 1914.

Mikhailov, M. "Peterburg i ego okrestnosti." *Severnoe siianie* 3 (1862): 162–168.

Mints, Z. G. "O nekotorykh 'neomifologicheskikh' tekstakh v tvorchestve russkikh simvolistov." In *Tvorchestvo A. A. Bloka i russkaia kul'tura XX veka. Blokovskii sbornik III. Uchenye zapiski Tartuskogo gosudarstvennoko universiteta* 459 (1979), 76–120.

Mut'ia, N. N. "Teatral'nost' russkoi salono-akademicheskoi zhivopisi vtoroi poloviny XIX veka." In *Nauchnye Trudy. Rossiiskaia akademiia khudozhestv. Institut im. I. E. Repina*. St. Petersburg, vol. 28 (January—March 2014): 58–67.

Nabokov, Vladimir. *Speak Memory. An Autobiography Revisited.* NY: Alfred A. Knopf, 1999.

Obatnin, Gennadii. *Ivanov-mistik. Okkul'tnye motivy v poezii i proze Viacheslava Ivanova (1907–1919).* Moscow: Novoe literaturnoe obozrenie, 2000.

Oksenov, Innokentii. Review of A. Ivanov, "Stereoskop." *Kniga i revoliutsiia* 7 (1921): 56–57.

Pyliaev, M. I. "Mody i modnitsy starogo vremeni." In *Staroe zhit'e,* by M. I. Pyliaev, 62–108. St. Petersburg: Tip. A. S. Suvorina, 1892.

Reischl, Katherine M. H. *Photographic Literacy: Cameras in the Hands of Russian Authors.* Ithaca, NY: Cornell University Press, 2018.

Ronen, Omry. *The Fallacy of the Silver Age.* Amsterdam: Routledge, 1997.

Rosenthal, Bernice, ed. *The Occult in Russian and Soviet Culture.* Ithaca, NY: Cornell University Press, 1997.

Shargorodskii, S. Commentary to A. P. Ivanov, *Stereoskop. Sumerechnyi rasskaz,* 54–63. Salamandra, P. V. V., 2013.

Tamarchenko, N. D. "Skrytaia tsitata kak otsylka k zhanrovoi traditsii." *Reosiayeongu* [Russian Studies, South Korea] 19, no. 2 (2009): 25–59.

Timenchik, Roman. "Peterburg v poezii russkoi emigratsii." *Zvezda* 10 (2003): 194–205.

Tolstoi, A. N. "Satir." *Solntse Rossii* 17, no. 116 (April 1912): 2–4.

Toporov, V. N. *Peterburgskii tekst russkoi literatury. Izbrannye Trudy.* St. Petersburg: Iskusstvo, 2003.

Tsiv'ian, T. V. "Kamen' v 'Stereoskope' Aleksandra Ivanova: Personazh ili anturazh?" In *Dialog s kamnem: ot prirody k kul'ture,* edited by M. V. Zav'ialova and T. V. Tsiv'ian. Moscow: MGU, 2016, 113–126.

Ungurianu, Dan. "Khranilishche. Zametki o topose muzeia v russkoi literature 1920–30-kh gg." In *Russian Literature and the West: A Tribute for David M. Bethea,* edited by Alexander Dolinin, Lazar Fleishman, and Leonid Livak,

2: 186–211. Stanford Slavic Studies, vols. 35–36. Stanford: Dept. of Slavic Languages and Literatures, Stanford University, 2008.

Ungurianu, Dan. *Plotting History: The Russian Historical Novel in the Imperial Age.* Madison: The University of Wisconsin Press, 2007.

Zhikharev, S. P. *Zapiski.* Moscow: Izdanie Russkogo Arkhiva, 1890.

Zhukovskii, V. A. *Spiashchaia tsarevna.* Lenigrad: Detizdat, 1939.

Zolotareva, Olga. "The Image Responds: Photographic Aura in Aleksandr Ivanov's 'Stereoscope.'" *Journal of Modern Literature* 45, no. 3 (2022): 53–71.

# About the Editor and Translator

**Dan Ungurianu** has a degree in history from Moscow State University and in Slavic languages and literature from the University of Wisconsin-Madison. He is Professor of Russian Studies at Vassar College.

**Elena Ungurianu** studies art history and linguistics at Yale University.

www.ingramcontent.com/pod-product-compliance
Lightning Source LLC
Chambersburg PA
CBHW070832020826
48982CB00015B/845
*9798887197647*